FINDING CHARITY

With one comprehensive sweep of his torch, Thanet took in the whole scene: the gaping suitcase in the middle of the path, a jumble of clothes spilling out, and, the focal point of it all, the crumpled body of the girl, lying at the foot of a door in the left-hand wall of the alley.

Thanet hurried forward, noting with relief that her clothing seemed undisturbed. Perhaps she had at least been spared the terror of a sexual assault—could even still be alive. He squatted down beside her and shone the light on her face. That blank, frozen stare left no room for doubt and the jagged gash on her right temple looked lethal. There was no whisper of breath, not even the faintest flutter of a pulse. He looked at the rounded, still childish contours of brow and cheek. This, he was sure, was Charity.

CRIME LINE Bantam Crime Line Books offer the finest in classic and modern British murder mysteries. Ask your bookseller for the books you have missed

CLOSE HER EYES

An Inspector Thanet Mystery

DOROTHY SIMPSON

BANTAM BOOKS

NEW YORK • TORONTO • LONDON • SYDNEY • AUCKLAND

ISBN 0-553-18518-7

TO ANNE

Stone walls do not a prison make
Nor iron bars a cage

Richard Lovelace
1618-58

CLOSE HER EYES

1

The news that a young girl is missing is likely to penetrate the armour of the most hard-bitten policeman, and Thanet was anything but that. The telephone receiver was suddenly slippery in his hand.

"How old?"

"Fifteen."

"And how long missing?"

"Since Friday morning." Lineham's voice was heavy with pessimism.

"Friday morning! But that's nearly three days ago! What the hell were the parents thinking of, not to have reported it till now?"

"It's a bit complicated, sir. The father says..."

"Save it. I'll be in as soon as I can."

Thanet glanced down at his stained knees, grubby shorts and grimy hands. He would have to make time for a quick shower. Taking the stairs two at a time he wondered why he was bothering to hurry. If the parents hadn't reported the disappearance for three days...

There could be a good reason, of course. They could have believed her to be spending the holiday weekend with a friend. She might even have gone off of her own free will. Fifteen was an especially vulnerable age, a peak time for traumatic rows at home... Nevertheless he was showered and dressed in less than ten minutes, slowing his pace only to peep in at Bridget and Ben, sound asleep with the bedclothes thrown back against the stifling warmth of one of the hottest Spring Bank Holiday Mondays on record.

Over the weekend all England had sweated and sweltered in the unseasonable heat. Motorists had taken to the road in record numbers, the sea exerting on them a magnetic pull which they were powerless to resist. As temperature and humidity soared hundreds of thousands of families had fretted and fumed away their precious holiday hours in traffic jams, trapped in their little metal boxes.

Thanet had had more sense. He and his mother-in-law had decided to pack the children into the car and spend the half-term holiday at her cottage in the country, trying to restore the garden to some sort of order. It wasn't the way Thanet would have chosen to spend one of his rare long weekends off, but he had felt that it was the least he could do. For the last two years, while Joan had been away at college completing her training as a Probation Officer, Mrs. Bolton had been looking after the children and running the house for Thanet. Very few women, he felt, would have been prepared to give up home and freedom as she had, and he still felt grateful to her for the sacrifice. In just under three weeks Joan would be home for good, thank God, and it was time to start thinking of ways to help his mother-in-law to take up the reins of her own life again. The cottage was only ten miles away from Sturrenden, the busy country town in Kent where Thanet lived and worked, and after the weekend Mrs. Bolton and the children could stay on for the remainder of the week's holiday while Thanet drove in daily to the office. But now it looked as though his time off was about to be curtailed.

He hurried out to the tiny, brick-paved terrace behind the house where the mingled scents of lilac and orange blossom, overlaid by the pungent odour of broom, hung heavy in the gathering dusk. Not a leaf stirred. The air was as suffocatingly hot and humid as if the entire garden were encased in a plastic dome.

Margaret Bolton was sitting limply in a deck chair, eyes closed, empty glass dangling from one hand. In repose she looked almost young again, the lines around eyes and mouth smoothed away, the fading light kind to the grey in the fair, curly hair so like her daughter's. For a fleeting moment it almost seemed to Thanet that he was looking at Joan herself twenty years hence, and briefly the sense of mortality ever-present in his working life spilled over into his private world, laying a cold hand upon his heart. He experienced a sudden and intense longing for Joan's warm, living presence. Then Mrs. Bolton opened her eyes, blinked at the transformation in his appearance, and normality was re-established.

"Work?"

"I'm afraid so."

She made to rise. "I'll make you a sandwich."

"No." Gently, he pushed her back. "I'll pick up something later. I'm not hungry anyway, it's too hot. Let me get you another drink before I go."

"I don't want one, thank you. Honestly." She smiled ruefully. "I hope you're not too tired to feel fit for work."

"Not at all. It's been a pleasant change, to do something physical." And it was true, he didn't feel in the least bit tired, despite the nagging ache in that troublesome back of his. A quarter of an hour ago he'd felt as exhausted as his mother-in-law now looked, but the adrenaline coursing through his veins since Lineham's call had miraculously restored him. He was impatient to be gone.

In a few moments he was on his way, winding along through country lanes adrift with the white froth of Queen Anne's lace and heady with the sweet, green scent of early summer. Already he had relinquished the tranquility of the cottage, the sleeping children, and was keyed up to meet the challenge ahead.

Detective Sergeant Lineham was waiting for him in the reception area and hurried forward to give him a précis of the facts.

Thanet listened intently. "Where is he?"

"In interview room three. PC Dennison is with him."

"What did you say his name was?"

"Pritchard."

As they entered the room, Thanet experienced a fleeting reaction of surprise at the embarrassment on the young constable's face before understanding the reason for it: Mr. Pritchard was kneeling on the floor, elbows on the seat of one of the chairs, forehead resting on clenched hands.

He was praying.

Thanet and Lineham exchanged a quick glance of uncomfortable astonishment. Never, in all his years in the force, could Thanet remember such a situation arising before. No wonder PC Dennison had been nonplussed. Dismissing the constable with a smile and a nod Thanet advanced into the room.

Clearly, Pritchard hadn't heard them arrive. The intensity of his concentration was such that it seemed to emanate from him in waves, etching upon Thanet's mind a black and white image of near-photographic clarity: dark suit, shiny across the

3

seat, with black mourning band stitched around one sleeve; white shirt, black hair divided by the white line of a centre parting so straight that it might have been drawn by a ruler.

Thanet hesitated. It seemed almost blasphemous to trespass upon such pious concentration. Then, telling himself that even at this late stage further delay could be a threat to the girl's safety, he laid one hand gently on Pritchard's shoulder and softly spoke his name.

Pritchard's eyelids snapped open in shock and he twisted his head to look up at Thanet. His eyes were very dark, almost as black as his hair and full of an agonised resignation. Slowly, he stood up, unfolding his long, thin body with the jerky, uncoordinated movements of a marionette.

Thanet found himself apologising. "Sorry to disturb you, Mr. Pritchard, but we have to talk." He introduced himself.

Pritchard hesitated. "I've been wondering if I was too precipitate. Perhaps I shouldn't have come."

Thanet frowned. "What do you mean?"

"I've been thinking it over. I'm afraid I panicked. I should have had more faith."

"Faith?"

"We are all in God's hands, Inspector. And we have to trust in Him. I can't really believe that He would have let anything bad happen to Charity . . . I'm sorry to have wasted your time." He gave a curious little half-bow and began to move towards the door.

Thanet couldn't believe what he was hearing. "Mr. Pritchard. Please . . . Wait a moment."

Pritchard paused and, with one hand on the door-knob, half-turned, eyebrows raised in polite enquiry.

Thanet moved a little closer to him. "Let me make sure I understand you. You mean, you don't want us to make any attempt to find your daughter?"

"That's right."

"Perhaps you've realised where she must be?"

Pritchard shook his head. "No. But I do believe that where ever she is, she must be safe in God's care."

It was incredible. The man really was prepared to let the matter rest there. Some might find such faith moving; Thanet, well-versed in man's inhumanity to man, thought it foolhardy to the point of insanity. Deliberately, he kept his voice low, his tone reasonable. "Then don't you think it might be

4

sensible to try to find her? Let's just sit down for a moment and discuss the matter.''

"There's nothing to discuss. I told you, God is sure to be watching over her.''

He was opening the door now and with a flash of combined inspiration and desperation Thanet said slowly, "Even God has to work sometimes through a human agency, Mr. Pritchard. Are you perhaps in danger of overlooking the possibility that He might have sent you here, to us?''

Pritchard hesitated. The dark eyes clouded and then bored into Thanet's as if trying to test the validity of his suggestion.

Thanet waited. The little room was stifling and he was conscious of the prick of sweat down his back and under his armpits.

Pritchard closed his eyes and remained motionless. A minute passed, then two. Thanet and Lineham exchanged anxious glances. Outside in the corridor there was a brief buzz of conversation, then a door closed, cutting it off. As if this were a signal, Pritchard relaxed a little, sighed, opened his eyes.

"You could be right, I suppose.'' But still he hesitated a moment longer before moving back to the table. "Very well,'' he said. And sat down.

Relieved, Thanet slipped off his jacket and hung it over the back of his chair before seating himself. He glanced at Lineham. The sergeant was ready. Careful now, Thanet told himself. This one will have to be handled with kid gloves.

"Sergeant Lineham here has given me the facts, very briefly, but I'd be grateful if you could go over them again for me in a little more detail.'' Then, as Pritchard hesitated, "As I understand it, your daughter was supposed to be spending the weekend in Dorset, with a friend.''

"Yes. They were going to one of the Jerusalem Holiday Homes. They were supposed to leave on Friday morning and get back tonight. They've been there before together, at Easter, and it all went off very smoothly, so there was no reason to think it wouldn't this time.''

"Let's take it a step at a time. What time did Charity leave the house on Friday morning?''

"About nine thirty, according to my wife. I was at work by then, of course.''

Little by little the tangled tale was unravelled. Charity and

5

her friend Veronica Hodges had planned to go to Dorset by train, catching the ten twenty-three to Victoria. Charity was to call at Veronica's house to pick her up on the way to the station. She found, however, that Veronica was unfit to travel, having woken up that morning with a high temperature.

"Didn't Mrs. Hodges try to contact you, to let you know Veronica wouldn't be able to go?"

"Neither of us is on the phone."

"I see. Go on."

According to Mrs. Hodges, Charity had taken the disappointment calmly and after spending a few minutes with her friend, had left. Knowing that the Pritchards would never have allowed Charity to travel alone and that the Holiday Home in any case insisted that girls under eighteen should travel in pairs, Mrs. Hodges had assumed that Charity had returned home.

"But she didn't?"

"Not as far as we know." Pritchard took an immaculately folded clean white handkerchief from his pocket and mopped at the sheen of sweat on his forehead.

"Why don't you take your jacket off, Mr. Pritchard? It's like an oven in here."

Pritchard shook his head, a sharp, involuntary movement, as if the idea offended him.

As well it might, Thanet thought. The man was so stiff, unbending, that it was difficult to imagine him ever relaxing in shirt sleeves.

Pritchard put the handkerchief back into his pocket.

"Soon after I got to work that morning, at about half past nine, I suppose, I had a phone call from my wife's sister in Birmingham. My mother-in-law had had a severe heart attack during the night and her condition was critical. I spoke to my employer and he told me to take the rest of the day off."

Pritchard, who worked as storeman in a wholesale stationery firm, had gone home to break the news of her mother's illness to his wife. By the time they had packed and given their next-door neighbour the Birmingham address where they could be contacted in case of emergency, it was too late for them to catch the same London train as the girls and they decided to leave a note on the kitchen table for Charity, in case she arrived back before they did. She had her own key and would be able to let herself in. They had expected that one or both of them would be back in time for her return this evening, but after lingering on over the weekend the old lady had died this morning and, wanting to stay on for the funeral, Mr. Pritchard had rung the Holiday Home to inform Charity of her grandmother's death and to suggest that she stay at Veronica's house for a day or two, until her parents returned home.

It had been a shock to learn that neither Charity nor Veronica had turned up, Mrs. Hodges having rung the Home from a phone-box on Friday morning to tell the Principal of Veronica's illness.

"Was your daughter mentioned?"

"Only in passing, apparently. It was taken for granted that she wouldn't be going. As I said, they're very strict about girls travelling in pairs. When you book, the parents have to sign a form, saying they won't allow their daughters to travel alone. Mrs. Hodges rang them quite early in the morning, and at that point even my wife and I didn't know we were going to be called away."

"Didn't you think to let Mrs. Hodges know, when you decided to go to Birmingham to see your mother-in-law?"

Pritchard dropped his face into his hands, and groaned. "If only I had. Looking back now, it was irresponsible—wickedly irresponsible, not to have been in touch with her before leaving. But it was all such a rush—so much to do, so many things to think of...We did leave a note next door, of course, I told you...And then we knew that Mrs. Hodges was here in Sturrenden in case of emergency...But you're right, of course you are. We should have thought..."

"Or if Mrs. Hodges had let you know that Veronica was ill..."

Pritchard's shoulders stiffened. "That's right." He raised his head and stared at Thanet, eyes glittering. "She should have, shouldn't she? If she had, Charity would simply have come with us, and we wouldn't be in this position now."

Thanet was sorry he'd made the suggestion. Wanting to alleviate Pritchard's sense of guilt by showing him that the responsibility had not been his alone, he had merely succeeded in giving the man a grievance which could distract him from the task in hand.

"We mustn't digress," he said firmly. "Can we go back to this morning, and your phone call to the Home, from

7

Birmingham? When the Principal told you that neither of the girls had been able to go because of Veronica's illness, what did you think had happened to Charity?"

"I assumed she'd gone home and found our note. We thought that, knowing how worried her mother would be about her grandmother, she'd hesitated to add to the burden by telling her that the holiday arrangements had fallen through."

"So at that stage you weren't really too worried?"

"Well, we were very upset to think she'd been alone in the house all over the weekend, of course. She is only fifteen, after all . . ."

"So what did you decide to do?"

"As there was no way of getting in touch with Charity, we thought I'd better come straight home and go up to Birmingham for the day on Friday, for the funeral."

"You didn't think of contacting Charity through us?"

"Through you?" Pritchard looked at Thanet as though he had suggested communicating through a creature from an alien planet.

"Well, we do often help members of the public out, in that sort of situation."

Pritchard shook his head. "It would never have occurred to me."

"So you came back to Sturrenden and went home, expecting to find Charity there."

"Yes." Pritchard wiped his forehead again, then transferred the handkerchief from his right hand to his left and began to pluck agitatedly at one corner with long, bony fingers. No doubt he was reliving the shock he had experienced upon finding the house empty.

"Was there any sign that she had been there at any time over the weekend?"

"No. The house was exactly as we'd left it, so far as I could see."

"No indication that she'd eaten, drunk anything?"

Pritchard put his hand up to his head, began to massage one temple. "No . . . I don't know . . . I didn't think to look in the larder."

"Or in the fridge?"

"We haven't got a refrigerator." Then, wearily, as if explaining something he had attempted to explain many times before, "We of the Children live very simply, Inspector, in a way which you would no doubt find incomprehensible."

"The Children?"

"The Children of Jerusalem." Even now, in the midst of his anxiety over his daughter, the dark eyes suddenly burned with religious fervour. "The true Church of God. We believe..."

From what Thanet had seen of the man he guessed that once Pritchard was side-tracked on to the question of religion he would be as difficult to stop as a runaway steamroller. Quickly, he intervened. "I see." He remembered what Lineham had told him. "So that was when you decided to go and see if she'd spent the weekend with the Hodges?"

Pritchard blinked. It was as if a switch had been clicked off in his head and there was a pause before he said, "Yes."

"You said just now that before Charity left the Hodges' on Friday morning she spent a few minutes alone with Veronica. Did she give Veronica any hint of what she was going to do now that their holiday was cancelled?"

"I don't think she could have, or Mrs. Hodges would have mentioned it. In any case, at that point Charity didn't know that we were going to be away. Otherwise she'd have told Mrs. Hodges, I'm sure, and Mrs. Hodges would probably have suggested she stay there for the weekend."

"You didn't actually speak to Veronica herself?"

"No."

"And then?"

"I came here. I told you, I panicked."

"Understandably, I think."

Pritchard frowned. "As I said, we must trust in God at all times, Inspector. I have to believe that He is watching over her."

Despite his words Pritchard gave Thanet a beseeching look and Thanet sensed his desperate need for reassurance. But what reassurance could he possibly give?

"Can you think of any other friends with whom Charity might have spent the weekend?"

"She didn't have any other friends."

Thanet bit back the questions which rushed into his mind concerning the girl's classmates, clubs, leisure activities. Time for all that later, when it was certain that they were necessary.

Pritchard dropped his head into his hands and groaned. "I just can't think where she might be."

Thanet stood up and Pritchard raised his head as the chair scraped the floor. His face was bone-white, the skin stretched taut, his eyes tormented.

"What are you going to do, Inspector?"

"First we'll go to your house, to check that she really hasn't been back at all over the weekend. Then we'll go and talk to Veronica. After that, well, we'll see."

As they ushered Pritchard down the stairs and into the car Thanet fervently hoped that after that they wouldn't be launching into a full-scale murder hunt.

2

It took them only ten minutes or so to reach Town Road, where the Pritchards lived; had it not been for the one-way system they could have done it in five. Sturrenden lies deep in the Kent countryside. It is a busy market town of some 45,000 inhabitants, the centre of a complex web of country lanes and scattered villages. The new traffic system has alleviated daytime congestion of the town centre, but older inhabitants still find it infuriating. Thanet's attitude was ambivalent: the policeman in him appreciated its benefits but the private citizen resented having to take twice as long to reach his destination, especially on occasions like tonight, when the streets were deserted and he was in a hurry.

Town Road was a long, narrow street of yellow-brick Victorian terraced houses with square-bayed windows upstairs and down. Cars were tightly packed along the kerbs on both sides of the road and Lineham was forced to park some little distance away from number 32.

All along the street light spilled into narrow front gardens from uncurtained windows, but the Pritchards' house was in darkness and Thanet and Lineham had to wait for a few moments while Pritchard fumbled with his keys. They followed him into a narrow passage and he switched on the light, an unshaded low-wattage bulb whose sickly glare revealed worn linoleum and bare walls.

"You take upstairs," Thanet murmured, and Lineham obediently moved towards the staircase at the far end of the passage.

Thanet asked to see the kitchen first and looked around him with disbelief. How many kitchens like this still existed? he asked himself. It was as though he had stepped back fifty years. Mrs. Pritchard still cooked at an old kitchen range. The fire was out and there was a reek of stale soot. A battered aluminium kettle stood on the hob above the side oven. There was a shallow stone sink with a single tap, an upturned white enamelled bowl inverted on the wooden draining board, a narow wooden table, its top bleached ivory with much scrubbing and a storage cupboard beside it, painted brown. There was a rag rug on the floor in front of the hearth and a wooden armchair into which Pritchard subsided with a groan.

"Go ahead, Inspector. Do whatever it is you want to do."

It certainly didn't look as though Charity had been back here, Thanet thought as he checked. The sink, the bowl, the dishcloth and tea-towels were bone-dry, the cast-iron range stone-cold. The larder was as spotlessly clean as the kitchen, despite the faint, sour smell of stale cheese. There was no bread, no butter, no milk. They had taken all three with them, said Pritchard, when they left for Birmingham. Thanet guessed that it would have seemed sinful to throw good food away.

Pritchard seemed to have sunk into a kind of stupor and Thanet went alone to take a quick look at the front room. People's homes, Thanet believed, were highly revealing. A man's sitting room is an expression of his personality—his choice of colour and patterns, his furniture, his *objets d'art*, his books, his records, all are evidence not only of his tastes but of his attitudes and habits.

What he saw here appalled him. Apart from a three-piece suite upholstered in slippery brown rexine and a heavy upright piano standing against one wall, the room was bare of furniture. The only ornament was a wooden clock placed dead in the centre of the mantelpiece, the only concession to comfort a small beige rug in front of the empty Victorian basket grate, the only wall decoration a religious text in a narrow black frame. *Thou, God, Seest Me*, it proclaimed in curly black letters on a white ground.

11

Thanet shivered. It was as if he had been vouchsafed a glimpse of the poverty of Pritchard's soul, of the barren rigidity of his outlook. What could Charity be like, he wondered, raised in an atmosphere such as this. Yet there was a piano. He crossed to glance at the neat stack of sheet music on top. *The Associated Board of the Royal Schools of Music*, he read. *Grade VII (Advanced)*. So Charity at least had music to enrich her bleak existence.

He heard Lineham coming down the stairs and went out into the hall to meet him.

"Anything up there?"

"Nothing. No sign of a suitcase in her room. Everything neat and tidy." Lineham grimaced. "The whole place gives me the creeps."

"I know what you mean. What about the bathroom?"

Lineham raised a quizzical eyebrow. "What bathroom?"

"No bathroom . . . Can't say I'm surprised, after what I've seen down here."

"Nothing downstairs either?"

"No trace of her. We'd better get over to the Hodges'. I'll just have a word with Pritchard first."

In the kitchen Pritchard was just as Thanet had left him, motionless in the armchair, hands on knees, head bowed, staring at the floor.

"We're just going over to see Mrs. Hodges now, Mr. Pritchard, and then we'll come back here. Are you all right?"

Pritchard raised dazed eyes and Thanet could see the effort the man made to concentrate on what Thanet was saying.

"Are you all right?" Thanet repeated.

"Yes. Yes, I'm fine, thank you."

"I'd like you to stay here in case Charity comes home while we're gone. But there's something I want you to do, while you're waiting."

"Yes?" A spark of interest, now.

"I'd like you to write down the names of all the people with whom Charity could conceivably have spent the weekend. Family friends, acquaintances, school friends, church members, anyone at all who is even a remote possibility. Could you do that?"

Pritchard pressed thumb and forefinger into his eyes. "Yes. Of course."

12

"Have you pencil and paper?" Thanet wanted Pritchard launched on the task before they left.

"Pencil and paper," Pritchard repeated, looking vaguely around. "Let me see." He heaved himself out of the chair. "Yes. In the table drawer. Here we are."

They left him to it.

"Doesn't look too bright, does it, sir?" said Lineham when they were in the car.

Thanet shrugged. The interview with Pritchard had alleviated some of his earlier anxiety. "We can't tell, yet. It's quite possible that after finding out that Veronica couldn't go to Dorset with her, Charity went home, found the note, thought I'm not spending the weekend in this dump by myself—and who could blame her?—and decided to throw herself on the mercy of one of her school friends."

"Why not go back to the Hodges' and ask if she could stay there?"

"I don't know. Perhaps she didn't like to ask, if Veronica was ill. Anyway, the point is, if she did spend the weekend with a friend, she wouldn't have felt it necessary to come back until this evening because she knew that her parents wouldn't be expecting her until then anyway. So she might well yet turn up safe and sound."

"True."

They slowed down to allow an ambulance to overtake them.

"How's Louise?" said Thanet, his memory jogged.

Lineham's wife was soon due to produce their first child.

"Oh, fine, thanks. The heat's getting her down at the moment, of course, and she'll be glad now when it's all over."

"How much longer is it?"

Lineham sighed. "Another four weeks."

Thanet grinned. "Cheer up, Mike. The first time's the worst. After that it gets easier every time."

"Some consolation at this stage!" Lineham swung the steering wheel. "Ah, here we are. Lantern Street."

More terraced cottages, but smaller and older this time, many of them boarded up or in disrepair. It looked as though the landlord had decided that the site was worth more than the rents.

Number 8, however, presented a brave face to the world.

Groups of scarlet tulips glowed like clustered rubies in the dusk and the brass door-knocker shone with much polishing.

The woman who answered the door was short and plump, with fluffy fair hair.

"Mrs. Hodges?" Thanet introduced himself. "It's about Charity Pritchard."

"Oh? What's the matter? What's wrong?"

"I thought you knew. She seems to have disappeared. Mr. Pritchard told me he'd been here earlier, this evening, that you hadn't seen her since Friday morning."

"Oh yes, but she's been here herself since then. In fact, she only left about a quarter of an hour ago. She should be home any minute."

"I see. Did she say where she'd been?"

"Staying with a friend, she said. I told her her dad had been round and she looked a bit upset—well she would, wouldn't she? I expect she'll be for it when she gets home."

Had he imagined that there had been a hint of satisfaction in her voice?

"So," said Lineham as they returned to the car. "You were right. All a storm in a teacup."

"Looks like it."

"All that hassle for nothing," Lineham grumbled.

"Let's just be thankful that it's turned out the way it has."

They drove back to Town Street in silence.

Pritchard opened the door to their knock almost at once, as if he had been waiting in the hall, and stood back wordlessly for them to enter. In the wan light his face was the colour of old parchment. Clearly, Charity wasn't home yet.

"It's all right, Mr. Pritchard," Thanet said gently, touching him reassuringly on the arm. "Charity is safe."

"She's all right?" Pritchard closed his eyes, swayed slightly and put one hand against the wall for support. "I thought . . . I was afraid . . ."

"I know." Thanet took him by the elbow and eased him along the passage into the kitchen, sat him down in the wooden armchair. "But it's all right. No harm has come to her. She'll be home any minute now."

"God be praised." Pritchard hunched forward, dropping his head into his hands.

"Mrs. Hodges said that Charity called in this evening on her way home. She'd spent the weekend with a friend,

14

apparently. We only missed her by fifteen minutes or so. I don't know how long it takes to walk from the Hodges' house, but she really should be here at any moment.''

Pritchard said nothing, did not look up, but Thanet could tell that he was listening. His body was tense, his breathing stilled.

"Would you like us to wait until she gets here?" Thanet offered. It wasn't really necessary for him to do so but by now he was rather curious about the girl. And they shouldn't have to wait long.

For a minute or two Pritchard did not respond. The silence stretched out and Thanet glanced at Lineham, who responded by raising his eyebrows and shrugging. Thanet was even beginning to wonder if Pritchard was so exhausted by the nervous strain of the last few hours that he had dropped off to sleep. Then the man stirred and slowly straightened up, sat back in the chair.

"Thank you," he said, "I'd be grateful if you would." His lips barely moved, as if even the effort of talking was too much for him and he had scarcely finished speaking before he closed his eyes and, head lolling back against the chair rail, dozed off.

With one accord Thanet and Lineham quietly left the room and went into the sitting room. It was the first time Lineham had been in here and as he looked around Thanet could see mirrored in his face the same incredulity which Thanet had felt at his first sight of the kitchen.

"My God," said Lineham. "Talk about Cosy Corner!"

"Shh." Thanet made sure the door was closed. "Not exactly a home from home, I agree."

They both sat down in the hard, slippery armchairs.

"How can they stand it?" said Lineham. "The bedrooms are the same, you know—lumpy flock mattresses which look as though they came out of the Ark, rusty bedsprings, bare lino on the floor...I just can't understand people being prepared to live like this."

"Perhaps they can't afford to do otherwise?"

"Oh come on, sir! It's not just lack of money I'm talking about, and you know it. It's the sheer drabness of it all. Just look at it! Anyone can buy a tin of emulsion paint and brighten things up if he wants to."

"Then obviously, the Pritchards don't want to. This, incredible as it may seem to us, must be how they like it."

15

"Like it!" Lineham's face was a study in disbelief.

"From what we've seen of Pritchard, I'd guess it's a question of religious principle. He probably thinks comfort is sinful, an indulgence of the flesh."

"Is that what they're like, these Children of Jerusalem?"

"I don't really know. I'm only judging by some of the things he's said, and by this place."

"They meet in that hall in Jubilee Road, don't they? The one with the green corrugated iron roof?"

"That's right."

"They can't exactly be thriving. The place looks as though it's about to fall down."

"They may be going downhill now, but at one time they were a force to be reckoned with in Sturrenden, I believe."

"How long have they been around?"

Thanet wrinkled his forehead. "I'm not sure exactly. But quite a time. I think I once heard, since the middle of the nineteenth century."

"As long as that! And presumably they're not just a local group, if they still have these holiday homes."

"Quite." Thanet shifted restlessly, aware that beneath the apparently innocuous surface of this brief conversation there had been a growing undercurrent of unease. He noticed Lineham glance surreptitiously at his watch.

"Mike, are you thinking what I'm thinking?"

"It's twenty past ten," said Lineham flatly.

"And she left the Hodges' at about nine thirty-five."

"Three-quarters of an hour."

"For a twenty-minute walk."

They looked at each other.

"I don't believe it," said Thanet. "Not with two policemen sitting in her own front room, waiting for her."

"We're clucking like a pair of mother hens," agreed Lineham.

"Suffering, no doubt, from residual anxiety."

They rose in unison.

The brief rest did not appear to have done Pritchard any good. His pallid forehead glistened with sweat in the dim light and his eyes were fixed, staring. The bones of his knuckles shone white through the skin where he gripped the arms of the chair. When he saw Thanet and Lineham he moistened his lips with the tip of his tongue. "You said she was all right," he said, in a near-whisper. And then, with a

16

suddenness that made them both start, he erupted from the chair. "If she's all right," he bellowed, raising clenched fists, "where is she? You tell me that!"

It was an effort of will not to flinch from that archetypal figure of despairing wrath.

"We were about to ask you, Mr. Pritchard," Thanet said calmly, "if there was anywhere she might have stopped off, on the way home."

The reasonableness of the question and Thanet's matter-of-fact tone punctured Pritchard's fear and anger and he seemed to deflate back to normal size. He shook his head in bewilderment. "I don't know."

"Which way would she have come?"

Pritchard frowned, his eyes unfocused. He shook his head as if to clear it, put one hand up to his temple. "Let me see . . . She'd have turned right out of Mrs. Hodges', then left at the end of Lantern Street into Victoria Road. Then, if she had any sense, she'd have gone to the end of Victoria Road, turned left into St. Peter's Street and left again into Town Road."

Thus describing a wide semi-circle, Thanet thought. "You said, 'If she had any sense . . .'"

Pritchard swallowed, as if to control rising nausea. "Half way along Victoria Road there's a short cut. A footpath."

A footpath. The word conjured up darkness, a narrow, confined space where shadows lurked at every corner. At this juncture the very word had a dangerous ring to it.

"Where does it come out?"

"Just along the road from here, about fifty yards away. But surely she wouldn't have . . . Not at night . . . in the dark . . ." Fear had dried Pritchard's throat and tightened his vocal cords. His voice was little more than a gasp, a whisper.

Unless she'd been in a hurry, Thanet thought, anxious to get home quickly and minimise her father's anger and anxiety. Of course, the opposite could be true. She might have opted for delaying tactics. He repeated his earlier question.

"I suppose she could have called in at my brother's," said Pritchard, his voice stronger now. "He and his wife live in Gate Street. There's another footpath linking Gate Street and the short cut we were talking about. But I really can't see why she'd have gone there instead of coming straight home."

"What number in Gate Street, sir?" asked Lineham.

"Fourteen."

"And your brother's full name?"

"Jethro Pritchard."

Lineham took it down.

"Could you tell us what Charity looks like?" said Thanet.

"Looks like..." Pritchard repeated. Once again he shook his head as if to clear it, passed his hand across his eyes as if brushing cobwebs away. "She's... not very big. Comes up to here." He laid his hand on his chest. "She's got brown hair, light brown. Long. Wears it tied back. Brown eyes..." Pritchard's lips worked and his face threatened disintegration.

"All right, sir, that's enough, I think." It would have to do, Thanet thought. With Pritchard in his present state too much time would be wasted trying to obtain either a more detailed description or a photograph. And time might be of the essence. The beat of urgency was back in his brain now, surging through his veins and tingling down into his legs, his feet. He shifted restlessly. "Sergeant Lineham and I will just stroll along and... meet her. We shouldn't be..."

"I'm coming too," Pritchard interrupted. "I can't sit about here doing nothing a minute longer."

Thanet didn't like this idea one little bit. The man looked dangerously near to cracking up, and if anything had happened to Charity...

"Wouldn't it be better for you to wait here, in case she comes home while we're gone?"

"No! I'll leave the lights on and the front door ajar if you like, to show I won't be long."

Thanet looked at him and empathy raised its inconvenient head. How would he himself feel if Bridget were missing in circumstances like these? He would be frantic to be up and about doing something, anything, to find her.

"As you wish. Let's go, then, shall we?"

3

Outside it was now marginally cooler and the air, though still humid, smelt clean and fresh after the stale, almost foetid

18

atmosphere of number 32. The street was deserted. Lineham fetched torches from the car and they set off in the direction of the entrance to the footpath.

After a few moments Pritchard stopped. "Here it is."

A narrow slit, barely three feet wide, flanked on either side by the blank side walls of two blocks of terraced houses. Dim light from a street lamp illuminated the first few yards. After that, darkness.

Thanet had already made up his mind. He dared not risk Pritchard stumbling across Charity's body alone. One of them would have to stay with him.

"Sergeant, you go the long way round with Mr. Pritchard. I'll cut through the footpath and wait for you at the far end."

Thanet half-expected a protest from Pritchard, but there was none. Perhaps he was by now incapable of further rebellion. He moved off obediently beside Lineham and Thanet switched on his torch and plunged into the black, yawning mouth of the alley.

Once past the houses the darkness thinned a little. The footpath now seemed to run between back gardens, and the six foot high close-boarded fence on either side was punctuated by wooden doors and gateways beyond some of which loomed the bulk of garden sheds of varying shapes and sizes. Thanet's footsteps beat out an irregular tattoo as he paused to check each entrance. Some were padlocked, others were not and if there was access he opened the gate as quietly as possible and shone his torch inside. The detritus of years seemed to have washed down the gardens and come to rest here. Wheel-less, rusting bicycle frames vied for space with broken toys, rotting cardboard boxes, unrecognisable pieces of machinery, neglected tools and legless chairs. It was impossible to search thoroughly at present, he had neither time nor justification and he forced himself to keep moving on, dissatisfied.

And all the while there was growing in him a sick certainty of what he was going to find, the apprehension that this time he would have no opportunity privately to prepare himself for the one moment in his work as a detective that he dreaded more than any other, his first sight of a corpse. He had never fully managed to analyse that split second of unbearable poignancy, compounded as it was of regret, compassion, sorrow, anger, despair and a sense of having brushed, however briefly, against the mystery of life itself and he had never talked about it, even to Joan, from whom he had no other secrets. For years he had fought against this weakness, had despised himself because of it until he had eventually come to realise that to do so was pointless, that this was one battle he would never win. And so he had in the end become resigned, had even managed to persuade himself that that one moment of private hell was necessary to him, the springboard from which he could launch himself whole-heartedly into an attempt to track down the murderer.

If Charity was dead...if he were to find her...His stomach clenched and, praying that she had chosen to go the long way around and was even now safely in the company of Lineham and her father, he softly opened yet another door and played his torch over the mounds of junk, his fearful imagination at once transforming a broken mop into a battered head, a discarded rubber glove into a severed hand...

Enough, he told himself severely. You're letting this get out of hand. Determined to keep his thoughts firmly under control he shut the door, turned away and began to walk more briskly.

After only a few steps his foot made contact with something that went skittering away across the path and hit the opposite wall. He focused his torch, advanced upon it frowning and bent to examine it.

It was a hairbrush.

He did not touch it, but quickly flashed his torch around it in ever-widening arcs. The immediate vicinity was clear but as the light probed the tunnel of darkness ahead the beam picked out a scattering of lightish splotches some ten to fifteen yards away.

Slowly, carefully, he advanced, the certainty of what he was going to find churning his stomach.

And yes, there she was.

With one comprehensive sweep of his torch Thanet took in the whole scene: the gaping suitcase in the middle of the path, a jumble of clothes spilling out of one corner; more clothes, strewn haphazardly about and, the focal point of it all, the crumpled body of the girl, lying at the foot of a door in the left-hand wall of the alley.

Thanet hurried forward, noting with relief that her clothing seemed undisturbed. Perhaps she had at least been spared the terror of a sexual assault—could even still be alive. He squatted down beside her and shone the light on her face. The brief flare of hope was at once extinguished. That blank, frozen stare left no room for doubt and the jagged gash on her right temple looked lethal. But, to be certain, he checked. There was no whisper of breath, not even the faintest flutter of a pulse. This, he was sure, was Charity. He looked at the rounded, still childish contours of brow and cheek and closed his eyes as the familiar pain swept through him. For a few seconds he remained motionless, abandoning himself to the protesting clamour in his head in the way that a patient resigns himself to the screaming whine of the dentist's drill. Then, jerkily, he stood up.

Now she was a case for Doc Mallard.

The thought reminded him of Lineham and the girl's father, waiting for him at the end of the footpath, and at once he realised his predicament. He dared not leave the body and risk someone else stumbling upon her. But if he didn't, Lineham and Pritchard would most surely become impatient and return along the footpath to meet him. And to think of Pritchard seeing his daughter lying there like that . . .

If only some passer-by would come along the alley it might be possible to despatch him with a message to Lineham, but on this Bank Holiday evening everyone seemed to be immersed in his chosen form of entertainment. Thanet hadn't seen a soul since leaving Pritchard's house. He glanced at his watch. A quarter to eleven. The pubs would soon be out. It was vital to get the footpath sealed before then. So, what to do?

His dilemma was resolved by the sound of footsteps, approaching from the far end of the alleyway. He listened carefully: yes, two pairs. Lineham and Pritchard? If so, he must warn Mike in time . . .

He waited tensely until the bobbing disc of light that was probably Lineham's torch had become visible around a bend in the path some fifty yards ahead and then he called softly, "Mike?"

There was a low answering cry and the footsteps accelerated.

Thanet switched off his own torch, hoping that Lineham would take the hint.

"Mike?" he repeated urgently, advancing to meet them. "Wait. Stay there. Switch off your torch."

But it was too late.

Involuntarily, Lineham had flashed his torch ahead, briefly illuminating the body of the girl and with a hoarse cry Pritchard rushed forward, shoving Thanet aside. Thanet staggered and put out a hand to hold him back and Lineham reached out, but the man's frantic impetus had already carried him to where the girl lay and before they could stop him he had fallen to his knees and with a cry of anguish had gathered her up into his arms.

Lineham made as if to pull him away but Thanet restrained him. "Leave it, Mike. The damage is already done."

Both men were painfully aware that forensic evidence might well have been destroyed before their eyes.

"Sorry, sir," Lineham's voice was thick with guilt. "I should have thought . . . I shouldn't have flashed that bloody torch."

Pritchard was weeping now, harsh, strangled gasps, his arms wrapped tightly around Charity's body.

Thanet turned to Lineham. "Go back to the car, get things organised as fast as you can. Stress the urgency, the pubs'll be out in a matter of minutes. I'll wait here, with him."

Lineham nodded and was gone, his receding footsteps soon no more than a hollow, echoing blur.

Pritchard slowly quietened down, the storm of tears gradually diminishing to irregular, sobbing breaths at ever-lengthening intervals.

Lineham was soon back.

"Everything's laid on, sir," he whispered.

"Doc Mallard?"

"Available."

"Good. I'd like you to get Pritchard away now, then. Fast. Stay with him till I come." Thanet knew that it would be only a matter of minutes before the first reinforcements arrived. He stepped forward, laid a gentle hand on Pritchard's shoulder.

The man stiffened, turned his head to look up.

"I'm sorry, Mr. Pritchard. Deeply sorry. But you must leave her, now."

Pritchard gave his daughter one last, lingering look, then laid her gently down and stood up, staggering a little. Thanet steadied him with a hand under one elbow.

"Sergeant Lineham will take you home."

Pritchard turned away without a word.

Thanet waited until they were out of sight, then flashed his

22

torch once more over the girl's body. Her sightless stare seemed to him a mute reproach, a silent protest against a life cut short.

He promised himself that the moment the photographers had finished with her he would close her eyes.

4

The bald patch on top of Doc Mallard's head gleamed in the light from the arc lamps as he knelt to examine Charity's body.

It was half past eleven and the secrets of this section of the alley were now laid bare, the harsh, merciless light probing into every crack and crevice. The last three-quarters of an hour had been packed with furious activity: the footpath had been sealed and a team of men despatched to inform the householders whose gardens backed on to it that it was temporarily out of bounds; photographs, sketches and preliminary searches had been made; Charity's pathetic belongings gathered up and borne away and various samples assembled in polythene bags by the Scenes-of-Crime Officer.

Now it was the turn of the police surgeon.

Thanet was leaning against the fence, patiently awaiting Mallard's verdict and jealously guarding a potentially vital piece of evidence. He knew better than to ask importunate questions. Ever since, some years ago, Mallard had lost his adored wife, he seemed to have lived in a state of imperfectly suppressed irritation. Thanet, who was fond of the older man and had known him since childhood, sympathised with Mallard's inability to come to terms with his grief and was tolerant of his testiness.

"Poor little beast," murmured Mallard at last, sitting back on his heels.

Thanet waited.

"Well," said the little doctor, heaving himself to his feet and dusting himself down, "for what it's worth, and with the usual reservations, of course, I'd say she's been dead for between one and two hours.''

"That fits. In fact, we can narrow it down further. She was last seen alive at about 9:35 and I found her at 10:40.''

Mallard looked gratified. "Hah! Thought you'd catch me out, did you?''

"Didn't work, though, did it?''

They grinned at each other.

"You found her yourself, you say?''

Thanet grimaced. "Yes.'' He told Mallard how this had come about. "Can you commit yourself as to the cause of death?''

Mallard frowned at Thanet over his half-moon spectacles. "You know I don't like committing myself at this stage.''

"We both know that,'' said Thanet equably, mentally castigating himself for his careless choice of words. "All the same, I'd appreciate . . .''

"A signed statement, no less!'' Mallard relented. "Oh, all right then, if I must. You've probably worked it out for yourself anyway. I'd say it was that blow to the right temple. I'd look for something fairly sharp and jagged, possibly metal.''

"This, for example?'' Thanet pointed to his bit of potential evidence, the rusted iron latch of the door at the foot of which Charity was lying. The projecting piece of metal which must be lifted to release such latches had been partially broken off and its jagged point glistened.

Mallard peered at it. "Highly probable, I should think. Right height, too, I should say.''

"That's what I thought.'' Thanet saw it all in his mind's eye: Charity walking along the dark footpath, suitcase in hand, the menacing figure of her assailant (lying in wait for her? Walking towards her? Running after her? Or even most hideous of all, accompanying her, in the guise of a friend?). He attacks her, Charity swings the suitcase at him but it bursts open, leaving her completely vulnerable; during the course of the ensuing struggle she is hurled against the door, striking her head against that wicked-looking metal spike . . . Thanet sighed. The Super wasn't easily going to forgive him for allowing Pritchard to interfere with the forensic evidence.

"What did you say the father's name was?''

"Pritchard.''

24

"Pritchard," repeated Mallard thoughtfully. "Pritchard, Pritchard. Rings a bell. Can't think why, though."

Thanet waited, but Mallard shook his head with finality. "It's no good, I can't remember. Perhaps it'll come back to me. Anyway, her pants and sanitary towel—she was menstruating—seem undisturbed, and there's no sign of violence, so it doesn't look as though she was raped. Might be some comfort to the parents, I suppose. She was fifteen, you said?"

"Yes."

"I'm surprised. I'd have said she was younger, even though she was physically mature. They'll be reaching puberty before they're out of their cradles soon, the way things are going."

"She does look younger," said Thanet thoughtfully. "I wonder what it is . . ."

Death, perhaps, he thought grimly, but no, it was more than that. The way she had done her hair, then, scraped back into a thick pigtail?

No, it was her clothes, of course. He didn't know much about young girls' fashions but Bridget had become very clothes-conscious of late and he now realised that Charity's clothes were dowdy in the extreme, strongly reminiscent of school uniform: dark skirt, plain white blouse buttoned up to the neck, plain dark cardigan, white ankle socks and Clarks' traditional-style school sandals. All in all, very odd clothing for a fifteen-year-old to be wearing on holiday these days, when cheap and pretty clothes are the rule rather than the exception. No doubt it was the religious influence. And from what he'd seen of the Pritchard household he would guess that there would be little sympathy for a desire to buy anything frivolous.

Once again he wondered what she had been like, this young girl whose future was now reduced to a dissecting table. Had she been content, satisfied to live within the limitations imposed upon her by her parents' religion? Or had she yearned for laughter, joy and beauty?

Thanet clenched his teeth. However much or however little potential Charity had possessed, she had had a right to live to fulfil it. As he stood looking down at her he could feel the determination stiffening the sinews of his body, filling him with a sense of purpose and an urgency that made him itch

25

now to be gone, to get on with his work, take the first steps towards bringing her killer to justice.

Doc Mallard picked up his bag. "I'll be getting along, then."

"I'll come with you." Thanet turned and nodded to the men who had been patiently waiting for Doc Mallard to finish. "You can take her away now."

As he and Mallard approached the canvas screen which had been erected across the entrance to the footpath Thanet heard a familiar sound, the hum of an expectant crowd.

"The ghouls are out in force, by the sound of it," murmured Mallard.

Thanet scowled, grunted agreement.

The noise increased as he and the doctor came into view. The crowd was enjoying this unexpected Bank Holiday late-night entertainment. The uniformed branch had done their best, stretching tapes across the road to right and left, carefully ensuring that the Pritchards' house was included in the empty section of the street, but even so Town Road was a very different place from the quiet thoroughfare Thanet had left a couple of hours previously.

Supressing a familiar anger at the public's relish of a tragedy, Thanet escorted Doc Mallard to his car, told the ambulance driver to back right up to the footpath entrance, then dealt briefly but courteously with the reporter from the *Kent Messenger* who had been awaiting his appearance, thankful that it was as yet too early for the national press to have arrived on the scene. His relationship with the media was good and he never made the mistake of under-estimating the value of the help they could give him or of the damage they could do if the police were deliberately obstructive, even though the thought of achieving personal publicity through another human being's violent end had always nauseated him.

Then he made his way swiftly to number 32.

Lineham came along the ill-lit passage to meet him as the uniformed constable on duty at the front door let him in.

"How is he?"

Lineham pulled a face. "Pretty distraught, I'd say. But I'm only guessing. He hasn't said much."

"Doctor been?"

"Refuses to have one. Against his principles, apparently."

Briefly, Thanet regretted having let Mallard go, but realised at once that it would have been pointless to detain him. There

26

was a deep stubbornness in Pritchard, an inflexibility which, even in these circumstances, would prevent him from abandoning his principles.

"Have you found someone to stay with him tonight?"

"I suggested his brother, but he said no, he didn't want anyone. He was going to spend the night in the company of the Lord. Anyone else would be superfluous."

"I presume you mean, in prayer."

"That's right. I told him we'd arrange for someone to break the news to Mrs. Pritchard."

Thanet nodded. An unenviable task, but it had to be done. "Where is he now?"

"In the kitchen."

Thanet peeped in. Pritchard was kneeling on the stone floor, elbows resting on the seat of the armchair, head in hands. He did not stir. Thanet withdrew.

"How long has he been like that?"

Lineham shrugged. "An hour or more, I'd say."

"You've done a search?"

"Yes. The only thing that looks even remotely promising is a diary. It's in Charity's school satchel, in her bedroom. I left it there, I thought you'd probably want to take a look around yourself."

"Right. I'll do that now."

Upstairs there were only two bedrooms and Charity's was the smaller, at the back. Here was the same drabness, the same total lack of interest in physical surroundings as downstairs. The walls were bare and so were the floorboards, save for a postage stamp of a bedside rug. The bed looked supremely uncomfortable and the door of the wardrobe would not stay closed without a small wad of paper to hold it in position. Thanet peered inside. Here hung Charity's school raincoat and blazer, both carefully buttoned up to hold their shape. It was the distinctive navy and yellow striped blazer of Sturrenden Girls' Technical School, Thanet noted. There were two or three skirts in sober colours, a couple of drab floral dresses and three pairs of shoes: black walking shoes, plimsolls, a pair of stout brown brogues. Two long drawers beneath the hanging space revealed underclothes, handkerchiefs, carefully folded blouses and sweaters, all utilitarian in the extreme.

There was no bedside table—reading in bed would perhaps

27

be considered self-indulgent?—and the only signs of human occupation were the school satchel Lineham had mentioned hanging on a hook behind the door and, near the window, a small wooden table piled with books. Thanet glanced through these: school textbooks, with only one exception, a black, leather-bound copy of the Bible. On the flyleaf was written *To Charity, on her tenth birthday, from her loving parents. Prov. 3:5-6.* Thanet flicked through the text, found the place: *Trust in the Lord with all thine heart; and lean not unto thine own understanding. In all thy ways acknowledge him, and he shall direct thy paths.*

Thanet winced.

The diary, it seemed, was his only hope and he plucked it out of the satchel with eager fingers, turned to the Spring Bank Holiday weekend. In Friday's space Charity had written, V. 9:50. The remainder of the weekend was blank. Thanet frowned. Strange that she hadn't noted the visit to Dorset.

He quickly leafed through the first half of the diary, to date. There were two regular entries each week, one on Tuesdays, one on Fridays. He opened the book at random to the third week in February and held it up to the dim central light in an attempt to decipher the pencilled scrawl. Tuesday's entry read: *Close next big hurdle, Gr. 7. Mr. M "great strides."* A music lesson, Thanet wondered, remembering the music on the piano downstairs. Friday's entry read: *Grp. v. int. tonight!* A religious group, he'd be willing to bet. Bible study, perhaps? But the exclamation mark surprised him.

So these had been the highlights of her life.

Sad, and not very promising from Thanet's point of view. They did however prove that Charity had had some outside interests and contacts, apart from school, and that her father's claim that she had no friends other than Veronica might have been exaggerated. Thanet put the diary in his pocket. He would study it at leisure later.

Meanwhile he would have to see if Pritchard were fit to be questioned.

Thanet always hated this business of interrogating people still raw with shock and grief, but it was necessary, indeed essential, to gather together as much personal information as possible about the victim, early in the case.

This house was the still centre of the hurricane of furious activity now raging in connection with Charity's death. This was where she had lived and it was here that her character had been formed. Perhaps it was her very innocence, her ignorance of the sophistications of the modern world that had left her unprepared to cope with one of its evil manifestations when it had come upon her.

In any case, it was Thanet's responsibility and his special skill to try to understand how this had come about, his firm conviction that except in cases of random violence (and this was a possibility he always bore in mind), if he could only come to understand *why* it had happened, the *who* would eventually become apparent.

And for that he would need Pritchard's help.

He checked that there was nothing hidden under the mattress and, remembering one of his earlier cases, that there was no trapdoor in the ceiling, and then took one last, lingering look around the room. As he gazed at Charity's monastic little cell there came unbidden to his mind a brief, vivid image of Bridget's room, of the bulging bookcases, overflowing cupboards, the pretty curtains, fitted carpet and walls crammed with posters, the whole rich, disorganised clutter which fed her imagination and catered to the needs of her expanding mind and personality. Raised in this bleak atmosphere, restricted and hedged about as she surely must have been with a father like Pritchard, what had happened to those hidden aspects of Charity's character? Had they shrivelled up and died? Or, starved of external stimulation, deprived of emotional satisfaction, had they turned in upon themselves, become warped and twisted and in some way led finally to Charity's death in that alley?

He was being fanciful, Thanet told himself as he closed the door softly behind him. She had probably, quite simply, channelled them into her music.

Well, time would tell.

5

When Thanet came down to breakfast next morning there was a note on the kitchen table: *Joan rang. Ask.*

He sat down, gingerly, for his back had stiffened up overnight, and waved the piece of paper at his mother-in-law, who was making toast.

"What time did she ring?"

"Ten fifteen. I told her you probably wouldn't be back till late."

Thanet frowned. Lately, he and Joan always seemed to miss each other when they phoned and he felt as though he hadn't spoken to her properly in months.

"How did she sound?"

"A bit tired, I thought. Abstracted."

Thanet knew what Mrs. Bolton meant, and he didn't like it. Theoretically there was no reason why Joan should not be relatively free now. She had finished her final placement—in a boys' borstal—some time ago, had handed in her final essay three weeks before. So, why was she so elusive? It would be a relief to have her home again where he could see her, talk to her, touch her, reassure himself of her affection. He'd even begun to wonder, of late, if the distance between them was not merely geographical, if Joan was slipping away from him. Once again he supressed the unbearable thought that she might even have met someone on the course who was proving more interesting to her than a husband whose attraction had been eroded by familiarity. The name of Geoffrey Benson, for instance, was cropping up far too often for Thanet's liking.

"Did she say when she'd ring again?"

"She said that if you were just launching into a new case, it might be easier if you rang her. She hopes to be in all evening."

"Good." Thanet sipped at his scalding coffee, hoping that it would clear his head a little. It had been after three this morning by the time he'd finally got to bed.

Bridget came skipping into the kitchen, cheeks flushed and eyes shining. She flipped his tie. "I thought you had one more day off, Daddy."

He kissed her back. "So did I, Sprig, but unfortunately it hasn't worked out like that. How's my girl, this morning?"

"Fine, thanks."

Already, at the age of ten, Bridget was springing up. It was another hot day and in her brief shorts her tanned legs were long and shapely. Thanet looked with a mixture of pride and alarm at the smooth oval of her face, the gleaming fall of

30

spun-gold hair; the policeman in him couldn't help feeling that these days beauty could be a mixed blessing.

"Does that mean we'll all have to go home today?" she asked with a frown.

"Do you want to?" he teased.

"Oh *no*. It's lovely here, isn't it, Ben? There's such lots to do."

Ben, two years younger, had just hurtled into the kitchen and skidded to a stop beside his father. Already, at seven thirty in the morning, his face was streaked with dirt, his jeans smeared with mud.

"Ben!" His grandmother was outraged. "What on earth have you been doing with yourself? Go and wash at *once*, do you hear me?"

Ben glanced sideways at his father who, unseen by Mrs. Bolton, gave him a consoling pat on the back before nodding. Ben departed, scowling, followed by Bridget. Inwardly, Thanet sympathised with his son. He and Joan had never made a fuss about dirt. Why bother, when it was so easily washed away? Rudeness, destructiveness, bad manners were different. Here, the Thanets had always been firm; spoiled children, they believed, grew up into unlikeable adults.

Mrs. Bolton, on the other hand, believed that children should look clean and neat at all times and it was not surprising that Bridget and Ben—particularly Ben—had found it very difficult to adjust to such different expectations.

"But it's only clean dirt, Grandma." Ben used to protest at first.

"Don't be silly, Ben. How can dirt be clean? I never heard such nonsense. Now, go and wash, at once."

Thanet, torn between sympathy for Ben and gratitude to his mother-in-law for stepping into Joan's shoes, had forced himself not to intervene. When Ben had complained he'd simply tried to explain that older people find it difficult to change and that as these arrangements were only temporary Ben would just have to grin and bear it.

Over the last few months there seemed to have been an increasing number of such minor conflicts. Patience was wearing thin on both sides as the time of Joan's return grew near.

Thanet finished his coffee and rose. "Don't keep supper for me, I expect I'll be late."

Bridget came back into the kitchen. "I've opened the front gate for you, Daddy."

"Thanks, poppet." He kissed her goodbye. "Where's Ben?"

"In the garden."

Outside Ben was wobbling away down the sloping drive on Mrs. Bolton's ancient sit-up-and-beg bicycle, which was of course much too big for him.

Thanet took in Ben's lack of control, the open gate ahead. Simultaneously he became aware of an ominous sound: out on the road, invisible because of the dense screen of trees and shrubs which fronted the cottage garden, a tractor was approaching.

The next few seconds were a blur. Thanet's shouted warning, Ben's futile attempt to stop, the flash of red as the tractor came into view, the heartstopping moment when the off-side wheel of the tractor slammed into the back wheel of the bicycle and Ben was catapulted over the handlebars . . .

Thanet pounded down the drive, fear drying his mouth and thundering in his ears. Ben's crumpled body seemed infinitely far away, as if he were looking at it through the wrong end of a telescope. Then, as he drew nearer, he saw with frantic hope that Ben had landed on the grass verge at the far side of the road.

Just before Thanet reached him, Ben rolled over and stood up.

He was all right.

By that mysterious alchemy peculiar to parents Thanet's anxiety and relief exploded into anger and before he could stop himself he had given Ben a resounding whack on the bottom.

"How many times have I told you *never* to ride down that drive when the gate is open!"

"He came right out under my wheels," said the tractor driver defensively, raising his voice to make himself heard above Ben's howls.

"I know. I saw. It wasn't your fault."

Bridget and Mrs. Bolton came running down the drive.

"What happened? Is Ben all right?"

Explanations and recriminations were soon over. Ben was sent to his room for an hour as punishment and before long

Thanet was on his way, shaken but thankful. When he thought how it could have ended . . .

In the office, mounds of reports awaited him. Lineham was already hard at work, sifting through them.

"Anything interesting?"

"Not so far. Reports from neighbours verify Pritchard's story. The house was deserted from the time they all left on Friday morning until Pritchard arrived back last night. They're not very popular, it seems."

"Actively disliked?"

"Pritchard is. No, I suppose that's not strictly true. Perhaps 'not liked' would be nearer the mark."

"And Mrs. Pritchard and Charity?"

"Neither has any friends amongst the neighbours. They keep themselves to themselves, don't mix, never take part in local activities. Apparently this is normal, amongst members of their sect."

"Mmm." Thanet was busy lighting his first pipe of the day and he waited now until it was drawing properly before saying, "Well, we'll skim through the rest of these and then get along to Town Road. Let's hope Pritchard is feeling more co-operative this morning."

Last night it had been impossible to get anything out of the man. In any case, Pritchard had so obviously been in a state of shock that Thanet had been unwilling to press too hard. Adamant in his refusal to see a doctor or to have anyone to keep him company through the night, Pritchard had clung stubbornly to his sole source of comfort. When they left he was still kneeling on the stone floor of the kitchen.

Thanet wondered if he was still there.

"Any news of Mrs. Pritchard, Mike?"

"A Sergeant Matthews rang this morning, from Birmingham. Someone went to break the news to her last night. If she was up to it, she was going to travel down early this morning."

"If. I shouldn't think we could count on it. Imagine what it must be like to lose both mother and daughter on the same day! Is someone coming with her?"

"I don't know. Of course, they're all tied up, up there, with the admin. to do with the death of the old lady."

The death round, thought Thanet, that infinitely depressing ordeal of the newly bereaved: death certificate, registry office,

33

undertaker. He couldn't see that Mrs. Pritchard would be in much of a state to be questioned this morning.

Surprisingly, he was wrong. It was she who answered the door and although her face was puffy and her eyes inflamed with weeping, she was composed.

"Come in, Inspector."

She was small and slight, her bony features and prominent nose accentuated by the way she wore her light brown hair, dragged back into a neat bun on the nape of her neck. She was wearing a shabby black dress and Thanet smelt mothballs as he and Lineham followed her down the passage and into the front room. The skimpy beige curtains were drawn and in the dim light filtering through them the room looked more depressing than ever.

"I'll fetch my husband."

Perhaps her presence had had a calming effect upon Pritchard. Although there were traces of fluff adhering to his neck where he had cut himself shaving, he appeared to be more in control of himself this morning. He looked unfamiliar in grey flannel trousers and a knitted cardigan.

Mrs. Pritchard glanced nervously from Thanet to her husband. It was obvious from their faces they were both apprehensive of what he was going to say. Perhaps they thought that he was bringing them news of their daughter's murderer. Thanet only wished he were. He decided to take the initiative.

"Perhaps we could sit down?"

The Pritchards backed away and perched side by side on the edge of the settee. Thanet and Lineham took the armchairs.

"Look, Mrs. Pritchard, Mr. Pritchard, I'm sorry to trouble you both at a time like this. I really mean that. But I'm afraid we're going to need your help."

They exchanged a brief, uneasy glance and Pritchard frowned. "What sort of help?"

"I need information—about your daughter's friends, associates, activities—"

"Activities?" Pritchard's voice was dull, lifeless.

"Meetings, hobbies, clubs . . ."

"Clubs?"

Mrs. Pritchard shifted restlessly on the settee. Since her husband had joined them she hadn't spoken a single word.

"Mrs. Pritchard?" said Thanet.

She glanced at her husband as if for permission to speak. But he did not look at her and she sighed, bowed her head.

"You were about to say something?" Thanet persisted.

"Leave my wife alone, Inspector." Pritchard's voice was heavy with despair. "She knows no more than I do. Hasn't she suffered enough?"

"Mr. Pritchard," said Thanet gently, "I know that she is suffering, that you are both suffering, but don't you see that if Charity's... if the person who is responsible for Charity's death is to be found, I really do need your help."

"What's the point? It won't bring her back. Nothing will bring her back..." Pritchard's eyes filled suddenly with tears and he dashed them angrily away, jumped up and crossed to stand with his back to them at the curtained window.

Thanet was filled with compassion. But pity, emotional involvement, were luxuries he could not afford. He needed this man's co-operation, had to have it if he was to get anywhere. He gave Pritchard a moment or two to recover and then said harshly, "Are you suggesting, then, that we should do nothing? Allow this man to go free? Perhaps to kill someone else's daughter?"

Mrs. Pritchard gave an inarticulate little moan of distress and pressed the knuckles of one hand hard against her mouth as if to prevent any more sounds escaping, and Pritchard swung around to face them. Thanet's severity had had the desired effect and jolted him out of his state of inertia. The black eyes were glittering with anger as he returned to the settee and put a protective arm around his wife's shoulders.

"What sort of a man are you?" he said in a low, furious voice. "Can't you see—?"

"No, Nathaniel." Mrs. Pritchard suddenly straightened her shoulders and sat up, laid a placatory hand on her husband's sleeve. "The Inspector's right, don't you see? We must help him. It would be dreadful if... I couldn't bear it if... It's our *duty* to do all we can to make sure this man is caught."

His wife's unexpected revolt had obviously taken Pritchard by surprise. His eyes widened and his mouth dropped open slightly. For a long moment he stared at her, searchingly. Then, slowly, he nodded. "Very well. I suppose you're right."

With Pritchard's capitulation the tension in the room slackened and Thanet heaved an inward sigh of relief. "Thank you. I'll try to be brief."

35

As Thanet had already noted, Charity had been a pupil at Sturrenden Girls' Technical School. Her parents had never received any complaints about either work or behaviour and her end of term reports had always been satisfactory. The one subject in which she excelled had been music.

"She passed all her grades with distinction," Mrs. Pritchard put in shyly. It was the first time she had volunteered any information.

"That's her music on the piano?" Thanet rose and crossed to glance at it, sensing that Mrs. Pritchard might respond to an interest shown in Charity's special gift.

"Yes. She was going to take her Grade Seven at the end of this term." Mrs. Pritchard's mouth began to go out of control and she bit her lower lip, hard.

"God gave her a great talent, Inspector," said Pritchard. "And she used it in His service. She used to play the organ for us at Sunday Service."

"Which day was her music lesson, Mrs. Pritchard?"

"On Tuesdays, after school."

So he had been right about the Tuesday entries in the diary. Small consolation, really, for the diary had yielded nothing else of interest. He had spent some time examining it last night, to no avail. "And was that the only day of the week she used to stay behind after school?"

"Yes."

"And she travelled?"

"By bicycle."

"With anyone?"

They both shook their heads. "No one else from around here goes to the Girls' Tech," said Pritchard.

"Could you tell me a little about out-of-school hours? What did Charity do in her spare time?"

Pritchard frowned. "She didn't have any 'spare time,' as you put it. The Devil always finds work for idle hands, Inspector, and Charity was brought up to use her time properly."

"Could you tell me what you mean by 'properly'? What did she do in the evenings, for example?"

"Do her homework. Help her mother in the house. Practise the piano."

"She always practised for at least an hour, every day, Inspector, sometimes more," put in Mrs. Pritchard.

36

"And she never went out in the evenings?"

"Only to Bible class on Fridays," said Pritchard.

"And where was that held?"

"At our meeting house, in Jubilee Road."

"Did she go alone?"

"In summer, yes. In winter I used to take her. And my brother, her uncle, used to walk home with her."

"He is a member of your sect?"

"Of course. My family has always belonged, as far back as we can remember."

"Does he work locally?"

"He's caretaker at Holly Road Primary School."

"And he attends this Bible class, presumably?"

"He is the leader. The group is for our younger members. It is essential these days to ensure that young people receive the correct spiritual food. There is so much evil in the world, so much temptation . . ."

Pritchard was getting that fanatical light in his eyes again. Quickly, Thanet interrupted him. "And Saturdays? What did she do on Saturdays?"

Pritchard gave a brief, angry parody of a laugh. "Well may you ask. She usually spent it with that girl."

"Veronica?"

"Yes. And look where it got her!"

"What do you mean?"

"It's obvious, surely. If she hadn't been friendly with that girl she wouldn't have been going to Dorset, she would have been safe with us in Birmingham, and none of this would ever have happened."

"You can't blame Veronica, though, Nathaniel," said Mrs. Pritchard timidly. "What happened to Charity . . . Veronica had nothing to do with that."

"Nothing to do with it! Nothing to do with it!" His solicitude for his wife apparently forgotten, Pritchard had turned on her with eyes blazing. "How can you possibly say that? How can you be so *blind*. I told you, didn't I? I warned you. I said that girl would be a bad influence on Charity and I was right!"

"What do you mean, bad influence?" said Thanet.

"In every way! You've only got to look at the girl to see what I mean, with her painted face and skirts halfway up her thighs. Disgusting, that's what she is, disgusting!"

37

"Are you suggesting, then that she..." Thanet didn't know how to put it tactfully. There *was* no way of putting it tactfully. "...that she contaminated Charity?"

Pritchard's face seemed to swell and a tide of bright colour ran up his neck and into his cheeks. "How dare you! How dare you come into my home at a time like this and make insinuations about my daughter! What right have you got, to..."

"I made no insinuations, Mr. Pritchard. You said that Veronica had had a bad influence on Charity, I was merely trying to clarify what you meant."

"You implied..."

"I implied nothing. I repeat, I was simply seeking to clarify what you were saying, that's all. Now look, Mr. Pritchard, all I'm trying to do is understand what Charity was like. You, as her parents, are best qualified to help me. I know that this must be very hard for you, but please, try to understand that I have no interest in drawing false conclusions. I merely want the truth."

"You were twisting my words. You were implying..."

"I repeat, I was implying—*am* implying—nothing. Simply asking for information."

But it was no good. Pritchard would not be pacified and, cursing himself for his tactless choice of words and, perhaps, for insensitivity for broaching such a predictably sensitive area so soon, Thanet decided to give up for the moment.

Mrs. Pritchard accompanied them to the door.

"Inspector," she whispered as she let them out, glancing back over her shoulder at the sitting room door. "If I can help, in any way..." Her eyes filled with tears. "You will ask, won't you?"

"Of course." Thanet touched her shoulder and smiled encouragement at her. "I promise."

She hesitated and Thanet sensed her reluctance to return to her husband. And who could blame her? he thought as he turned away. And yet...it took collusion, to establish that kind of relationship. Pritchard's domination could not have been achieved without aquiescence on the part of his wife. Did she enjoy playing the submissive role, Thanet wondered, or had she, over the years, adopted it for the sake of peace?

"Difficult customer," said Lineham.

"Pritchard? They don't come much more prickly, that's for sure. And I had to put my foot in it, of course."

"Bound to happen sooner or later, with someone like him. Anyway, it was obvious we weren't going to get anywhere. I shouldn't have thought they've have had much more to tell us."

"You may be right." Thanet paused to extract pipe and matches from his pocket.

"So, what now, sir?"

"Time for you to improve your mind, I think. Do a bit of research." Thanet grinned as he saw Lineham's expression. "Come on, Mike, you know you quite enjoy ferreting for facts, once you get down to it."

"So what do I have to do?"

"Go down to the library, see if you can dig anything up on the Children of Jerusalem. They've been around quite a long time, as I told you, so you should be able to glean something."

"And you, sir?"

"A word with Pritchard's brother, I think. Then with Veronica. I'll see you in the Hay Wain, around one, and we'll swop notes. You can take the car, I won't need it."

"Right, sir."

Thanet watched him drive off, then allowed himself an indulgent smile. Naturally Lineham would have preferred to accompany him; interviews were much more interesting than dusty archives. Nevertheless, he had a feeling that this particular piece of research could be important. Lineham would have to put up with the disappointment as best he could.

Thanet turned and walked briskly up the street towards the entrance to the footpath. A quick check, first, on whether a daylight search had turned up anything interesting, then he'd visit Jethro Pritchard.

He was rather looking forward to that.

6

The search was still going on, but as yet nothing of interest had turned up. Thanet stopped for a word here and there and then walked on, past the spot where Charity's body had lain. According to Pritchard there was a footpath which linked Gate Street, where his brother lived, with this one. He found the entrance to it on the right about a hundred yards further on, just beyond the bend around which Lineham and Pritchard had come into view last night. It ran between the side walls of two blocks of gardens and was only about seventy-five yards long. If he had come this way, Charity's assailant could have been well away in a matter of minutes.

The front door of number 14 was flung open with such force that it rebounded from the wall. Square in the opening stood a formidable woman; legs planted apart and arms akimbo she reminded Thanet of a picture of the Genie from Aladdin's lamp in one of Bridget's books of fairytales.

Her expression, however, was anything but benevolent.

"Mrs. Pritchard?"

"We are sick and tired of being pestered like this. Persecution, that's what it is, persecution."

"My name is . . ."

"Whatever you've got to say, I don't want to hear it. Go away, or we'll call the police."

Thanet fished in his pocket.

She was still in full flood. "I meant what I said. Scavengers, that's what you are, scavengers. We haven't had a minute's peace since daybreak. And there's no point in waving that thing in my face. Press cards don't cut no ice with me. I said, if you don't go away I'll call the . . ."

"POLICE," said Thanet, holding his warrant card up in front of her nose. And then, more quietly, "I *am* the police."

She snatched the card from him, held it away to peer at it long-sightedly, then sniffed, her mouth twitching sideways.

"Why didn't you say so?" She held the card up, comparing photograph and original. "Why aren't you wearing uniform, then?"

For a moment Thanet could not believe that she was serious. Was it possible that anyone these days could be unaware of the existence of plain-clothes policemen? But of course, the Jethro Pritchards were also of the Children. Perhaps, if one never watched television or even, for all he knew, read a newspaper or listened to the radio, it was just conceivable . . .

"I'm from the CID—the Criminal Investigation Department. We all wear plain clothes."

She pushed his warrant card at him and reluctantly stepped back.

"I suppose you'd better come in."

She lingered to scowl up and down the street before closing the door behind them.

"In here." She opened the door of the front room.

Here was the same drabness, the same musty, unused odour that had characterised the sitting room of the house in Town Road. Thanet was surprised to see that there were two people in it, a middle-aged man and an old woman, and that despite the heat of the day there was a small fire burning in the hearth; in his experience such rooms were kept exclusively for occasional visitors.

The man had risen.

"My husband," said Mrs. Pritchard ungraciously. "And my mother-in-law."

Then Thanet understood. The three of them were wearing black. This was the official face of mourning.

What had they been doing before he arrived? he wondered. Presumably, at such a time it was considered unseemly to go about one's daily business as if nothing had happened. Yet there was no reading matter lying about, no radio, no sewing or knitting . . . And looking at this ill-assorted trio he simply couldn't visualise them engaged in amiable conversation.

Jethro Pritchard was a small, stooping, sepia version of his brother. They shared the same bony facial structure, but Jethro's hair was brown and thinning, carefully combed in separated strands across his baldness, his manner timid and placatory. After shaking his clammy hand Thanet had consciously to restrain himself from wiping his palm on his trouser legs.

The old lady was sitting close to the fire, her legs swathed in a rug, her shoulders draped in a black, knitted shawl. She did not acknowledge Thanet's greeting, but simply went on gazing at him with faded, rheumy eyes in which there was no flicker of acknowledgement or response.

"You'd better sit down, I suppose." But Mrs. Pritchard remained standing, arms folded. This interview, her posture indicated, was going to be very brief.

Thanet had no intention of being browbeaten and he sat back as comfortably as possible in his armchair's inhospitable embrace and prepared for battle. An imp of mischief urged him to take out his pipe and relight it, but he resisted temptation. No point in arousing unnecessary antagonism, there was enough here already.

But why? That was the interesting question.

Mrs. Pritchard was still glowering at him. "I can't think why you need to bother us again anyway. We've been through it all once already."

"Were you fond of your niece, Mrs. Pritchard?"

The unexpectedness of the question caught her off-balance. She hesitated and, before she could suppress it, some fierce emotion glittered in her eyes. She blinked and it was gone.

"Well . . . of course."

But her initial response had betrayed her. She had disliked Charity, had felt positive hostility towards her. Now why was that? Thanet wondered.

"Then you will naturally wish to co-operate with the police to the fullest possible extent," he said blandly.

She stared at him for a moment longer, then crossed to sit beside her husband. "We're all very upset this morning."

Thanet recognised self-justification when he heard it. Still, he pretended to take it at face value.

"Understandably," he said.

Jethro Pritchard made a small, choking sound in his throat. His hands were tightly clasped in his lap, his lips clamped together as if he were afraid of what would emerge if he opened them. A thick, worm-like vein across his temple pulsated in a rapid, regular rhythm. He caught Thanet's eye.

"She was like a daughter to us," he said.

Old Mrs. Pritchard suddenly stirred. "Jethro, what's that man doing here?" Her voice was shrill, querulous.

Jethro looked at his wife as if for guidance and licked his lips. "He's from the police, mother. Charity's had an . . . accident."

The old woman stared at her son without comprehension.

"You remember Charity, mother? Nathaniel's girl?"

"I don't like it in here," she said. "I want to go back in the kitchen."

Jethro glanced at his wife, who nodded.

"I want to go back in the kitchen," repeated old Mrs. Pritchard. "I don't like it in here."

42

"Would you mind, Inspector?" said Jethro, half-rising. "I'm afraid once she gets an idea in her head . . ."

"Carry on, by all means."

"Come along then, Mother. I'll take you back. Up we come . . ."

It took several minutes for Jethro to lever his mother out of her chair, manoeuvre her out of the room and get her settled in the kitchen, all the while keeping up a flow of solicitous encouragement.

"All right then, Mother?" Thanet finally heard him say, and a moment later he returned. It was at once apparent that the old lady's dependence had somehow given him strength. He was moving briskly and his facial muscles had relaxed.

Damn, thought Thanet.

"We are particularly interested in tracing Charity's movements last night and over the weekend," he said, when Jethro was settled again.

"Over the weekend?" Mrs. Pritchard's eyes stretched wide. "But we know where she was over the weekend."

"Oh? Where?"

"In Dorset. With that Veronica Hodges. At one of the Jerusalem Holiday Homes."

"But that's the point, Mrs. Pritchard. She wasn't."

Pritchard and his wife exchanged a puzzled glance.

"Veronica was ill, and couldn't go to Dorset. Therefore Charity couldn't go, either. Because of the rule about young girls not travelling alone."

"Quite right, too," put in Jethro. "But doesn't Veronica know where Charity was over the weekend?"

"Apparently not."

"Perhaps she was at home?"

"She wasn't."

They both were silent, staring at him with identical expressions of blank incomprehension.

"She must have stayed with a friend," said Mrs. Pritchard.

"Do you happen to know the names of any of her friends?" They shook their heads.

Thanet looked at Jethro. "What about the Bible class?"

"What do you mean?"

For a moment Thanet could have sworn he'd seen a hint of panic there. Had he been mistaken?

"Well, I understand that you lead a Bible class on Friday

43

evenings, and that Charity was a member. Was there anyone in it with whom she was particularly friendly?"

"Only Veronica."

Thanet was beginning to feel that all roads led to Veronica.

"Are there any boys in the class?"

Jethro said stiffly, "Two."

"How old?"

"Ten and eleven."

"I see." Much too young to be of interest to a girl of fifteen. "Did Charity ever speak of a boy friend, to either of you?" He knew it was a pointless question, but it had to be asked.

"Charity didn't have any boy friends." Mrs. Pritchard had sucked her lips in disapprovingly.

"Maybe not in the accepted sense of the word. But did you ever hear her refer to a boy, even in passing?"

More headshaking.

"She knew no young men at all?"

Again, negative—though there had been a flicker of some indefinable emotion in Mrs. Pritchard's eyes.

"You're sure?" Thanet pressed.

They were sure.

"We know that Charity left Veronica Hodges' house at around 9:35 last night, and she wasn't found until 10:40. We were wondering if by any chance she called in here on her way home?"

Jethro turned to his wife, eyebrows raised interrogatively.

So, thought Thanet. Jethro had been out last night.

Mrs. Pritchard frowned. "Why should she have wanted to call here?"

Thanet shrugged. "If she was like a daughter to you . . ." It was difficult not to let a hint of sarcasm creep into his voice.

Mrs. Pritchard's shoulders twitched impatiently. "Well, she didn't."

"You were here?"

"Of course I was here," she snapped. "Where else d'you think I'd be at that time of night? Anyway, I can't leave my mother-in-law by herself."

"I'd have thought an old lady like that would be tucked up in bed pretty early."

"If you knew anything at all about old people, you'd know they need very little sleep. My mother-in-law may go to bed

44

early, but she's often still awake when we go up. There's always the danger she might start wandering around and fall down the stairs or something."

"And you were out, I gather, Mr. Pritchard?"

"There was a meeting at the school—I'm caretaker at Holly Road Primary."

"On Bank Holiday Monday?"

Jethro flushed. "It was a special occasion. They're supposed to be closing the school down, and the parents have been up in arms about it. They've been trying for months to get Peter Hannaway to come and hear their case and in the end he said the only date he could manage was Bank Holiday Monday." Peter Hannaway was the local MP. Jethro gave a cynical little jerk of the head. "Some of the parents thought he only suggested that date because he hoped most of them would be too busy off enjoying themselves to turn up, but if so he was disappointed. The hall was packed."

"What time did the meeting end?"

Jethro hesitated fractionally. "About 9:30."

And you got home at . . . ?"

"Quarter past ten," said Mrs. Pritchard, with a long-suffering glance at her husband.

"I didn't get away till after ten," said Jethro defensively. "There's always a lot to do after a meeting—tidy up, switch all the lights off, lock up . . . And there're always a few people who don't seem to have homes to go to."

So Jethro had been out and about for part of the relevant time . . . Thanet had already familiarised himself with the geography of the area and was aware that at one point, just before Charity entered the footpath, Jethro's route would have touched on hers. "On your way home, did you see Charity?"

Jethro shook his head vehemently. "If I had, I'd have told you, wouldn't I?"

That depends, thought Thanet.

"Not even a glimpse in the distance?"

"No! And it was dark by then, remember."

"And you're both absolutely certain that you can't think of anyone with whom she might have spent the weekend?"

They couldn't. No point in wasting any more time here at present. Thanet left.

All the same, he thought as he set off briskly for Lantern Street, the interview had been interesting, if not particularly

45

informative. Mrs. Pritchard's hostility to himself, for example. Was it because she had taken an instant dislike to him? Because that was how she treated everyone? Or—much more interestingly—because she had been on the defensive in this particular situation?

One thing was certain. Whatever Jethro had felt about his niece, Mrs. Pritchard had disliked her intensely. Thanet remembered that hint of satisfaction in Mrs. Hodges' voice last night, when she had said that Charity would be in trouble at home after her weekend's absence, and he began to wonder: what was it about the girl, which had provoked dislike? It could be very important to find out. Dislike magnified over and over, can become hatred, and in hatred may lie the seeds of murder.

Perhaps Veronica would be able to enlighten him.

7

"What a terrible thing, Inspector!" burst out Mrs. Hodges as soon as she saw who was on the doorstep. She gestured to him to come in.

"Your constable called to tell me just before I heard it on Radio Medway. Veronica doesn't know yet, she left very early on a trip to Boulogne. She'll be ever so upset, when she hears. I can't bear to think about it. I mean, it must have happened when Charity was on her way home from here...Oh, do sit down."

By daylight, Mrs. Hodges was revealed as short and plump, her ample curves inadequately corseted into a tight, pink crimplene dress. Her frizzy blonde hair haloed a round, pleasant face, a face which somehow lacked definition, like a jelly which has been poured into one mould and then, when it was almost set, transferred to a different one. She was wearing fluffy pink bedroom slippers and exuded a faint odour of fresh perspiration overlaid with cheap talcum powder.

"Would you like a cup of tea? Or coffee? I was just going

46

to have one, the kettle's already boiled. Oh dear, it seems awful to be talking about cups of tea, when . . .''

Thanet smiled. ''That's very kind of you. I'd love a cup of coffee.''

''Won't be a minute.''

One glance at this room had told Thanet that, whatever Veronica's religious convictions, Mrs. Hodges did not belong to the Children. The morning sun, streaming through the gap between the frilly net curtains, reflected off the row of brass ornaments on the mantelpiece, gleamed upon the surface of small, highly polished tables and glowed through vases of coloured glass filled with garish plastic flowers. A vivid print of a Spanish dancer with a rose between her teeth took pride of place above the fireplace.

Thanet looked thoughtfully at Mrs. Hodges as she returned with the coffee. Owner and room were strangely at variance. He would have expected the creator of all this exuberance to have a natural gaiety, but now that he looked at her more closely he could see in her face a settled sadness which he felt had nothing to do with the shock of Charity's death.

''Here we are, then,'' she said.

She had exchanged the slippers for high-heeled shoes which gave her a jerky, stiff-legged gait reminiscent of the pigeons in Trafalgar Square. Thanet was touched to see that she had taken trouble with the tray. There was a starched linen cloth of dazzling whiteness and a plate of homemade biscuits. He took one.

''Mmm. Delicious,'' he said.

She looked gratified. ''Veronica's favourites.''

''She gone on a day trip to Boulogne, you said?''

''Yes. With some friends from school. Four of them. Of course, as I said, she hadn't heard the news or I don't suppose she'd have gone.''

''What time will she be back?''

''I'm not sure. They're catching the four o'clock boat, that's all I know.''

''Did she happen to mention which friend Charity had been staying with, over the weekend?''

Mrs. Hodges shook her head.

''Or where the friend lived?''

''No.''

''I'd very much like a word with her. Would you mind if I

came back this evening? You can stay with us while we talk, of course.''

"If you think it'll be any help..."

"Thank you ... Was Charity supposed to be going on this trip?"

"Oh no. Her father would never have let her. Anyway, I don't suppose she'd have wanted to. She never was one for a crowd.''

"Veronica was her only friend?"

Mrs. Hodges shrugged. "So far as I know. And..."

"Yes?"

"Well, to be honest, I've never really been able to understand why Veronica took up with her in the first place. Mind, they've known each other for years, ever since they were kids. They went to Dene Road Primary together.''

"But they weren't particularly friendly at that time?"

"No. That wasn't till after..." She shook her head, looked away from him.

"After what?"

She compressed her lips. "After Veronica's dad died."

Thanet knew the value of silence. He waited.

Mrs. Hodges sighed, shook her head again, sadly. "I suppose it was all down to me—Veronica taking up with Charity, I mean. When Jim—my husband—was killed in a road accident two years ago...It was such a shock. I just couldn't take it in. He went off to work one day and...never came back.''

Lineham's father had died in similar circumstances. Thanet vividly remembered the sergeant speaking of the experience in just these tones.

Mrs. Hodges gave Thanet a shamefaced glance and then looked away again, out of the window, eyes glazed with memory. "It hit me so hard I just went to pieces. And Veronica...poor kid, she just used to shut herself up in her room, for hours at a time. And I was so busy feeling sorry for myself I just didn't see she needed comforting just as much as I did.''

She fell silent.

"And that was when she became friendly with Charity?"

"Yes." Mrs. Hodges gave a rueful grin. "And, would you believe it, at the time I was grateful to her for taking Veronica off my back!''

48

"You mean, you later regretted encouraging the friendship?"

"Did I just!"

"Why?" said Thanet softly.

She looked full at him then, a fierce, assessing stare. He could almost hear her thinking, *Will he use anything I tell him to hurt Veronica?* He held her eyes steadily with what he hoped was benign reassurance and after a moment he saw her shoulders relax as she sat back a little in her chair.

"Because she had far too much influence over Veronica, that's why. You wouldn't believe how much Veronica's changed since she started going around with Charity."

"In what way?"

"She used to be full of fun, always laughing. But now, well, you're lucky even to get a smile out of her."

"Adolescents are often moody, I believe."

"I know that! I'm not just talking about moods, this is *all* the time. Veronica used to have loads of friends, this place used to be full of kids in and out all day long, but now...today's the first time she's done anything with anybody but Charity for ages, and she took an awful lot of persuading before she said she'd go, I can tell you." Mrs. Hodges was really launched now. "Then there's that Jubilee Road lot..."

"The Children of Jerusalem, you mean?"

"That's right. Downright peculiar they are, I can tell you. And once they get hold of you...I'm not saying anything against religion, mind. I go to church regular myself, at Christmas and Easter, and people are entitled to their own opinions, but that lot...No telly, no boy friends, no make-up, no dancing, no pictures, Bible classes once a week and church all day on Sundays...It's not natural and Veronica's heart wasn't in it, no one can tell me otherwise."

"Then why did she go along with it, do you think?"

"Beats me. To please Charity, I suppose. And yet..."

"Yes?"

"Well, you might think this sounds stupid, when they used to spend so much time together, but I never really felt Veronica *liked* Charity."

"She must have, to a certain extent, surely. They've even been away on holiday together, haven't they?"

"Just a weekend at Easter, to the Jerusalem Holiday place in Dorset. And that's another thing. I didn't think Veronica had

49

enjoyed it that much at Easter but there she was, begging to go again. Went on and on about it till I said yes..."

"As it turned out, she couldn't go because she was ill. That's right, isn't it?"

"Had a temperature of 103 on Friday morning. I took one look at her and said, 'That's it, my girl. You're not going anywhere today and that's that.' And d'you know, after all that nagging to allow her to go, I could have sworn she was relieved! I ask you! It's beyond me, I can tell you."

"She's all right again now, I gather."

"Yes. I don't know what it was, but by Saturday she was back to normal."

"How did Charity take it when she found that the holiday was off?"

"Didn't say much. But she wasn't very pleased, I could tell. Well, I could understand that, when she was all packed up and on her way, it was bound to be a disappointment, wasn't it? But there wasn't much she could do about it, was there? And she didn't say a word about her parents going away."

"She didn't know herself, at that point, that they were going to."

"Ah. I see. Well anyway, when she did find out she could easily have come back here. I'd willingly have put her up for the weekend."

"Even though you didn't like her?" said Thanet softly.

"I didn't say that, did I?" She caught Thanet's eyes, gave a rueful little smile. "No, well, I suppose it's pretty obvious. I didn't, and that's the truth."

"Why not?" Thanet was very gentle. This could be important.

Mrs. Hodges wrinkled her nose. "I feel terrible, talking about her like this, with the poor girl barely cold..."

"But...?"

"But I can't help the way I feel, can I?"

"No one can."

Again, he waited, and once more his patience was rewarded.

Mrs. Hodges twisted her hands in her lap and said, "I don't know why it was, really, I've never tried to put my finger on it before. She was always very quiet, polite, well-behaved..." She stopped, looked surprised.

"You've just remembered something?"

"Yes. I'd forgotten. It was so long ago. When they were

50

quite little—six or seven, perhaps—Charity was forever in hot water at school. I remember now, Veronica was always coming home with tales of what Charity'd been up to. Then, suddenly, it stopped.''

"You don't know why?"

"I never thought to ask, at the time. But now, looking back, it does seem a bit odd. I mean, knowing Charity as she is now—was, I mean—I just can't imagine her as naughty as that. D'you see what I mean?''

"Yes." Thanet was thoughtful. If true, this was interesting. But there was always the possibility that Veronica had been fantasising. At a certain age naughtiness has a fascination for many children.

"You were trying to explain what it was you didn't like about Charity."

"Yes . . . But it's so difficult to pin down. She just made me feel . . . uncomfortable, that's all.''

"How do you mean, exactly?''

But try as he would, Thanet could not get her to be more specific. Finally, there was just one other question he wanted to ask. He should have put it to Charity's parents, but he'd forgotten.

"Just as a matter of interest, if the girls had gone to Dorset as planned, what time would they have got back last night?''

"Same time as Charity got here. They were going to catch the 7:20 from Victoria.''

"I see. Thank you." Thanet arranged to return at 9 pm to see Veronica.''

Lineham was already waiting for him in the car park of the Hay Wain.

"Looks as though it's under new management," said the sergeant as they walked into the public bar.

"Very nice, too." The place had been redecorated and recarpeted, but the old high-back oak settles had been retained and none of the atmosphere sacrificed on the altar of modernity.

The food looked good, too: homemade soups, pâtés, pies and quiches, interesting salads and even desserts. Thanet chose a wedge of cold game pie packed with a variety of meats, Lineham a slice of tuna and tomato quiche. Both added a baked potato, with butter.

51

"I'm surprised the place isn't packed out," said Lineham, chewing appreciatively.

"I expect it soon will be, once the word gets around."

They had found a corner table where they could talk without fear of being overheard.

"How did you get on, then, Mike?"

Lineham pulled a face. "All right. Not exactly riveting stuff, though."

"Well?"

Lineham took out his notebook.

"Children of Jerusalem: started in the mid-nineteenth century by one Jeremiah Jones. According to the books I found, many troubles—unspecified—were sent to test him and at the end of this time of trial he had a vision of God and the Holy City and started the Children of Jerusalem. His mission, and that of the sect after his death, was to carry the flame of Truth and pass it on to each succeeding generation."

"And the Truth was . . . ?"

Lineham consulted his notebook. "That only the Children will go to Heaven, the rest of us will be dragged straight off to the other place; that God is one person, Jesus and Jeremiah Jones his prophets, that . . ."

"Wait a minute. They're not Christians, then? They do not accept that Christ was the Son of God?"

"Nope. They believe that the only way to be saved is to repent of one's sins and to strive to obey God according to the laws of the Old Testament. Sickness, according to them, is the penalty for sin. Healing is forgiveness. God is the only physician. And the Devil, Satan, is the chief of evil spirits, the personification of evil."

"So salvation lies in . . ."

"Well, repenting of one's sins, as I said, and then giving a tenth of one's income to the Church. No smoking, drinking, dancing, no cinema or television, no boy friends or sex before marriage, marriage partners to be found only within the sect . . . They see life as a continual war against the power of the Devil."

"Anything else?"

"Worship: a typical Sunday will include a morning service comprised of sermon, hymns, prayer and witness—that's a sort of extempore statement of one's experiences in relation to one's religious beliefs—followed in the afternoon by discussion groups and in the evening by a confession service, known as The Shriving...Doesn't leave much scope for people to enjoy themselves, does it! Enough to drive anyone off the rails, I should think, especially the youngsters.''

"Mmm." Was that what had happened to Charity, Thanet wondered. If so, there had been no indication of it as yet. But if it had...

"What about you, sir? What did you get from Veronica?"

"I didn't." Thanet explained, then went on to fill Lineham in on the interview with Mrs. Hodges. "No doubt about it, there's something very odd going on there, Mike.''

"Between Charity and Veronica, you mean?"

"Yes. Mrs. Hodges is far from being a perceptive woman and of course, she's very partisan. Veronica's her only chick and she's fiercely protective. Jealous of Charity, too, so we have to take everything she says with a grain of salt. All the same, there do seem to be grounds for thinking that Veronica was almost forced into agreeing to go to Dorset with Charity, against her will.''

"You mean, because she begged her mother to allow her to go and then seemed relieved when she couldn't?"

"Yes. It even occurs to me that the so-called illness might have been psychosomatic.''

"Genuine, though?"

"Oh yes, but with an emotional rather than physical origin. I should have thought it was unusual for girls of that age to throw such a high temperature one day and then be perfectly fit the next. Young kids, yes, but at fifteen...''

"You're suggesting she was actually *afraid* to go?"

"Well, it does rather seem that way to me. I think it might be an idea for you to have a chat with the Superintendent, Principal or whatever he's called, of the Holiday Home, see if anything happened to upset Veronica when she was there at Easter. Do it this afternoon.''

"Right. But in any case, the implication of all this is that Charity had some sort of hold over Veronica, which she was using to make her do something she didn't want to do.''

"Precisely. And if so, it'll be very interesting to find out what that hold was. Even more interesting is the avenue of investigation it would open up. If Charity was capable of exerting that degree of pressure on one person, she was presumably capable of exerting it on another.''

53

"You don't think you're being a bit, well . . ."

"Yes, Mike?" Thanet grinned. "No, don't bother, I'll finish for you. 'Fanciful' is what you were going to say, I believe?"

Lineham gave a sheepish grin, but stuck to his guns. "Well, don't you?"

Thanet had a sudden, vivid mental image of that small crumpled body in her shcoolgirlish clothes. He sighed. "I know what you mean. And God knows, it's difficult to see where she could have found opportunities for blackmail, with the sort of life she was leading. By the way, there was another interesting point . . ." Thanet told Lineham what Mrs. Hodges had said about Charity's reputation for bad behaviour while at primary school. "Come to think of it, it might be worth having a word with the Head of Dene Road School, at some point. If he or she is still there, of course. It was seven or eight years ago."

"Yes. Though it shouldn't be too difficult to trace him, even if he's retired. Unless he's moved right out of the area and bought himself a cottage with roses around the door in the West Country."

"Anyway, we might be able to get to the bottom of all this when we see Veronica herself. I've arranged to go back this evening. Want to come?"

"You bet," said Lineham fervently. "And what about the Pritchards? The Jethro Pritchards, I mean."

"Yes, well, that was interesting too." Again, Thanet gave a brief account of the interview.

"Are you saying you think Mrs. Pritchard might be a candidate, then?"

"She certainly didn't hold any brief for Charity, that's for sure. I know she claims she was in all evening, but whatever she says, once her mother-in-law was tucked up in bed, Mrs. Pritchard could easily have slipped out."

"You mean, with the intention of waylaying Charity on her way home?"

"Perhaps."

"But what possible motive could she have had?"

"I can't begin to guess at the moment. And the same goes for Jethro. But he was definitely out and about at the crucial time, and we must remember that they could easily have found out what time Charity was expected back. They weren't to know the arrangements for the weekend had been called off."

"And in any case, Charity obviously planned to arrive home at the same time as she'd originally intended."

"Quite. I wonder where she was, over the weekend."

This was still one of the most intriguing questions of all. There had been no clue in Charity's shoulder bag—no tickets, receipts, nothing to indicate whether she had stayed locally or travelled further afield, and no word as yet from the "friend" Charity had mentioned to Veronica.

"Come on, Mike, let's get out of here. I could do with some fresh air."

Outside the sun was at its zenith and heat shimmered on the tarmac of the car park.

"Wonder how long this is going to last," said Thanet.

"All summer, I hope." Lineham, like Thanet, thrived on hot weather. "Anyway, you think it's worth keeping the Jethro Pritchards in mind."

"They were certainly holding something back. Though it could be quite irrelevant, of course."

"What about Mrs. Hodges?"

"Mmm, well, we can't dismiss her entirely, I feel. If she thought Charity was a serious threat to her Veronica, she could be pretty fierce, I should imagine."

"But in that case, she surely wouldn't have told you any of that stuff about their friendship being peculiar, would she?"

"I don't know . . . Come on, Mike, enough speculating for the moment. We'll just have to wait and see."

Back at the office there was a message for Lineham: *Your wife rang from the hospital. She's being kept in. Could you pick up her suitcase (ready-packed in bedroom) and bring it in?*

Lineham showed it to Thanet. "They must have kept her in after the clinic this morning. Oh God, what if something's gone wrong?"

"Come on, Mike, no need to imagine the worst. Perhaps they're just being careful. And even if she's gone into premature labour, there's an excellent chance that the baby'll be fine. She's thirty-six weeks, you said?"

Lineham nodded. "Yes, but . . ."

"There you are, then." Thanet could hear the heartiness in his own voice and hated himself for it. Nothing would reassure Lineham but the sight of Louise in apparent good health. Fortunately Louise, a qualified nurse herself, was a sensible girl, not liable to panic in circumstances such as these. Thanet fervently hoped that nothing was seriously wrong. He glanced at Lineham's still, set face. He could imagine how he was feeling. Becoming a father for the first time was no joke even when everything was running smoothly. And when it wasn't ...

"Well, what are you waiting for?" he said gently. "Go on, on your way."

8

Thanet lit his pipe, sat back in his chair and drummed his fingers thoughtfully on his desk. The last hour had not been very productive. After Lineham's departure he had worked his way through the fresh reports awaiting his attention (nothing interesting there), made an unproductive telephone call to the Holiday Home in Dorset (the Principal had been out) and had despatched DC Carson to the railway station to enquire about arrivals last night (so far without result).

So, what now?

What he really needed was to talk to someone who could give him an assessment of Charity's character which was both unbiased and perceptive. Also, someone who could provide information about possible friends. Ah, yes ... he reached for the telephone directory.

He decided to try the school first. In his experience the Heads of large secondary schools invariably spent a considerable part of any holiday catching up on paperwork.

He was in luck. Yes, Miss Bench was working today, the secretary informed him. And yes, she was free to see him if he so wished. Thanet said that he would be right along.

His spirits rose as he set off. This was the part of his work that he enjoyed most, the interviewing. No two individuals are alike and the same person may be interviewed by two different people with completely different results. The variables are infinite. This, then, is the detective's testing ground. Here he must sharpen his perceptions and develop his skills in order to coax out of his witness that one (with luck, more than one) little nugget of information which may appear irrelevant at the time but which might eventually prove crucial to his understanding of the case.

It had taken Thanet a long time to realise that it wasn't simply a matter of interviewing technique—though that was important—but something much more subtle: interaction between questioner and questioned. Slowly and painfully, through years of trial and error—especially error—he had come to understand that an interview is rather like an iceberg; only a fraction of it is visible above the surface. A significant aspect of the detective's task is therefore to watch out for and interpret the minute, unconscious signals which rise to the surface like bubbles of gas in lemonade and betray what lies beneath. Only occasionally did he have the good fortune to come across a witness who was both honest and direct.

This time he was in luck.

Miss Bench rose as he was ushered into her study. He had not met her before and his first reaction was one of surprise as his preconceived notions of a headmistress shrivelled and died an instant death. She was a little younger than he—in her early thirties, he guessed, tall and slim. Elegant, too, in a narrow dress of dark blue linen with floppy lace collar and cuffs. Her straight fair hair was cut in what has become known as the Princess Diana style. If Thanet had seen her in the street he would have guessed her to be a high-powered secretary. No, he corrected himself, not a secretary, however high-powered. There was an unmistakable authority in those calm, pale blue eyes, an assumption that the world would shape itself to her command. There'd be no problems of discipline in this school, he thought. He was disconcerted to see that her smile had more than welcome in it, there was amusement, too. She was aware of the effect her appearance was having upon him and was enjoying it.

They settled themselves in easy chairs on either side of a low coffee table. Evidently she did not need her desk and chair, props of her authority, to bolster her self-confidence.

She came straight to the point.

"It's about Charity Pritchard, I suppose."

"Yes." There was obviously no need to beat about the

bush. "I wanted to talk to someone who could give me an impartial opinion of her."

"Oh dear." Her mouth tucked wryly down at the corners.

"You don't consider that you qualify for that description?"

"I'm afraid not. I'm sorry to disappoint you."

"You disliked her?"

"Yes. Oh, I can't say that it doesn't grieve me to think of the way she died. It does. I wouldn't wish that on my worst enemy." There was pain in her eyes, in her quick, fierce frown. "But it would be hypocritical to say that I shall mourn her." She gave a self-deprecating little smile. "I know that teachers are supposed to be above likes and dislikes and I would certainly hope that no personal preferences or prejudices would ever show in my behaviour or distort my judgement. But there it is. Contrary to popular belief, teachers are human, after all."

"Like policemen." Thanet grinned.

She smiled back. "Exactly."

"Tell me why you didn't like her."

Miss Bench sighed, plucked abstractedly at a loose thread on one of the lace cuffs. "Ah, now there's the problem. It's so difficult to say. Don't think I haven't asked myself why, I always do, when I discover an antipathy towards a pupil."

Thanet said nothing, waited.

"Usually it's relatively simple to pinpoint the reason. But in Charity's case . . . She's . . . she was a model pupil, you see—conscientious, hard-working, well-behaved, I can't ever recall having to take her to task for bad behaviour. In fact, thinking about it now, I suppose she was almost unnaturally well-behaved. One expects to find even the most decorous of girls occasionally lapsing into some minor breach of discipline. But not Charity."

She paused, lips pursed and eyes narrowed. "Why didn't I like her . . . ?" She shrugged. "It was a purely emotional reaction."

"A gut-reaction." But for the first time he sensed that she was being less than frank with him.

She looked amused. "Not quite how I would encourage one of my girls to put it. But yes, that's it, exactly."

"Hmm." Thanet was silent for a few moments, thinking. Miss Bench waited calmly, sitting back into her armchair and crossing her legs.

Temporarily distracted, Thanet forced his attention away from those shapely planes of nylon-clad flesh (her shoes were prettily feminine too, he noticed, high-heeled, strappy sandals) and tried to feel his way into understanding the qualities for which this woman would have an instinctive dislike. They would probably be character traits diametrically opposite to those which she valued in herself. Which would be . . . ?

He saw her blink, no doubt at the intensity of his gaze.

"I was thinking," he said.

"So I gathered." She gave a wry grin. "Did you reach any conclusions?"

He had. "Would you say that Charity was devious?"

She hesitated. "I suspect she was," she said reluctantly.

"Untrustworthy?"

"I suppose so. Well, yes, then. Potentially, anyway. Oh dear." She gave a shamefaced little laugh and lifted her hands helplessly. "I can't help feeling rather guilty, talking about her in this way."

"Because you don't like speaking ill of the dead, you mean?"

So that was the reason for her reticence just now. He had thought her too objective to be influenced by so universal an irrationality.

She turned in disconcertingly on what he was thinking. "I know you'll say it's irrational to feel this way, but I'm not so sure. One is always aware that the dead have no right of reply, that they can't defend themselves and never will be able to again. And when someone has died as Charity did, a victim of violence, it almost seems as though one is compounding the crime by blackening all that is now left to her, her reputation."

Strange that he had never thought of it in quite this way before. He was impressed by her natural delicacy, almost felt himself rebuked for insensitivity. Not that he could allow himself to be influenced by such scruples, of course—his job would become virtually impossible if he did—but he was inclined to respect hers. Ignoring the little voice which whispered that he could afford to be magnanimous because he had got what he wanted and forced her to betray her true opinion of Charity, he said, "We'll talk about something else, then. Tell me about her friendship with Veronica."

This was easier for her. She relaxed.

"It's interesting that you should ask about that. It has always puzzled me, that friendship. On the surface they're so very different—or perhaps I should say, *were* very different. I'm not using the past tense because of Charity's death, you understand."

"Veronica changed, you mean?"

"Yes."

"Because of Charity's influence?"

Miss Bench considered. "I'm just not sure." She hesitated again. "It's difficult to tell. Certainly the initial change was . . . Perhaps I'd better explain. I took up my post here two years ago last September. It was my first Headship and of course it was a busy time for me, picking up the reins and generally establishing myself. For some months most of the girls were just a blur—we have over seven hundred pupils here and it is quite impossible to get to know them all at once. But I did notice Veronica because she was always bubbling over—a bit silly, giggly, but invariably bright, cheerful. She was always the centre of a noisy group—I suppose her high spirits were infectious. And then, towards the end of that first term, early in the December, her father was killed. It was a hit and run affair and the man was never caught. A very sad business altogether. I understand that they'd been a very close family, the Hodges, that Veronica was the only child and they'd both adored her. The suddenness of her father's death absolutely devastated her. Overnight she became quiet, withdrawn—sullen, almost. I talked to her, of course, tried to help her, but without success. I told myself that time would help, that she'd come out of it gradually, but somehow she never has."

Miss Bench sighed. "I'm afraid I feel somewhat responsible. With so many girls to look after, it's a question of priorities and Veronica did seem to be coping, she didn't become clinically depressed. The only excuse I have for not giving her more attention is that at that time I suddenly found myself with a whole crop of problems to deal with. One of the fifth form girls was found to be pregnant, there was a spate of petty thieving and to cap it all there was an outbreak of German measles which decimated not only pupils but staff, too. I can tell you, by that first Christmas I was beginning to wonder if I was going to survive . . .

"Anyway, the point is, that when I emerged from this

period of frantic activity I realised that in the interim Charity and Veronica had become friends. Frankly, I didn't think it would last. I believed that as time went on and Veronica regained her natural ebullience, she would revert to being one of the crowd again, but she never has. And I still don't understand why the friendship has lasted.''

"Had Charity any other friends?"

"Not to my knowledge, no. Before Veronica, she was always a rather solitary creature. Rather pathetic, really.''

"I wanted to ask you . . . I believe Dene Road Primary School is in your catchment area."

"That's right, it is.''

"So you know the present Head?''

"Mr. Hoskins, you mean? Yes.''

"Do you happen to know how long he's been there?''

"I can easily find out.''

Miss Bench's secretary quickly came up with the information that Mr. Hoskins had become Head of Dene Road five years previously, when the former Head had retired, a Miss Foskett.

"Foskett . . .'' said Miss Bench thoughtfully. "I'm sure I . . . Ah yes, I remember now. I met a retired Headmistress called Foskett a few months ago, at some local Department of Education function.''

With any luck it would be the same woman. Good. With a relatively unusual name she shouldn't be too difficult to trace.

Thanet's thanks were sincere. It had been a useful interview. There was one scrap of information in particular that had given him food for thought.

Outside the sun was still beating relentlessly down and the sky overhead was a very pale, unclouded blue, shading off to a whitish glare at the limits of vision. A blast of stored-up heat gushed out at him as he opened the car door. Thanet took off his jacket, which he had donned for the interview with Miss Bench, and slung it on to the passenger seat.

He wondered how Louise was, and whether Lineham was back from the hospital yet.

9

"DS Lineham back yet?"

"Came in about half an hour ago, sir."

And the news wasn't good, by the look of it, thought Thanet, as he entered his office. Only a couple of hours had gone by since he had last seen the sergeant, but in the interval the planes of Lineham's face seemed to have sharpened and there was a taut, stretched look about his eyes.

"How is she?"

Lineham grimaced, shook his head. "She *says* she's fine, but I think she's putting on an act for my benefit. Underneath I think she's scared to death."

Thanet sat down, prepared to listen. Joan had had two trouble-free pregnancies, thank God, but each time she'd been in hospital there had been others less fortunate. Thanet had heard enough stories to know that the maternity wards had their own share of tragedy.

"What's the trouble, exactly?"

"High blood pressure. Therefore possible toxaemia."

"Which means?"

"The oxygen supply to the baby diminishes, might be cut off. And of course, if that happens..."

Oh God, thought Thanet. To carry a baby for eight months and then to lose it, at the eleventh hour... "So what is happening?"

"She's been put on complete bed-rest, suitable medication, to see if they can get her blood pressure down."

"And if they don't succeed?"

"They'll induce. Fortunately, as you pointed out earlier, she's thirty-six weeks already and the baby'd have an excellent chance of survival."

"It's a first-rate maternity unit, Mike. They'll keep a very close eye on her. They would with any patient, but with one of their own they'll give just that little edge of special care, I'm sure."

Until four months ago Louise herself had been a ward sister at Sturrenden General.

"That's what I keep telling myself."

"Look, would you prefer me to put you off the Pritchard case, give you something less demanding?"

"You mean, I'll be no good to you, in this state?"

"Oh come on, Mike, I hope you know me better than that. If that was what I'd meant, I'd have said so. You know perfectly well that there's no one I prefer to work with. It's just that I thought you might prefer to be relatively free for the next day or two." But even as he spoke, Thanet knew that it had been a stupid suggestion. With nothing but his anxiety to dwell on, Lineham would be far worse off than he was now.

"I'd go round the bend. If you don't mind, I'd really prefer to stay on."

"Good. But if at any time you change your mind . . . "

As if to demonstrate his ability to set his personal worries aside, Lineham picked up some of the papers spread out before him and said, "There've been one or two interesting developments while you were out."

"Oh?"

"DC Carson's report . . . "

"On his visit to the railway station?"

"Yes, sir. Apparently the ticket collector on duty last night says that he saw Charity get off the London train."

"At what time?"

"Eight fifty-eight."

"Did he, now! How sure is he?"

"Dead certain, apparently. But here's the best bit. She was with a man."

"*With* him?"

"That's what the ticket collector says. Claims they got off the train together, walked along the platform together, left the station together. He remembers, he says, because that's a pretty dead time of the evening and there were very few passengers."

"Let me see."

Lineham handed the report over and Thanet read it through quickly and then again, more slowly. "Of course, it could just

63

have been someone she knew, someone she met by chance on the train. In which case it would have been quite natural for them to leave the station together. Still, we'll follow it up, obviously. Quite a good description, isn't it? Pretty distinctive, too . . . 'Mid-thirties, medium height, fair hair, pebble-lensed glasses, carrying an orange rucksack.' And there's always the interesting fact that we now *know*—assuming the ticket collector is right—that she was away from Sturrenden yesterday, at least.''

"He does sound pretty positive on the identification, don't you agree, sir?"

"I do indeed. Good. There was something else, you said?"

"Yes. While I was waiting for you to get back, I rang the Holiday Home, as you asked.''

"Ah yes, I tried a couple of times earlier on, but the Principal was out.''

"Well he was back, and I managed to talk to him.''

"And?"

Lineham hesitated—deliberately. Thanet recognised that look. He'd seen it before when the sergeant had managed to unearth a particularly intriguing piece of information.

"Of course, there might be nothing in it . . ."

"Mike!"

"It could just be that both families happened to forget to mention it . . ."

Thanet sat back, clasped his hands and began to rotate his thumbs around each other in a gesture of mock impatience.

Lineham grinned. "Apparently Veronica and Charity did not stay for the entire weekend at Easter. They were called home a day early, by telegram—well, a tele-message, as they're now called—addressed to Charity. One of her family was ill, apparently.''

"Is that so?" Thanet considered. Lineham could, of course, be right. Both the Pritchards and Mrs. Hodges might just have happened to forget to mention the fact, the incident having been driven out of their minds by shock, or grief, or both. Or it simply might not have occurred to them to mention it because they did not consider it to be of any significance. He said so. "All the same, it is just possible that neither family mentioned it because neither knew about it. In which case . . ."

"The girls could have sent the telegram to themselves! Look, sir, I've been thinking about it while you were out.

They could have been bored stiff, wanted to get away early. Perhaps they originally intended going straight home, perhaps not, but in any case, when they found they had a whole day—and night—of freedom, to do whatever they wanted to without their families knowing . . . Well, Charity's parents were pretty strict, weren't they? The temptation may have been irresistible."

"What are you suggesting they did?"

Lineham shrugged. "Could have been something perfectly innocuous, like going to the cinema—even that would have been living it up, by the Pritchards' standards—or, just possibly, they could have decided to be a bit more daring, pick up a couple of boys."

Thanet remembered that still, childish figure. How attractive to the opposite sex would Charity have been? But then, some men were really turned on by young girls, the younger-seeming the better . . .

"They could even," concluded Lineham triumphantly, "have arranged to meet them again last weekend!"

They could indeed. Thanet remembered Veronica's apparent ambivalence over returning to Dorset. If Charity had been the ring-leader in all this, if Veronica had not enjoyed the exercise, had dreaded going through it all over again . . . Yes, Lineham was right. This would certainly have to be followed up.

Lineham was watching him eagerly. "What do you think, sir?"

"You don't think, Mike, that you're being a little, well . . . fanciful?" Thanet teased.

"Perhaps it's catching, sir. Like measles." Lineham gave an impish grin.

"Anyway, yes, you're right. It's definitely worth looking into. But don't raise your hopes too high. There might be a perfectly innocent explanation."

"The man she got off the train with. He could be . . ."

Thanet held up his hand. "No, Mike. Let's take it one step at a time, wait until we've established a few more facts."

"We'll go and check with the Pritchards?"

"Mrs. Hodges, I think. I don't really want to bother the Pritchards any more today, if I can help it."

"I'll go, if you like, sir." Lineham was already getting up.

"Mike! Hold your horses!" Thanet could understand

Lineham's need to stifle anxiety with action, but had no intention of allowing it to precipitate him into rash behaviour. "I think we ought to discuss tactics, first."

"I'm not sure I follow you, sir. It's a fairly straightforward enquiry, surely."

"It's a question of timing. Consider the implications. We have here a piece of information which may be useless. The girls may quite legitimately have been called home a day early. In which case, timing wouldn't matter. But, if the parents know nothing about that telegram, if the girls were involved in some sort of deception, then that information is potentially valuable, could open up important avenues of exploration. But, and this is the point, only one person could give us access to them."

"Veronica."

"Exactly. And we have an appointment with her in—let me see—just under four hours from now. Now think. If, meanwhile, we went to see her mother, discovered that she knew nothing about all this . . ."

"The first thing she'd do when Veronica got home would be to tackle her about it and we'd not only lose the element of surprise, she'd have time to think up a story, too . . . Good grief! Did you say just under four hours from now?" Lineham consulted his watch, leapt out of his chair. "It's a quarter past five, already, and I promised Louise I'd pick one or two things up for her before the shops close this afternoon. Would you mind . . . ?"

Thanet waved a hand. "Carry on. There's nothing urgent, here. You still want to come to the Hodges' this evening?"

Lineham grinned. "Try and stop me."

"See you there, at nine, then."

When Lineham had gone Thanet sat back in his chair and closed his eyes. At once his mind was full of confused images and snatches of conversation from the many interviews he had conducted today. His impressions of Charity were gradually gaining substance; outwardly conformist, abiding faithfully by the rigid rules laid down by her overbearing father, she had lived a life apparently blameless in the extreme. And yet . . . underneath, there was more to it, he was sure. There had, for instance, been something about her which invariably provoked dislike—antipathy, even. Aunt, Headmistress, friend's mother, all had felt it in varying degrees, and her one friend had been a friend in name only, it seemed. How had this come about? What had gone wrong in the life of this young girl, to make her incapable of forming good relationships with others?

"Charity was forever in hot water at school."

Mrs. Hodges' remark returned once more to intrigue him. If this were true, what had happened to change the child so radically?

He opened his eyes and reached for the telephone directory. As he had expected, there were very few Fosketts and only two were local. One was a man, the other an E. V. Foskett. Address, Jasmine Cottage, Nettleton. Nettleton was on his way home...

The voice at the other end of the telephone was brisk, businesslike. E. V. Foskett, it seemed, was indeed the former Head of Dene Road Primary School. Yes, Charity had been one of her pupils and certainly, Inspector Thanet was welcome to call if he thought she could be of any help.

"I'll be with you in about fifteen minutes," he said with satisfaction.

10

Jasmine Cottage was quite the tiniest cottage Thanet had ever seen. Tucked away in a little lane off the main street of Nettleton village, its minute leaded windows, timbered walls and crooked chimney would have elicited murmurs of admiration from any foreign tourist. The garden was to scale. There was a pocket-handkerchief of a lawn, surrounded by low stone walls topped with cushions of yellow alyssum and a delicately woven tapestry of aubretia in palest pink, red, purple and mauve. Trained against the house wall was a rare Banksia rose, with its clusters of tiny golden blossoms. Thanet inhaled their scent appreciatively as he waited for the door to open.

After all this miniature beauty Miss Foskett was a surprise.

Square and chunky, with iron-grey hair cut in an uncompromising bob, she almost filled the low doorway.

"Do come in," she said with a smile. "This is exciting. I've never had a policeman on my doorstep before. Though I deplore the circumstances which have brought you here, of course."

The sitting room displayed the same diminutive charm: low ceiling, spindly occasional tables, a small Persian rug on the floor of polished red brick.

Miss Foskett waved him into a pretty Victorian spoonback armchair and seated herself in the only sizeable piece of furniture in the room, a large wing chair beside the inglenook fireplace. He was disconcerted to find that her eyes were twinkling with amusement.

"I know what you're thinking," she said. "We don't match."

I don't believe it, thought Thanet. Two perceptive witnesses in one afternoon... He smiled back. "Well, to be honest..."

"I can always tell, when someone's clever enough to spot the discrepancy. It doesn't happen often, but when it does I always feel I owe them an explanation. The truth is, I inherited it all, lock, stock and barrel, from a truly minuscule aunt who died at the ripe old age of eighty-nine, last year. I was living in a rather dreary bungalow at the time, and frankly, I couldn't resist. The whole place was so delightful I decided to keep it exactly as it was. Except for this chair," and she patted the arm as if it were a dog, "my nice roomy bed and a few odds and ends with sentimental associations." She frowned and her eyes grew sombre. "So you want to talk to me about Charity Pritchard, poor girl."

"Yes."

"I don't see how I can possibly help, but of course I'm willing to try."

Thanet decided to come straight to the point.

"I've been talking to Mrs. Hodges, Veronica's mother..."

"Just a moment. Hodges... Ah yes, I remember Veronica. A fluffy, rather silly little girl, as I recall. But I don't quite see..."

"She and Charity have been close friends for the last couple of years, by all accounts."

"Really? You do surprise me. Chalk and cheese, those two."

"According to Mrs. Hodges, at one time, while the two girls were pupils at Dene Road, Charity was always in hot water. Veronica was forever coming home with tales of Charity's escapades. And then, apparently, the stories suddenly stopped. Is this true?"

Miss Foskett sighed. "I'm afraid so."

"Would you tell me about it?"

"Certainly. Though I must confess I don't like dwelling on my failures any more than the next man."

"What do you mean, failures? No, sorry, perhaps you could ignore that for the moment. I'd like to hear about Charity's behaviour, first."

"Charity *was* my failure. Look, are you sure you want me to go into all this? It's all water under the bridge now, and rather a long story."

"It's why I've come."

She shrugged. "If you think it will help . . ."

Thanet sat back and prepared to listen.

"It's difficult to know where to begin, really . . ." She caught his eyes, smiled. "I know . . . at the beginning. Very well . . . Soon after she started school, it became obvious that Charity was going to be a difficult pupil—disobedient, lacking in application and concentration, rebellious, uncooperative, often downright naughty. She was bright, mind, but whatever we did we couldn't seem to harness her abilities, get her to use them constructively. We tried everything—praise, admonition, condemnation, punishment, but nothing worked. I kept on hoping she would settle down, find her feet, but to no avail."

"You spoke to the parents about this?"

"Initially I didn't want to make an issue of it. It was the mother who used to turn up at parents' evenings, and I did try tackling her about it, but nothing happened. She was a quiet, ineffectual little woman and I guessed she simply didn't have the strength of character to get Charity to toe the line. Having met her, and having been aware all along that there must be some reason for so young a child to be so troublesome, I concluded that either the father was as ineffectual as the mother, and Charity had always been allowed to have her way unchecked, or that he must be a very powerful, repressive person who kept Charity so firmly under control at home that at school she was reacting against being over-disciplined. Ah,

I can see from your face, you've already met him. Of course, you would have, in the circumstances. You'll understand what I'm going to tell you, then...

"Well, eventually I reached the point where I decided that I must have a word with him, and the next time Charity was in trouble I told her that that was what I had decided to do. I can assure you that I've never seen that particular warning have so powerful an effect. The child was petrified. She must have been—oh, let me see—about six and a half at the time. She begged me not to send for him, promised there'd be no more misbehaviour."

"So you didn't see him?"

"Not at that point. I thought that the threat alone might have achieved the desired outcome and indeed, for a while, Charity was much better behaved. But gradually she began to slip back into her old patterns of behaviour. Now I didn't like ruling a child by fear, and I don't like making threats which are never put into practice, because obviously they lose their efficacy. I gave her one or two gentle warnings and privately decided that if this went on, I would have to talk to Mr. Pritchard, if only to satisfy my own need to know the right way to handle Charity. I thought, if we could have a sensible discussion together, we might be able to help her."

Thanet could see what was coming.

"Well, things came to a head about six months later. Charity's form teacher came to me and told me that she'd caught the child red-handed, pouring ink over a set of brand-new text books. Those particular books had been on order for months, and the entire class knew it. I called Charity in, told her I'd definitely decided to ask her parents to come and see me. She became hysterical. She screamed, she sobbed, she swore she was sorry, that she'd never, ever put a foot wrong again... It was so distressing. I felt in something of a dilemma. If I back-pedalled now, I would undermine my authority and destroy my credibility, make Charity think that she could always manipulate me if the need arose. On the other hand, the child was clearly so terrified at the prospect... Anyway, I finally decided to go ahead, on the grounds that there was clearly something radically wrong in her relationship with her father, and that if I were to be able to help her, I needed to know what it was. I can see, you've guessed what's coming, haven't you?"

"Possibly. But I want to hear it all the same. In detail. So do go on."

Miss Foskett shook her head sadly. "The interview was a disaster, from start to finish. I talked, they listened. I'm not exaggerating when I say that Mrs. Pritchard did not say a single word, from beginning to end. Any questions I asked were countered by further questions from Mr. Pritchard. There was no discussion, as such, at all. I really did try very hard, but soon realised that it was pointless. The man had a completely closed mind . . . You know they belong to that sect called the Children of Jerusalem?"

"Yes."

"I've had difficulties in dealing with the children of families belonging to it before, but never in quite such an extreme form. As soon as I saw that there really was no point in continuing, I brought the interview to a close." Miss Foskett shivered, hugged herself as if she were cold. "And do you know what he said, as he went through the door?"

Thanet waited.

"I've never forgotten it. He turned, looked at me with those very dark, burning eyes of his and said, 'Thank you, Miss Foskett, for bringing the matter to my attention. The Devil walketh about, seeking whom he may devour.'"

"And then?"

"They left."

"What did he mean, do you think?"

"Presumably, that the Devil was responsible for Charity's behaviour, that he had seduced her into evil, so to speak . . ."

"And the result?"

"Disaster, to my mind. Charity was away for a week and when she came back she was a different child—really different. Apart from being painfully thin, she was polite, quiet, well-behaved, industrious . . . You'll probably ask what I'm complaining about, when this was precisely the effect I'd been struggling to achieve, but to my mind . . . How can I explain? After this incident she was . . . lifeless. There was no vivacity, spontaneity, responsiveness . . . And yet, I still don't see how else I could have handled the situation constructively. As I told you, I still think of Charity as one of my worst failures—perhaps the worst failure of all. And I would like to assure you that I'm not given to self-castigation. It's so unconstructive to brood on failure. Better, by far, to learn

71

from it and forget it. But in Charity's case . . . I suppose you
might say that that child has haunted me, over the years. And
now . . . '' Miss Foskett shook her head regretfully and then
added briskly, ''Well, that's about it. I can't really see why
you wanted to hear all this rigmarole, but for what it's worth,
there it is.''

Thanet did not feel that this was either the time or the place
to embark upon a dissertation on the importance of understanding the victim's character in a murder investigation such
as this. He merely assured Miss Foskett that what she had told
him was extremely helpful to him and that he was grateful to
her for being so frank.

Before she closed the front door behind him she said, ''You
know, I'd have given anything to know just what he did to her
in that week she was away from school.''

And so should I, thought Thanet. So should I.

What was more, he was going to have a damned good try
at finding out.

11

''She's in the front room.''

It was precisely nine o'clock and Mrs. Hodges had clearly
been waiting for their knock; the door had opened almost
before the reverberations had died away. In the narrow hall
she hesitated. ''She's ever so upset. You won't . . . ?''

''I do understand that, Mrs. Hodges,'' said Thanet. ''And
I'll be as gentle as I can, I promise.''

This seemed to satisfy her and she opened the door, led the
way inside.

The girl huddled in the armchair facing them raised blank,
terrified blue eyes. She was very like her mother in build and
colouring, with a bush of elaborately frizzed hair haloing a
round face puffy with weeping. Beside her, on the arm of the
chair, lay a damp, wadded face-flannel. Thanet had a brief,
vivid image of Mrs. Hodges kneeling on the floor beside her
daughter, murmuring soothing words and sponging away the

tears as if Veronica were a little girl again and had hurt herself while playing in the garden.

But the marks of this injury were not going to be so easily eradicated, he thought as they all sat down. Crouching on the edge of her chair with fixed, stricken gaze, hugging herself as if she were afraid that her body might be about to fly apart, Veronica reminded him of a wounded bird waiting for the vultures to descend upon her and tear at her vulnerable flesh with their sharp beaks.

If he was right, she was more sinned against than sinning, and had had a pretty bad time over the last two years. But her evidence was crucial, of that he was convinced, and somehow he must win her confidence sufficiently to obtain it.

He glanced approvingly at Lineham, who had positioned himself behind the girl's line of vision, on a small upright chair. Louise's condition was apparently unchanged and the sergeant seemed marginally more cheerful this evening. He was as aware as Thanet of the importance of this interview and clearly his mind was on the job.

Mrs. Hodges had seated herself protectively on the arm of Veronica's chair, with an arm around the girl's shoulders.

"I really am sorry to have to bother you at a time like this, Veronica—I may call you Veronica?"

He waited for her tight, wary nod before going on.

"I do appreciate what a terrible shock this must have been for you. But I'm sure you'll want to do all you can to help us."

She bit her lip and he cast about for a reassuring opening. Every line of questioning seemed fraught with potential menace for the girl.

"Your mother tells me you've known Charity for a long time? Since you were at primary school together, I believe?"

"Yes."

It was barely audible, but a beginning. For the next quarter of an hour Thanet concentrated on putting her more at ease, chatting innocuously about Dene Road School, then about the Girls' Technical School, and gradually he was rewarded by seeing Victoria relax a little, speak more readily.

When he judged that the time was right, he said, "Now I know that you might find some of the questions I have to ask you a bit upsetting, but I want you to remember that I'm not out to browbeat or frighten you—in fact, that's the very last

73

thing I want to do, and if at any point you feel you'd really rather call it a day, you only have to say so and we'll stop. Though it's only fair to warn you that in that case we'd have to resume some other time. It'll be up to you. I'm trying to be completely frank with you, you see."

She was listening intently. So was her mother.

"The other thing I want to say is that whatever you may have to tell me about your friendship with Charity, we're not here to judge you. We're not out to find a scapegoat, merely to try to find out a little more about her. Charity didn't seem to have many friends and we really do feel that you might be able to help us perhaps more than anyone else can. You follow me?"

A small, tight nod. She was frightened again but, Thanet judged, prepared to be co-operative, within limits. Here goes, then, he thought. He had no choice, really, he had to begin with the business of the telegram. So much of his subsequent questioning would depend on whether or not there was an innocent explanation. If there wasn't, he hoped that Mrs. Hodges' reaction to the news of the girls' duplicity would not interfere with the course he wanted the interview to take. If only he could have seen Veronica alone . . .

"Perhaps we could begin by going back to last Easter, when you and Charity went to Dorset."

This was unexpected and she didn't know whether to be reassured or alarmed. Her eyes widened slightly and she glanced up at her mother, who squeezed her shoulder.

"When did you leave Sturrenden?"

"On the Friday morning."

They had arrived at the Holiday Home soon after four. They had been in a group of twenty-four young people from all over the country. Ages ranged from fourteen to eighteen and most of them were girls. The three boys, like Charity and Veronica, were among the youngest. All of them had been expected to make their own beds in the dormitories, to follow a rota system for laying the tables and washing up, to follow the tight schedule of Bible classes and discussion groups and to participate in the organised games in the afternoons.

"You enjoyed the weekend?"

"Yes, of course." But her voice lacked conviction.

"So why did you leave a day early?" His voice was mild and he had phrased the question very carefully, leaving the way open for a straightforward explanation of telegram and family illness, if that was the way it had been.

Her eyes told him at once that it had not. That quick, agonised upward flicker in the direction of her mother only just preceded Mrs. Hodges' reaction.

"A day early?" she said sharply. "What do you mean, a day early?"

"I'm sorry, Veronica," said Thanet. "But I'm afraid all this really does have to come out."

Mrs. Hodges' face had gone red. "What do you mean, sorry? What are you talking about?" And then, to Veronica, "What'll all have to come out?"

"No!" Veronica began to shake her head wildly. "No no no no no..." Then she buried her face in her hands and began to cry without restraint, rocking to and fro as if noise and motion together could block out awareness of the ordeal now facing her.

Mrs. Hodges, looking shocked and bewildered, slid off the arm of the chair, knelt before her daughter and, putting both arms around her, tried to calm her.

Lineham raised his eyebrows at Thanet. *Delaying tactics?* he mouthed.

Thanet shook his head. He had been expecting just this reaction and had decided how to deal with it. He waited until the girl's sobs had begun to abate and then, raising his voice, said, "Veronica, there's no need to be so upset. Your mother's not going to blame you, you know, when she hears the whole story."

As he had hoped, this gave her pause. Slowly, she raised a streaming face from her mother's shoulder and looked at him.

He met her gaze squarely. "I really mean that."

She wanted to believe him, he could see. She looked doubtfully at her mother, who was now sitting back on her heels.

It was Mrs. Hodges who clinched the matter. Levering herself up with one hand on the arm of the chair, she scrambled to her feet. Then she put her hands on her hips.

"Well, I haven't the foggiest idea what all this is about, but if you're worried about what *I* think, love, forget it. Anything's better than all this palaver. And if you do know anything that'll help the police, well, you owe it to Charity to tell it."

"Owe it to Charity!" Veronica burst out. "But that's just the point, Mum. I don't owe her anything, not a bloody thing!"

"Watch your mouth, girl! You know your dad couldn't stand women swearing."

"Oh all right, Mum, I'm sorry, but honest, you just don't know what you're talking about."

"Well how am I supposed to, if you won't explain!"

But still Veronica hesitated before taking the plunge. She glanced from Thanet to her mother and back again. Then she shrugged and said, "It was Charity's idea. The telegram."

"What telegram?" said Mrs. Hodges.

Thanet raised his hand. "Please, Mrs. Hodges, I think Veronica would find this easier if you could just listen, for the moment. I know it won't be easy for you, but if you could wait, save your questions till later..."

"All right." She was reluctant, but seated herself on the arm of Veronica's chair again and prepared to do as he asked.

"You might prefer to tell us in your own way, Veronica," said Thanet. "If you get stuck, I'll help you out."

Veronica shifted restlessly.

"You were bored, I suppose," prompted Thanet.

"Out of our minds!"

"Then why...?" Mrs. Hodges caught Thanet's eye, subsided.

"Never a minute to yourself," said Veronica as if her mother had not spoken. "Lights out at ten o'clock, jolly hockey sticks every afternoon, washing up for thirty-odd, including the staff, who never lifted a finger to help...And the atmosphere of the place! Long faces, everyone in dead earnest all the time...So in the end, Charity said, come on, let's get out of here, I've had enough."

"This was when?"

"On the Sunday afternoon. We were supposed to be staying until Wednesday morning. Well, I'd had enough too and we talked about it for a bit. I knew Mum wouldn't mind if I got home a couple of days early. But we haven't got a telephone here and we knew they'd never let us go without permission from our parents. So Charity suggested the best way would be to send ourselves a telegram, pretend there was some emergency at home. There was a pay-phone booth at the Home and we had just enough change between us, so we decided to send it right away, but when we enquired we found that although you can phone in a telemessage any time up to eight in the evening, they're not actually delivered until the next first class post in the area. And there was no post next day, being a Bank holiday. So we had to wait to send it until the Monday and it came first thing Tuesday morning.''

"And it worked?"

"Oh yes, no problem. We were away by mid-morning.''

Veronica paused, glanced uneasily at her mother.

Mrs. Hodges opened her mouth to speak, closed it again as Thanet shook his head. *Wait,* his eyes signalled. *You'll find out soon enough.*

"Go on, Veronica," he said gently. Then, as she still hesitated, "Let me help you. When you were on the train you were upset to find out that Charity had no intention of going straight home. Instead, she was suggesting that you should make the most of the unexpected day's freedom, live it up a little . . . Am I right?''

Thanet heard Mrs. Hodges' sharp intake of breath as Veronica nodded miserably.

"How was I to know she was going to suggest anything so crazy!" Veronica burst out. "We hardly had any money left after paying more than three pounds for the telegram and naturally I thought we'd be going straight home. But no! The minute we sat down in the train she started on me. She had it all worked out. We'd pick up some boys on the train or, failing that, in London, and get them to pay for everything . . . Don't look at me like that, Mum! You needn't worry, I didn't go along with her, though believe me, you ought to give me a medal for holding out. She just went on and on and on . . .''

"So what did you do, in the end?" asked Thanet gently.

"We split up. When we got to London I didn't know what to do . . . In the end I looked up the YWCA in the phone book. They've got an accommodation and advisory service. I couldn't stay in one of their hostels because I was broke, but they managed to fix me up just for the night in one of their emergency hostels . . . It was *awful,* having to throw myself on their mercy like that. I've never felt so humiliated in my life . . .'' Veronica shook her head as if to erase the memory and rubbed her eyes.

Thanet could see that Mrs. Hodges was again bursting to

ask a question and again he knew what it was: *But why didn't you just catch a train, come straight home?* Thanet gave her a quick, fierce frown. *Later*, he mouthed. He had his own reasons for not wanting to put that particular question at this point.

"And Charity?"

"Went off with some fella she picked up on the train. She was mad with me, of course. In the end she saw I wasn't going to budge and she said if I wouldn't go along with her she'd bloody well—sorry, Mum—do it by herself. So off she went to the buffet car and that was the last I saw of her till Paddington."

"She did pick someone up, you say?"

"You bet."

"You saw him?"

"Yes. When we got to London. They got off the train together."

"How far away were you?"

"About fifty yards, I suppose."

"Did you get a good look at him?"

"Not really. Only a side view."

"Can you give me a description?"

Veronica frowned, recalling. "Young—early twenties, I suppose. Black hair and beard."

"Tall? Short?"

"Medium. He had his arm around Charity's shoulders and they were laughing . . . He was a few inches taller than her and she's . . . she was the same height as me, five four."

"So, five eight or nine, then?"

"Yes."

"What sort of clothes was he wearing?"

"Jeans and a black leather jacket."

"Anything else you can remember?"

"No. Sorry. Oh . . . just a minute, yes . . . He was carrying a crash helmet. Yellow, it was."

"Was he wearing glasses?" Thanet had to ask, though he knew that the question was pointless, really. The description was quite different from that of the man who had got off the London train with Charity last night.

She shook her head.

"Did she ever tell you anything about him, later?"

"No. She liked being mysterious about him. She was

always going on about how terrific he was, how crazy about her, what a marvellous time they'd had, that sort of thing . . .''

"Did she spend the night with him?"

"Yes." Veronica was studiously avoiding her mother's eye.

"Did she say where?"

"No."

"Did she tell you where he lived?"

"Sorry, no."

"Whether she was going to meet him again?"

Veronica hesitated.

"Was she going to meet him again?" said Thanet softly. "Last weekend, for example."

Veronica bit her lip. "I'm not sure."

"But Veronica!" burst out Mrs. Hodges, unable to keep quiet any longer.

Thanet leaned across to lay a restraining hand on her arm. "Mrs. Hodges, look. I do appreciate how difficult this is for you. But I've nearly finished, now. If you could just bear with me . . . When we've gone, you and Veronica will be able to talk as much as you like."

Mrs. Hodges compressed her lips, scowled at him. "It's all very well for you. It's not you sitting here listening to your daughter telling you . . .''

"I know. But I won't be much longer, I promise. This really is very important."

He took her silence for assent, turned back to the girl.

"What were Charity's plans for the weekend?"

Veronica glanced nervously at her mother. "To book up at the Holiday Home again, then, on the morning of the day we were due to arrive, ring to say one of us was ill. That would mean neither of us could go because of this rule they have about girls travelling in pairs. Then we'd go to London, have a good time . . .''

"Pick up some men again, you mean?"

"That's what she said, but . . .''

"But what?"

"Well, I just didn't know whether to believe her or not. You never knew, with Charity. She could tell lies and look so innocent about it that you'd believe every word she was saying. It was ages before I cottoned on to that."

"So what made you think she wasn't telling you what her real plans for the weekend were?"

"I don't know. It was just an impression. And a letter came for her, three or four weeks ago, from London."

"It came here, you mean?"

"Yes. Inside an envelope addressed to me. She'd even had the nerve to tell him he could write to her here!"

"The man she met at Easter, you mean? I see, so you suspected that they might have made arrangements to spend the weekend together, and that you were going to be—how shall I put it?—ditched, when you got to London."

"That's right. But do you think I could get her to admit it? Whenever I tried, she'd just laugh, say I was imagining things."

"But when you saw her last night, when she called in on the way back from the station . . . Didn't she tell you where she'd been, over the weekend?"

"London, that's all. With a friend. As a matter of fact, I had the impression the weekend hadn't been much of a success."

"What do you mean?"

"I thought she looked tired. And a bit . . . subdued, depressed. Though I suppose that could have been because Mum had told her her father'd been round here looking for her and she knew she'd be for it when she got home. No . . . I still think there was more to it than that."

"Do you happen to know if Charity knew a man who wears pebble-lensed glasses?"

The question had taken her by surprise. Thanet glimpsed shock and recognition before she shook her head, a little too hastily.

"I'm afraid not, I'm sorry."

She was lying. Should he press her? The girl was looking exhausted and he had the feeling that she couldn't take much more. No, he'd leave it for the moment. There was one other question he wanted to ask before he had to stop. He'd saved it until last because he had the feeling that it was the one Veronica would find most difficult of all to answer, especially in her mother's presence. He hesitated, wondering how to phrase it tactfully.

Mrs. Hodges beat him to it. Taking his brief silence as an indication that he had finished, she leant forward and said, "But Veronica, love, I don't understand. Why go along with all this, if you didn't want to? Why go on being friends with

80

Charity at all, if that's what she was like?" Mrs. Hodges gave a little shiver of distaste. "Your dad would've had a thousand fits if he'd been here listening to all this."

Veronica's gaze slid away from her mother's. Her hands, until now lying loosely in her lap, curled into fists and Thanet saw her feet move slightly as her toes bunched up inside her shoes. He had been right. This was the question she had feared most of all.

"Veronica?" said her mother sharply.

"I was sorry for her," Veronica muttered.

"Sorry for her? *Sorry* for her? So sorry that you had to go begging for somewhere to spend the night in London, rather than come home a day early?" Mrs. Hodges' pent-up bewilderment and frustration suddenly erupted into anger. She jumped off the arm of the chair and stood over her daughter, feet apart, hands on hips, eyes blazing. "You really expect me to believe that? That you begged me to allow you to go to Dorset again knowing that you had no intention of doing so . . . that you deliberately set out to deceive me—me, your own mother—just because you were *sorry for Charity*? What kind of a fool do you take me for?"

Veronica had shrunk back in her chair, desperate as a cornered animal. Poor kid, thought Thanet. She couldn't defend herself without giving herself away. Her only resort would be to react angrily, use the quarrel as a smokescreen.

As if she had read his mind Veronica sprang to her feet and shouted furiously, "So that's what you think of me, is it! I'm a liar, am I?"

"Well, what else am I to think? You knew what she was planning, yet you agreed to go along with it. You *begged* me to let you go. You'd even packed your suitcase! If you weren't going to Dorset and you didn't intend doing what she wanted you to do, what *did* you plan to do? Spend the entire weekend with tramps and drop-outs at an emergency hostel in some grubby part of London?"

"But I didn't, did I? I *didn't* bloody go! Just remember that, will you?"

And, bursting into tears, Veronica ran out of the room. They heard her pound up the stairs, then there was silence.

For a few moments Mrs. Hodges stood rigid, staring blankly at the door. Then, moving very slowly, she lowered herself into the armchair Veronica had vacated and slumped back into it. "That's done it," she said ruefully. "Now I'll never find out. I shouldn't have lost my temper, should I?"

"I shouldn't give up hope," said Thanet equably. "Give her time. She's in a pretty fragile state at the moment, remember. She's just had a very bad shock, learning about Charity's death, and then, on top of that, having to be questioned . . ."

But Mrs. Hodges was still shaking her head. "Time was, I'd have agreed with you. We were so close, Veronica's dad, her and me . . . If you'd told me it would ever come to this . . ." Her eyes clouded, became almost opaque. "If I'd had any idea what was going on, I'd have . . ." She stopped, passed her hand across her face as if brushing cobwebs away and seemed to become aware of their presence again. "And I don't suppose she'll ever forgive me for shouting at her like that in front of you . . . I should have listened to what you said, kept my mouth shut until you'd gone . . . I'm sorry, I suppose you . . . Had you finished? Your questions, I mean?"

"Most of them. But there were one or two small points . . ." Not to mention the delicate issue over which the interview had broken down. "I'll have to come back tomorrow morning, I'm afraid. If that's all right by you."

Mrs. Hodges gave a resigned shrug. "I suppose if you must, you must."

Thanet waited until he and Lineham were in the car before asking him for his impressions of the interview.

"Looks as though we were right. Charity did have something on her. I wonder what."

"As a matter of fact, I've got a good idea. It was something her headmistress said . . ." Thanet explained his theory.

Lineham whistled. "Could be . . . That would be just the sort of thing she'd be terrified would come out. But I was thinking, while I was listening, back there . . ."

"Yes?"

"Well, we haven't had the PM report yet, of course, but I think you'll agree that from what we saw of the circumstances of the murder, last night, it did look as though it could have been an unpremeditated job."

"Possibly, yes."

"I know he could have been lying in wait for her with the deliberate intention of attacking her—or anyone else, for that matter—but he could simply have been waiting for her for some innocent reason—he may have wanted to talk to her about something.''

"True."

"Or, he could have been walking with her, and they had a quarrel during which he gave her a violent shove, causing her to fall against that lethal bit of iron.''

"Agreed."

"Or,'' said Lineham slowly, "he could even have followed her, caught up with her and then ditto. I'm saying 'he,' but of course, it could equally have been 'she.' It wouldn't have taken that much strength . . .''

"So what are you suggesting?''

"Well, as I said, while I was listening, I was thinking . . . Supposing Veronica had had just about as much as she could take, from Charity. Suppose that after Charity left her last night she thought about it for a minute or two and then decided to follow her, tell her just that.''

Thanet didn't like it. But he had to concede that Lineham could, just possibly, be right. Perhaps Veronica's desperation, which he had attributed to fear of her mother finding out the reason why Charity had had a hold over her, had really been terror of discovery. As Lineham had suggested, Charity's death could well have been an accident, the unfortunate result of a jagged piece of metal being in the wrong place at the wrong time. But would Veronica then have gone calmly off on a day trip to Boulogne?

He put this to Lineham.

"How do we know it was calmly?'' said Lineham. "I think you'll agree, sir, that Mrs. Hodges would do anything to protect Veronica. It could have happened like this . . . After the accident Veronica rushes home to Mum, in a state of shock. Mrs. Hodges calms her down and they discuss what they are going to do. They decide it would be best to behave as though nothing has happened, that Veronica should go on her trip as planned. It'll give her a breathing space, a chance to get over the shock a bit . . .''

"So that performance we just witnessed was just that, a performance?''

"Not entirely,'' said Lineham eagerly. "Mrs. Hodges might genuinely not have known anything about the business with the telegram at Easter . . . But I haven't quite finished, yet, sir. Or . . .''

"You're brimming over with theories tonight, Mike. Don't tell me there's another one coming up!"

"Well, it did just occur to me . . ."

"Come on, then, let's have it."

"Well, it could equally well have been Mrs. Hodges—who killed Charity, I mean. After all, we've only got her word for it that Charity left there at 9:35. All we know—if the ticket collector is right—is that Charity got off that train at 8:58. I'd guess it's about ten minutes walk to Lantern Street, so she would have got there about ten past nine. If Mrs. Hodges is telling the truth, Charity must have spent about twenty-five minutes there, but for all we know it was nothing like as long as that, it could have been ten minutes, or even five. Now, say during that time Mrs. Hodges overhears something between Charity and Veronica—an argument, anything which tells her that Veronica is getting desperate about her relationship with Charity . . . Mrs. Hodges could have decided to have a word with Charity on her own, follow her and have it out with her. She catches up with her . . . they quarrel . . . we have that fatal shove . . . and Mrs. Hodges rushes home, just getting back in time to look innocent when we arrive on the doorstep asking where Charity is . . ." Lineham paused, took his eyes off the road long enough to glance hopefully at Thanet.

"Could be . . ." Again, it was possible. Mrs. Hodges had obviously disliked Charity, resented her influence over Veronica. But, enough to kill her . . . Though she might not have *intended* to kill her . . . "We'll do some checking on their movements tomorrow."

They were in the car parked now and Lineham reached for his notebook.

"Starting with a house to house in Lantern Street?"

"Yes. Covering the earlier period, too—say from nine o'clock onwards."

"Right. Incidentally, Veronica was lying, when you asked about the man in glasses, wasn't she?"

"You spotted that too. Yes, I'm certain of it. I'll have to have another go at her about that, when we see her tomorrow. And we must both set our minds to working out how to trace either of the two men."

"The one she picked up at Easter could be tricky, sir. He could be anywhere in the country by now—or abroad, for that matter."

84

"Come on, Mike. Let's just regard it as a challenge to our ingenuity."

Lineham grinned, gave a mock salute. "Yes, sir. Right, sir. Any other homework for tonight?"

On the way home Thanet pondered the sergeant's suggestions. Could Mrs. Hodges or Veronica be guilty? If so, his own antennae had let him down badly during that interview. Perhaps he had been to preoccupied with trying to ask the right questions in the right order, and with preventing Mrs. Hodges from messing the whole thing up. This, after all, was one of the main reasons for having an observer: a non-participant had a much better chance of seeing what was going on beneath the surface. Had his own perceptions really been so dulled, tonight?

It was a sobering thought, but it was pointless to dwell upon it. He began instead to consider the task he had set Lineham: how to trace either of the shadowy male figures of whom they had been given such tantalising glimpses.

He tried to picture Charity with the young man Veronica had described, but somehow he couldn't do it. That virile, male image in jeans and black leather jacket simply didn't go with Charity's schoolgirlish style of dressing. And the clothes at home and in her suitcase had been much the same—dull, sober, juvenile. Perhaps Veronica had been telling a pack of lies? Perhaps it had been she who had been the prime mover in the Easter escapade and it had been Charity, not she, who had spent the night in a hostel.

Thanet shook his head unconsciously. No, he didn't believe that. It was Charity who had been murdered and besides, Veronica's story had rung true, had fitted in with the emerging picture of Charity as a girl whose rebellion against her repressive father, driven underground during her childhood years, had recently begun to manifest itself in much more devious and dangerous ways. He frowned. The trouble was, she just hadn't *looked* the part. If she had been dressed differently, now . . .

Inspiration came as he swung into his mother-in-law's drive. Of course!

He cut the engine and the dense, country silence enfolded him. He sat for a few minutes, thinking. If he were right, it would explain so much—how Charity had so completely hoodwinked her parents, for example, and why she had called first at Veronica's house, instead of going straight home from the station . . .

Yes, it all the made sense.

Why on earth hadn't he seen it before?

12

Thanet slammed the receiver down in frustration. He'd already tried twice to get through to Joan earlier on this evening, before leaving for Veronica's house.

"No luck?" His mother-in-law had just come into the room with two cups of tea balanced on a tray.

"Still out." Thanet sat down heavily on the settee and essayed a smile as he accepted the tea. He didn't feel in the least like smiling. A quarter to eleven and Joan was still out, after saying she'd be in all evening. Where the hell was she?

It was above all at times like this, when he had had a demanding day and was in need of the solace which she had never failed to give, that the fear of losing her—or perhaps having already lost her—surfaced most strongly. They'd known that this time apart would be difficult, of course, and had both been aware that it would be harder for Thanet and the children than for her. She would be working towards a goal, would be expanding her knowledge and experience, breaking new ground all the time, whereas he would remain in the same situation, conscious only of his sense of loss, of the yawning gap left by her absence.

What he had not anticipated was the burgeoning crop of fears: that her taste of freedom from family ties and domesticity would give her an appetite for more; that she was drifting further and further away from them; that he might even lose her for good.

Above all, he had not anticipated this gut-twisting jealousy, the terror that she might have found a more congenial lover. In his more rational moments he knew that he was a fool even to entertain the idea. Joan, unfaithful? Never. They had always been very close, had valued their relationship, taken care to nurture it. Thanet had believed that they had been moving into that satisfying stage when marriage becomes a liberating force, when each partner, secure in the knowledge that he is fully accepted and understood, becomes free to develop in ways undreamt of earlier on in life. Not that there hadn't been disagreements, of course, but somehow they'd always managed to take them in stride, been ready to compromise . . .

He shook his head cynically. Compromise, indeed! Look where compromise had brought him! But, if he had held out, over this? If he had refused to listen to Joan's plea to be allowed to train for a satisfying career of her own? He would have lost her anyway, or at best theirs would have been a relationship crippled by bitterness and resentment on her side, possessiveness and stubbornness on his.

No, he really didn't see how he could have acted otherwise. All the same, it was sometimes very difficult to convince himself that he had done the right thing.

"I shouldn't worry." Margaret Bolton was watching him sympathetically. "You know the sort of crises that are always cropping up in her sort of work . . . It's just unfortunate that yours is equally unpredictable."

" 'Never the twain shall meet,' I know." Thanet sipped at his tea, made an effort to pretend nonchalance. He had never discussed his marriage with anyone and had no intention of starting now. Joan would soon be home for good, he told himself once more. Until then, he'd grit his teeth and hang on.

Mrs. Bolton sighed, leaned her head against the back of her chair and closed her eyes. She looked very tired, Thanet thought guiltily. Joan's absence was taking its toll of her mother, too.

"Children been difficult?"

She opened her eyes, smiled ruefully. "A bit. I just don't seem to have as much energy as I used to. And it's been so hot . . ."

It still was. The French windows were wide open and the sweet scents of the garden had drifted into the room. There was another smell, too, Thanet realised: furniture polish. He looked about him and realised that his mother-in-law had been taking this opportunity to give her house a good clean; the furniture was shining, the copper coal scuttle and brass

87

fire-irons in the inglenook fireplace gleaming. After all that gardening over the weekend, too . . .

He looked at her anxiously. "All this is taking too much out of you, isn't it? Two houses to run, two gardens, the children to look after . . ."

She shook her head. "I don't mind. It's only for a little while longer, after all. Another couple of weeks and Joan'll be back."

So she was counting the weeks too.

"We don't tell you often enough how much we appreciate what you're doing."

She smiled. "Nonsense. Joan's my daughter, after all. And at my age it's good to feel needed from time to time, believe me."

But his words had pleased her, he could tell. He made a mental note to have a word with the children, try once more to get them to understand that their grandmother didn't have endless reserves of energy to draw upon. But they were so young, and it was a difficult time for them, too . . .

"I think I'll go to bed now," said Mrs. Bolton.

"Me too. You go on. I'll lock up."

After making the rounds Thanet made one more attempt to ring Joan. She was still out.

Just over two more weeks, he told himself as he climbed the stairs. Seventeen days.

Next morning he and Lineham arrived in the car park simultaneously.

"How's Louise?"

"The specialist is seeing her this morning. She had a reasonable night, apparently."

Which was more than could be said of Lineham, by the look of it. The taut, stretched look was back and the skin beneath his eyes was dark with the bruises of insomnia and anxiety.

"What time are you supposed to ring again?"

"Not before twelve, they said."

Inside they were greeted with the news that the post mortem on Charity was scheduled for this morning and that Doctor Mallard had arranged to be present. The unofficial results should be through in an hour or so.

They had just settled down to work their way through the reports on the previous day's work when the phone rang.

"Mr. Pritchard is here, sir. Wants to see you. It's urgent, he says."

"Do you know what it's about?"

"No, sir. He won't say. But he's in a bit of a state."

"Send him up. Pritchard," Thanet explained to Lineham. "In a state, apparently."

"I wonder what he wants."

They would soon find out, thought Thanet as Pritchard was shown in. The man was bursting with barely suppressed emotion. The immaculate black hair was ruffled and his eyes blazed with a feverish light.

"I've just seen Mrs. Hodges."

"Do sit..."

"It's not true, is it?"

"Please, Mr. Pritchard, do sit down."

Pritchard came across the room in a rush and, leaning on Thanet's desk, bent forward and shouted into Thanet's face, "I have a right to know!"

"Mr. Pritchard, no one is..."

"How dare you withhold information from me, her father!"

"Mr. Pritchard! If you would just calm..."

"It's outrageous! It's..."

Thanet stood up so abruptly that his chair crashed over on to the floor. "Mr. Pritchard!"

Pritchard recoiled, his mouth hanging slightly open.

Thanet was sorry for the man, could understand his distress, but this sort of performance was intolerable. "I refuse, categorically, to be bullied and harangued in my own office. If you're prepared to sit down and discuss this matter in a civilised fashion, then do so. Otherwise, I'm afraid I shall have to ask you to leave."

For a moment Pritchard stood motionless. Then, without another word, he subsided on to the chair Lineham brought forward.

Thanet calmly righted his own, followed suit. "Now then, perhaps we could start again."

Pritchard ran his hand through his hair and, controlling himself with difficulty, said, "I've just seen Mrs. Hodges."

"And?"

"She told me some tale about a telegram, about Charity

and Veronica leaving Dorset a day early at Easter . . .'' Pritchard faltered, stopped.

''Yes?''

''Is it . . . is it true?''

''I'm afraid so.''

''But it can't be! It's impossible. Charity would never have . . . That girl has made it all up.''

''Veronica, you mean?''

''Yes. She's evil, through and through. I told them. I knew it from the start. She's been a bad influence on Charity right from the beginning. But they wouldn't listen, they . . .''

''Veronica didn't make it up,'' said Lineham.

The new voice penetrated Pritchard's diatribe. His head swivelled in Lineham's direction. ''How do you know?''

''It was Sergeant Lineham who talked to the Principal of the Holiday Home,'' said Thanet gently.

''Mr. Harrison, you mean?''

Lineham nodded. ''That's right.''

''You know him?'' Thanet asked Pritchard.

''I have met him, yes.''

''And would you say that he is the kind of man to fabricate a story like this?''

Pritchard avoided a reply by turning to Lineham. ''You spoke to Mr. Harrison himself?''

''Yes.''

''What . . . what did he say?''

''That on the Tuesday morning, a day before they had been due to leave, Charity received a telegram saying . . .''

''It was addressed to Charity, not Veronica?''

''Yes.''

''What did it say?''

''That someone in the family was ill,'' said Lineham patiently. ''Charity's grandmother, Mr. Harrison thought. And that Charity should return home immediately.''

Pritchard ran his hand over his face, rubbed his eyes as if to erase his confusion. ''Who was it supposed to be from?''

''Mr. Harrison wasn't sure. But he rather thought . . . from you, sir.''

''Me!''

''You didn't send it?'' interrupted Thanet.

''I did not.'' Pritchard's eyes glittered like faceted jet. ''Really, Inspector, it's obvious, isn't it? Veronica sent it.

And she addressed it to Charity so that if the truth ever came out, it would be Charity who got the blame. Which is precisely what has happened . . .'' His eyes narrowed, glazed.

"Something has occurred to you, Mr. Pritchard?"

"What?"

"I wondered if you'd thought of something just then."

Pritchard's stare was as blank as if Thanet were speaking a foreign language. Then he shook his head, made a visible effort to refocus his attention. "I was simply explaining what must have happened." His voice was flat.

"If something did occur to you, then it really is your duty to tell us," persisted Thanet.

"I don't know what you're talking about, Inspector. And I think I'm entitled to an apology, don't you?"

Thanet gave up. He couldn't force the man . . . "Apology?"

"And an explanation. Why I haven't been told any of this before. Me, the girl's father! Why I had to find out myself, by accident, come around here and have to drag the information out of you . . . ''

Once more Pritchard seemed to be working himself into a rage. But this time, thought Thanet, it was different. For some reason the fire had suddenly gone out of him. Disillusionment, perhaps?

"I agree, it was unfortunate that you should hear of it second-hand . . . ''

"Unfortunate!"

'' . . . as we had every intention of telling you ourselves, later on today. No, Mr. Pritchard, please let me finish. When we first heard about this telegram, yesterday afternoon, we didn't go around to your house to question you about it for one reason and one reason only. We thought that you and Mrs. Pritchard had had just about as much as you could take, for one day. We judged it kinder to wait. Furthermore,'' Thanet went on, raising his voice as Pritchard opened his mouth to interrupt again, "furthermore, I must make it clear here and now that although we shall obviously keep you informed of the progress of our investigation, we have no *obligation* whatsoever to report to you every new development that comes along.''

"Indeed!" Now the indignation was genuine once more. "You don't consider that we, as Charity's parents, have a right to know what is happening?"

91

"Not if imparting that information could prejudice the progress of the case, no, I'm sorry."

"Don't lie!" roared Pritchard. "Sorry, indeed! And *case* . . . Yes, that's all it is to you, isn't it? A *case*." His voice suddenly dropped and, piercing Thanet with a look of entreaty, he said, "But she was my *daughter*, my only child . . . Can't you see, I *need* to know." His eyes filled with tears. "Can't you understand that?"

Thanet could, only too well. The man's despair hammered at the wall of professionalism which was his only defence at such times. He shook his head, said gently, "I'm sorry, Mr. Pritchard. I truly am. All I can promise is that we'll keep you as fully informed as possible."

Pritchard stared at him for a moment longer and then rose, blundering out of the room so clumsily that he almost knocked Doc Mallard over.

"I did knock," said the little doctor plaintively, clutching at the doorpost to regain his balance, "but there was so much noise . . ."

"Come in, Doc. Yes, sorry about that, the poor man was in rather a state . . . PM finished yet?"

Mallard ignored the question. He scowled and advanced into the room, straightening his half-moon spectacles. "Who was that, anyway?"

"Charity's father. Nathaniel Pritchard, to be precise. Doc, have you got the . . ."

"*Nathaniel?* I thought that went out with the Victorians."

"With the Old Testament, more like," said Lineham with a grin. "The Pritchard clan all sound as though they came out of the Ark." He shuffled through the papers on his desk, picked one up. "Hannah Pritchard—that's Charity's mother; Jethro Pritchard, Pritchard's brother; sister-in-law, Mercy Pritchard . . ."

"And that's a misnomer if ever there was one," said Thanet, recalling Jethro's formidable wife. "Look, could we discuss the . . ."

"Jethro," said Mallard thoughtfully. "Now that is an unusual name. Rings a bell . . ."

Pointless to ask any more questions about the post mortem, Thanet realised. Mallard would impart the information in his own good time, was probably enjoying keeping them in suspense. "You said that before, about 'Pritchard,' when you were examining the body."

"Yes, I did, didn't I?"

"You haven't remembered why?"

"I'd have told you, if I had," said Mallard irritably. "What was Pritchard shouting about, anyway?"

"He thinks we ought to keep him fully informed about the progress of the case. And he was upset because he'd just discovered his daughter had been deceiving him." Thanet told Mallard Veronica's story of the telegram and Charity's subsequent behaviour. "You don't seem surprised," he commented, when he had finished.

"Not really, no. Not in the least, in fact."

"The post mortem!" said Thanet.

Mallard nodded sagely. "If Pritchard was as upset as that about the business at Easter, I can't imagine how he'll react when he hears this."

"Hears what?" cried Thanet, patience giving out at last.

But there had been no need to ask, really. Suddenly the knowledge was clear and cold within him and Mallard's reply, when it came, merely echoed the words in his mind.

"She'd just had an abortion."

13

So that was that, Thanet thought. He had wanted proof to support his theory about Charity and now he had it. Her innocent image had finally shattered into a thousand pieces. It was true that, so far at any rate, he had not found her at all likeable, but now he was suddenly filled with pity for her. To have been in that particular situation with Pritchard as a father...She would never have dared tell him. How desperately alone she must have felt.

"So that's where she was over the weekend," said Lineham. His voice was tight with barely suppressed emotion and Thanet realised why: with Louise in danger of losing their

93

baby, the thought of an abortion must at this particular moment be especially abhorrent to him.

Mallard nodded. "Must have been."

"But surely she couldn't have had an abortion without her parents knowing?" objected the sergeant. "She was only fifteen, after all."

Mallard sighed. "I'm afraid it's only too possible. The medical profession is still divided on this issue of confidentiality. If a young girl comes to you and you confirm that she is pregnant, what do you do? Many of my colleagues feel bound to respect her confidence. They'll . . ."

"I think that's positively irresponsible!" said Lineham.

Thanet glanced uneasily at Mallard. How would he react to such an attack on his profession? Would he realise the reason for Lineham's unwonted rudeness? Apparently he had. The little doctor gave the sergeant a sharp, assessing glance over his half-moons before saying testily, "As I was about to say, they would naturally try to persuade her to confide in her parents, but if she refuses point-blank . . . What can they do? And," Mallard raised his voice as Lineham opened his mouth to answer what had been merely a rhetorical question, "if she does refuse to tell her parents and is determined about wanting an abortion, what then? Again, many of my colleagues would feel that she has the right to make up her own mind."

"But how can a kid of that age possibly make up her own mind about something like that?" Lineham burst out.

"She isn't allowed to make the final decision in a hurry, believe me. First, she'd have to have counselling . . ."

"Counselling!" said Lineham scornfully.

Mallard looked as though he would explode any minute now. He took a deep breath and in a voice taut with anger said, "Look, sergeant, I've neither the time nor the inclination just now to go into the ethics of abortion. I'm simply trying to give you the facts. And the facts are that with sufficient determination, yes, Charity could have got an abortion without her parents' knowledge or consent. Either on the National Health, if she were lucky . . ."

"Lucky!" muttered Lineham.

"Or," Mallard went on, turning his back on Lineham and addressing his explanation to Thanet, "at a clinic, if she could have afforded it. There are plenty of clinics which are prepared not to ask too many questions, provided the patient can pay.''

"Well *I* think . . .''

"That's enough, Mike," Thanet snapped. There was a limit to what he could allow Lineham to get away with, even in these circumstances.

Lineham frowned rebelliously, but clamped his mouth shut.

"Anyway," Thanet went on, "I should think it highly unlikely that Charity would have been able to pay, even if her parents had known about it, and I'm pretty certain they didn't . . . If she'd had it done on the National Health, Doc, would it have been done locally?"

"Not necessarily. It would depend on who she saw initially, what he was able to arrange in the way of a second opinion and so on. Anyway, couldn't the baby's father have provided the money?"

The man she met at Easter? The timing would be right. "It's possible, I suppose," said Thanet doubtfully.

Mallard stood up. "Well, I'll leave you to it. It's your problem now. Just thought you ought to hear right away. You'll get the full report later, of course, but I don't think there was anything else of much significance."

"Cause of death?" said Thanet with a grin.

Mallard smote his forehead. "You'll have to pension me off soon, I must be getting senile . . . As a matter of fact, it was rather interesting. Contre-coup."

"Really?" Thanet had heard of this, of course, but had never actually come across it in one of his cases.

Lineham was looking puzzled. "It rings a bell, but . . ."

Mallard loved expounding. "Very interesting type of head injury." He picked up an ashtray. "Imagine this is your victim's skull. Now in the classic blow to the stationary head with a blunt instrument," and he demonstrated by clenching his fist and hitting the side of the ashtray, "you have a rather nasty fracture, with bits of bone being driven into the soft brain tissue lying directly below the area of impact. This is the most common type of head injury, the 'coup' injury— 'coup' meaning 'blow,' of course. But in *contre*-coup you have an injury to the *opposite* side from the point of impact, and this occurs when you have a *moving* head coming into contact with a stationary surface." He demonstrated by strik-

95

ing the ashtray on Thanet's desk and putting his finger on the rim at a point directly opposite the site of impact.

Lineham was working it out. "So you're saying that the damage to Charity's brain was on the opposite side from the injury from the latch."

"That's right. It is believed that what actually happens in this type of injury is that you have compression of brain tissue when it strikes the inside of the skull and also a kind of tearing effect on membrane and blood vessels due to rotational forces which cause the brain to go on moving inside the skull after the head has come to rest."

"So she must have been thrown against the latch with considerable force," said Thanet.

"Not necessarily. If she'd been off balance, for example, with most of her weight resting on her right foot, the side of the injury . . ."

"Was there any evidence of the blow, shove or whatever it was that threw her against the door?"

"Only a slight bruising across the right side of her face and neck."

"Caused by?"

"Ah, now here we enter the realm of speculation," said Mallard, getting up. "And that's your job, not mine. I must be off, I'm late already."

"Just one more point," said Thanet quickly as Mallard headed for the door.

Mallard stopped, turned to peer at Thanet over his spectacles. "What?"

"Were there any traces of make-up on her face?"

"As a matter of fact, there were. Very slight traces, mind. Eye make-up, chiefly. Mascara and so on. Why do you ask?"

"Just wondered. Anyway, thanks for coming up, Doc."

"Er . . . Doc." Lineham was on his feet, looking sheepish. "Sorry I got so worked up just now."

Mallard twinkled at him over his spectacles. "If I apologised for every time I'd lost my temper, I'd be a rich man. Forget it."

Thanet was glad that Lineham had saved him the trouble of a reprimand in somewhat delicate circumstances. He gave the sergeant an approving nod and said, "Now then, Mike . . ."

"Just a minute, sir. Before we start talking about something else, why *did* you ask? About make-up."

"Think, Mike. Do you recall seeing make-up of any description in her belongings? In her bag? In her suitcase? In her room at home?"

"No. So I still don't get it. What did make you ask?"

Thanet stood up. "Come on, I'll tell you on the way to Lantern Street. We've got an appointment to see Veronica again, remember."

"You see, Mike," he went on, when they were in the car, "last night on the way home, I was thinking..."

Lineham groaned.

"What's that supposed to mean?"

"It was a groan of despair. When you say you've been thinking, I know that I'm going to hear something I should have thought of, if I'd only had the wit to do it."

"You'd rather not hear?"

"On the contrary. I can't wait. I'm a masochist."

"Well you did ask..."

"So?"

"Well, as I said, on the way home last night, I was thinking. About Charity. Trying to assimilate all the stuff we learned yesterday."

"I did that, too," said Lineham resignedly. "But it didn't lead me to questions about make-up."

"Are you going to listen, or aren't you? If you want to go on beating your breast, then fine, go ahead and do it. If not, just listen and apply that brain you're forever saying you haven't got."

Lineham's self-deprecation always irritated Thanet. He knew it ought not to, because he had long ago realised that it was a kind of barometer of the sergeant's state of mind. When Lineham was feeling good it was conspicuous by its absence. When things were going badly at him, or in his relationship with his difficult, demanding mother, the sergeant's confidence seemed to crumble away. At the moment, of course, he must be frantic about Louise.

"You see," said Thanet, "what puzzled me most was that if Charity had been going off the rails in the way Veronica described, why hadn't it shown in her appearance? The answer was..."

"She wouldn't have dared let it show. Her father would have been down on her like a ton of bricks."

"Exactly. But all the same, I somehow just couldn't picture

her behaving as she was supposed to have behaved looking like a twelve-year-old schoolgirl.''

"There are plenty of men who like little girls."

"Maybe. But the man Veronica described, the one Charity picked up on the train, just didn't sound that type."

"That's true. Too young, for one thing. And his clothes . . . Sounded the sort to fancy himself with the girls, didn't he?"

"Quite. So then I thought, but suppose she *had* looked different. Put her in jeans, let her hair down, put some make-up on her and she'd have been transformed."

"You're suggesting she actually did have other gear, then?"

"I am. And if she did, where would she have kept it?"

"I *see* . . . Veronica's, of course!"

"Exactly."

"Which was why she went there first on Monday, instead of going straight home from the station. She had to change."

"Right. Of course, we didn't think to ask Carson to check how she was dressed, when he was making enquiries at the station."

"Nor to ask Veronica, last night."

"It hadn't occurred to me, at that point."

"She didn't mention it herself, though—that Charity had left some stuff at her house."

"Scarcely surprising. She was in rather a state, with one thing and another."

"Let's hope she's calmed down a bit by now." Lineham parked neatly in front of the Hodges' house and they both got out.

By day, Lantern Street was even more depressing than by night. It looked as though only four or five out of the forty or so houses were occupied. The minute front gardens, surrounded by crumbling brick walls, were gateless and rubbish-strewn. Broken gutters leaned crazily down over walls stained green with algae and the rows of boarded-up windows imparted a slightly sinister air to the place.

Lineham grimaced. "Pretty grim, isn't it?"

"Infested with vermin, too, I shouldn't be surprised. I wonder why they stay here."

"Cheap? It's not easy, being a widow, with a child to bring up."

Lineham would know all about that particular struggle, Thanet thought. The sergeant had been only six when he had lost his father and Mrs. Lineham had never remarried. "Perhaps. Possibly the council won't re-house until the tenants are actually homeless."

Mrs. Hodges opened the door on the chain.

"I thought it might be Mr. Pritchard back again," she explained as she let them in. "And there was no way he was going to get over my doorstep again."

"Yes, we heard he'd been round to see you this morning."

"According to him I'm the one who's to blame for Charity's death, because I didn't let him know Veronica was ill on Friday morning! As if it wasn't just as much his fault, going off to Birmingham like that without a word to me. And you should have heard him, ranting and raving about Veronica corrupting his precious Charity, who of course was as pure as the driven snow. Well I soon put him straight on that one, I can tell you. I really let him have it, believe me!"

"So we gathered."

She pulled a face. "Oh dear. Did he go round and start on you? I am sorry. Please, sit down, both of you."

She looked exhausted, Thanet thought. Her skin was the colour of a tallow candle and her eyes were red-veined with lack of sleep. And yet, there was a lightness about her which had not been there yesterday.

"We've come to see Veronica, Mrs. Hodges," he reminded her gently. "How is she, this morning?"

Her hands tightened in her lap. "She's still in bed, I'm afraid."

"I'm sorry. It really is important that we see her."

She gave him a long, considering look. "Perhaps you ought to know . . . We had a long talk after you went, last night, Veronica and me."

Thanet said nothing, waited.

"I couldn't let it go like that . . . She was so upset. When I went up, I could hear her crying . . . I knew I wouldn't sleep. And I thought, well, she must think she's done something terrible, to be so afraid of me finding out. But she is my daughter, after all, and she's all I've got. We can't go on like this, what have I got to lose? So I went in to her. At first she wouldn't listen, put her hands over her ears, but in the end I managed to make her see that I didn't care what she'd done, it wouldn't make any difference to the way I felt about her . . . So then she came out with it."

Mrs. Hodges hesitated. "You may think it's a silly thing to get so worked up about, but then, you didn't know Veronica's dad. Straight as a die, he was, and honest as the day is long. I think that's why she felt so bad about it . . . She felt she'd let him down, as well as me . . ." Mrs. Hodges sat up a little straighter and looked defiantly at Thanet. "She'd been stealing, you see."

Thanet nodded. "At school."

She looked astounded. "You *knew*?"

"I guessed. I went to see Miss Bench the other day and amongst other things she mentioned that there'd been an outbreak of stealing at the school, shortly after she went there as Headmistress. And as you'd already told me about Veronica's distress and your inability to cope, at the time . . ."

"Miss Bench doesn't know, about Veronica?" said Mrs. Hodges in alarm.

"Oh no. Certainly not. As I say, the matter was only mentioned in passing and not in connection with Veronica at all, I assure you."

Mrs. Hodges sagged a little, with relief. "Thank goodness for that. Veronica couldn't have borne it coming out at school."

"Charity found out, I suppose, and blackmailed her into going along with her?"

"Yes. She caught her at it one day. She didn't say anything at first, but gradually she started tagging along with Veronica and Veronica didn't dare say she didn't want to be friends with her . . . Veronica was terrified, all the time, that Charity might give her away, and gradually it got so that Charity was expecting her to spend all her free time with her, go around with her at school . . . It was just as I thought, Veronica didn't like her at all, she only went along with her because she was afraid of what would happen if she said she didn't want to. And all this time, the matter was never mentioned between them, not openly . . . Veronica said it was just the way Charity would look at her . . . And then the crunch came, a month or two before Easter. Charity wanted her to go on holiday with her, to Dorset. Veronica didn't want to go. She wanted to stay here with me, she knew I'd be all on my own, otherwise, right over the holiday . . . But Charity wouldn't take no for an answer. And that was when she finally threatened her. Oh, not directly, openly, 'I'll tell,' that sort of thing. But slyly, nastily. 'What a pity it would be if your mother found out...' Then, another time, 'Wouldn't it be awful if Miss Bench found out... if the girls found out...' So in the end Veronica gave in. She simply could not *bear* the thought of being branded as a thief.'' The muscles along Mrs. Hodges' jaw tightened as she clenched her teeth. "If I'd known what was going on..." she said balefully.

Then what? Thanet wondered. Would Mrs. Hodges have been so furious with Charity that it could have happened as Lineham had suggested? A quarrel, a blow struck in anger...

But if so, Mrs. Hodges was putting on a superb performance. He wouldn't have thought her capable of such dissimulation. Still, there was a lot at stake, for her. The most ordinary person is capable of extraordinary feats when the whole fabric of his life is threatened.

Mrs. Hodges was shaking her head in bewilderment. "I don't understand any of it. I still can't believe that Veronica could have... But she told me herself, so I suppose I must believe it. I can't imagine what got into her. Stealing... her dad would have turned in his grave.''

"Mrs. Hodges,'' said Thanet gently. "You remember when I came to see you, yesterday?''

She nodded.

"You remember telling me how your husband's death hit you so hard that later you blamed yourself for not understanding just how badly Veronica was taking it?''

"Yes, but I don't quite see...''

"Mrs. Hodges, did you know that if a previously honest child suddenly starts stealing, it is often regarded as a cry for help?''

"What do you mean?''

"It's a bid for attention. It often begins with stealing from the parent whose affection is desired. Did you notice whether you yourself lost any sums of money around that time?''

Mrs. Hodges passed a hand over her face. "Now that you mention it... Yes, I do remember. I just put it down to me. I mean, I was in such a state I didn't really know whether I was coming or going...''

"Presumably, when Veronica found that that didn't work, she started stealing at school.''

He watched as understanding afflicted her. "Are you saying... you're saying it was my fault, then.''

101

Thanet shook his head with impatient compassion. "I think that at this stage it is irrelevant—it doesn't matter—whose *fault* it is. The important thing is to understand what went wrong, and why. Then you can pick up the pieces and start again. I'm simply saying that I'm sure Veronica is not by nature a thief—the very fact that she has gone to such lengths to keep it from you shows how upset and ashamed she is of what she did—and that her behaviour at that time was the result of a particularly distressing set of circumstances. I honestly don't think anything is to be gained by dwelling on whose fault it was. From what you say it sounds as though you and Veronica have got the chance of a fresh start, and who knows, the fact that you've been through difficult times together may bring you closer than you ever were before."

Mrs. Hodges was listening intently. Oh God, he thought, just listen to me preach. Thanet the social worker again. When I start off on that tack there's no holding me. If Lineham starts grinning I swear I'll ... but a glance out of the corner of his eye told him that the sergeant was listening with apparent solemnity.

"Yes ... " said Mrs. Hodges. "Yes, I can see that ... " She was silent for a few moments and then said, "Well, you've certainly given me something to think about, Inspector. Thank you."

All in the day's work, said an ironic little voice in Thanet's head. But he simply smiled, said, "Good."

"There's just one thing, though," said Mrs Hodges anxiously.

"What's that?"

"There won't be any need for Miss Bench to know, will there?"

"I should think it extremely unlikely. But I think I can promise you that if it did become necessary for her to know, Miss Bench wouldn't even consider making the matter public. She's a very understanding woman."

"You really think so?"

"I do. And now, Mrs. Hodges, if we could see Veronica ... "

She jumped up, her movements suddenly buoyant. "I'll go and see if she's up. If she's not, she may take a few minutes."

Thanet smiled. "Don't worry. We'll wait."

As soon as the door had closed behind her, Lineham said, "Bull's-eye again!"

"What are you talking about?"

"The stealing. You were right, yet again. Sickening, that's what it is, sickening. First you guess about the stealing, then about the make-up... It's enough to give anyone an inferiority complex."

"Oh come on, Mike, aren't you laying it on a bit thick? They're both very minor matters, after all."

"Minor! Well, OK, they might be minor in themselves, but the one put you on to the fact that Charity might be a blackmailer, the other on to where she stashed her gear..."

"We don't *know* that yet, Mike, we're only guessing."

"It's your guessing I'm complaining about. Some guess! I bet you a fiver you're right.. No! I take that back. I can't afford to throw fivers away like confetti, I'll bet you a pint..."

Thanet laughed. "Done!"

"What am I doing? I must be crazy. We both know you're right."

"We're about to find out."

They grinned at each other as footsteps were heard on the stairs. Thanet felt his stomach clench in anticipation. He had to be right. He needed Charity to have left her belongings here. There was no telling what he might find...

A moment later Mrs. Hodges entered the room, followed closely by Veronica. Like her mother the girl looked pale and very tired. Without the make-up she had been wearing last night she looked much younger.

"Ah, Veronica," said Thanet with a reassuring smile. "I hope you're feeling better, this morning?" Then, without waiting for an answer, "We've just come to collect Charity's things."

"Things?" said Mrs. Hodges. And then, with relief in her voice, "Oh, her jeans and so on... Run up and fetch them, will you, love?"

Veronica disappeared with alacrity.

Lineham, behind Mrs. Hodges, rolled his eyes at Thanet in mock despair.

Thanet ignored his clowning with difficulty. "You knew she left stuff here?"

"Well of course. Why shouldn't I? There's only one small bag... I felt sorry for the girl," she added defensively. "I may not have liked her, but I did feel sorry for her, with a

103

father like that. She could hardly blow her nose without asking his permission first. As for doing any of the things girls usually do . . . And she did ask my permission—didn't she, love?'' She turned to Veronica, who had just returned, a large nylon shoulder bag dangling from one hand.

"To do what, Mum?"

"To leave that here." Mrs. Hodges nodded at the bag.

"Yeah, sure."

"It was only a few bits and pieces of clothes. Some jeans and that . . . and some make-up. Her father would have locked her up rather than let her wear trousers, wouldn't he, Veronica, and as for make-up . . . He'd have thought she was on the streets or something."

"So when did she wear them?" said Thanet. "She could hardly have gone out in them, in case it got back to her parents."

"Indoors, mostly," said Veronica. "She'd come round on a Saturday, change into her jeans, put some make-up on and we'd play pop records."

"To tell you the truth," said Mrs. Hodges, "I encouraged it. Made me feel she was more normal. It was just a harmless bit of fun, that's all."

Harmless? Thanet wondered. Or had it fed Charity's fantasies, encouraged her secret rebellion? Had those stolen moments been so heady, spiced as they were by the knowledge that she was breaking out of the rigid guidelines laid down by her father, that she had grown to hunger for more dangerous ways of defying him?

"You said, 'Indoors, mostly' . . . "

"Well, she did wear them on the way home from Dorset at Easter," said Veronica. "She couldn't have worn them at the Holiday Home, trousers weren't allowed for girls."

Mrs. Hodges made a clicking sound of disgust. "Ridiculous," she muttered.

"She changed in the toilet, on the train," Veronica added.

"And this weekend?"

"She wasn't wearing them when she left, but she was when she came back."

"And presumably she changed back into her normal clothes when she called here on the way home from the station?"

"Yes. And washed her make-up off."

Thanet held out his hand for the bag. "May I see?"

She handed it over. Thanet could feel Lineham's attention riveted to the bag with the quivering anticipation of a terrier watching a rat-hole. Normally, at this point, Thanet would have left, returned to the office to examine its contents at leisure. But today he didn't. He rather thought—hoped—that he would have to question Veronica about something that was in it. He lifted it on to his knees, unzipped it and rummaged about inside. Ah yes, here it was...His fingers closed triumphantly over the small oblong shape and withdrew it.

The other three stared at the wallet as if mesmerised.

Turning aside a little so that its contents were not visible to the two women, Thanet flicked through it, his calm, unhurried movements betraying nothing of his inward agitation. If he was right, this small leather object could hold the key to the riddle of Charity's death. He *had* to be right...But it didn't look as though it had. The letter he had hoped to find was not there, and the wallet contained only a bundle of five-pound notes (he'd check how much, later) and, in a separate compartment, a Polaroid photograph. Perhaps this would help...

He took it across to the window, to have a look at it in better light. Charity smiled up at him. She was wearing jeans and a yellow crash helmet and was sitting astride a motor cycle. And yes...He gave a satisfied nod. The registration number was clearly visible. He handed the photograph to Lineham, who immediately saw the point. They exchanged a gratified glance.

"Let Veronica take a look, will you, Sergeant?"

Thanet waited while Mrs. Hodges and the girl studied the photograph together.

"Do you know whose motor cycle that is?"

Both women shook their heads.

"Unless..." said Veronica.

"Yes?"

"It could belong to the chap she picked up at Easter. She told me he had one—and he was carrying a crash helmet when I saw him at Paddington, I told you."

Thanet retrieved the photograph. No point in wasting time asking questions. It would be a simple enough matter to check. There was just one other point he wanted to bring up, though.

"I asked you last night if Charity knew anyone—a man—who wears pebble-lensed glasses."

Even before he had finished speaking Veronica was shaking her head. "I told you, no."

"I wondered if, having had time to think about it overnight . . . ?"

But she was equally emphatic. No. And he was equally certain she was lying. It was pointless to persist at the moment, she obviously wasn't going to budge.

He thanked them both for their help and left.

"Why d'you think she's lying about the chap with glasses?" said Lineham, when they were in the car.

"Protecting him, perhaps?"

"But why would she?"

"Fellow feeling? He could be another of Charity's victims. Blackmailers rarely stop at one, once they get a taste for it. If Veronica knows him, likes him, even, and is aware that Charity had some sort of hold on him . . ."

"Could be, I suppose. Bit of luck with the photograph though, sir, wasn't it?"

"Being able to read the registration number, you mean. Yes. As soon as we get back, you can ring Maidstone, get them to run it through the computer."

"With any luck, we've got him!" Lineham exulted.

"Perhaps." Over the years Thanet had learned that it was safer not to expect too much.

All the same, he knew the excitement in Lineham's face was reflected in his own when the sergeant put the phone down and said triumphantly, "Got it, sir! David Williams, 10, Bryn Mawr Terrace, Cardiff."

14

"There's the Severn Bridge, sir."

Thanet knew that the note of satisfaction in Lineham's voice was caused not by their first glimpse of the famous suspension bridge but by what it signified: they were nearing the end of their journey.

He eyed the soaring, swooping curves appreciatively. "Impressive, isn't it?"

As soon as the computer had come up with Williams' address, Thanet had decided to drive down to South Wales that very afternoon. Lineham had been against the idea from the start.

"What's the point, when we know he lives in London?"

"But we don't know where, do we? This seems as good a way as any, of finding out. So just get a move on and arrange clearance for us, will you? I'd like to be away between one and two, if possible."

"But...two hundred miles there and two hundred back, just for an address?"

"It's not quite as simple as that."

"But why can't we just get Cardiff to check it out for us, sir?"

"I agree, we could. But I'd prefer to go myself."

"But..."

"If you say 'But' just once more, I'll...Look, Mike, we're going, and that's that. At least, I am." Then, more gently, "Mike, I appreciate that this is not a good time for you to be out of Sturrenden. If you'd prefer not to come with me, I'd quite understand."

Lineham flushed. The gynaecologist had confirmed that an induction would be necessary, but had refused to commit himself as to timing. Louise would be kept under constant observation, her case under daily review, and that was all he was prepared to say at present.

"It's not that, sir. Oh, hell, to be honest, I suppose it is. Not that they'll do anything now before tomorrow."

"You're thinking of not being able to visit her tonight, I suppose?"

Lineham nodded miserably.

"In that case, why not stay here? I can easily get another driver."

"But I'd like to come, sir..."

Thanet swallowed his exasperation. "Look, why don't you nip along to the hospital now, see if they'll let you in to see Louise for a few minutes?"

"Do you think they would?"

107

"You can but try. They might well, in the circumstances . . ."

They did, and three-quarters of an hour later Thanet and Lineham were on their way. They shared the driving, changing over when they stopped for a quick cup of coffee at Membury Service Station, and so far the journey had gone without a hitch. The M25 had been almost deserted and although the tedious stretch along the A322 through Bisley, Bagshot and Bracknell had been slow, once they were on the M4 they'd been able to keep up a steady 70 mph and were now only half an hour from their destination.

"They say people used to queue for hours to cross on the old ferry, before the bridge was built," murmured Thanet, gazing out across the glittering expanse of water.

"Why did you say, 'It is not quite as simple as that'?" said Lineham suddenly.

"What?"

"When I said it wasn't worth driving two hundred miles there and two hundred back, just for an address . . ."

"Ah, yes . . . Well, if you don't mind, I'd rather tell you later. On the way back. I may be wrong . . ."

Lineham frowned. He hated being kept in the dark. Thanet, equally, hated giving explanations before he was ready for them. And it was rather a long shot, after all . . .

Thanet once more gave his attention to the scenery. He'd never been to Wales before and now he regretted that he was approaching it at such speed and on such an errand. Road signs in Welsh began to flash by, giving him a sense of entering a foreign land, and already the character of the landscape was changing. Hills dotted with sheep loomed ahead and he began to sense the nearness of the mountains. Even the grass in the fields looked tougher, coarser, less groomed, subtly creating the impression of a greater wildness to come.

As they skirted Newport Thanet thought how much pleasanter it would have been if Joan had been with him and they had been setting off on a holiday weekend, just the two of them, and they could have made a more leisurely approach, through Chepstow, perhaps . . .

"Cardiff," said Lineham with satisfaction. "This is where we turn off."

"Straight through the city centre, they said. Though we haven't exactly chosen the best time of day, have we?"

It was a quarter to five and the traffic was thickening by the minute. They crawled along the Newport Road into the heart of the city, paid their courtesy call and emerged with directions to Bryn Mawr Terrace. They reached it just before six o'clock.

"Don't think much of the local architecture, do you?" Lineham said.

"Depends what you're used to, I expect."

This, Thanet supposed, was the Welsh version of the Victorian Terrace: narrow little houses built of ugly rough stone blocks, with the window surrounds picked out in a variety of garish colours. Number ten sported a particularly virulent shade of orangey-pink. The net curtains at the downstairs window twitched as Thanet knocked at the door.

"Mrs. Williams?"

The woman peered up at him like a suspicious sparrow. She was middle-aged, her sharp face and skinny body all knobs and angles. Her head was encased turban-style in a blue chiffon scarf punctuated by the ridges of plastic rollers.

"What do you want?"

"We'd like a word with Mr. David Williams, please." Thanet introduced himself, offered identification.

She glanced up and down the street. "You'd better come in a minute."

The hall was so tiny that there was barely room for the three of them to squeeze into it, but she did not offer to show them into the sitting room. She shut the front door behind her and turned to face them, folding her arms across her chest.

"What do you want with our Dai?"

Thanet had no intention of telling her in any, but the vaguest terms and there followed a few minutes of sparring, each of them in his own way enjoying the contest. Eventually she capitulated.

"He works at a garage round the corner," she said grudgingly. "Mechanic. He'll be home any minute now."

Thanet carefully avoided giving Lineham a "told you so" look.

"You'd better wait in here." She squeezed past them to open a door, led them in.

A motor cycle roared up the street, cut off outside.

"That'll be him." She scuttled off, closing the door behind her, and there was a murmur of voices in the hall. When she came back in, followed by her son, she was carrying a sheet of plastic which she draped over one of the armchairs.

"I'm not having you dirtying my nice clean chair with that filthy old pair of jeans."

She was determined to stay and listen ("It's my right, he's my son, isn't he?") and it wasn't until Thanet courteously pointed out that he, too, had his rights and one of them was to take the boy away and question him at the police station that she reluctantly left them in peace.

David Williams was in his early twenties and certainly fitted the description Veronica had given them. Thanet could see why Charity would have been attracted to him. He was a well-built, good-looking boy with an air of slightly swaggering virility. He had adopted an almost aggressively nonchalant pose, sitting well back in his chair with the ankle of one leg resting on the knee of the other. He was chewing gum with the non-stop, rhythmic movements of a cow chewing the cud.

Thanet decided that he couldn't be bothered to waste a lot of time in preliminary skirmishing. He and Lineham still had a long drive ahead of them tonight. He produced the Polaroid photograph.

"That your motor cycle?"

Williams' jaw stopped moving for a moment, then began again, more slowly.

"What if it is?"

"Oh come on, Williams. Don't you read the newspapers?"

The boy's eyes narrowed. "What're you talking about?"

He really didn't know, Thanet was prepared to swear it.

"That girl, in the photograph . . . She's dead." He caught the flash of relief in Williams' eyes before the boy said disbelievingly, *"Dead?"*

"To be precise . . . Murdered."

Williams stopped chewing altogether and for a moment his jaw hung down. Then he sat up and with an impatient movement took the gum from his mouth and flung it in the direction of the empty fireplace. It landed on the hearth where, thought Thanet, its presence would no doubt later earn Williams a sharp rebuke.

"You're having me on."

Thanet shook his head. "And as we found that photograph amongst her belongings . . ."

" 'Ere, what you getting at?"

110

"...we'd like you tell us about your relationship with her."

"Relationship!" Williams gave a bark of sour laughter. "Oh boy, I like that. Relationship! Look, Inspector, that bird was a good screw, that's all. A one-night stand, no more, no less."

"People don't write letters to a one-night stand," said Thanet. He shook his head reprovingly. "Most unwise, to commit yourself to paper like that."

Williams was looking frightened now. Thanet glanced at Lineham.

"Of course," said the sergeant smoothly, "we don't make snap judgements. We can't afford to. Especially in murder cases."

"I didn't even know she was dead till you told me, a minute ago! I told you, I only ever met her once, and that was months ago."

"Once could be more than enough, in certain circumstances," said Thanet.

"What...cricumstances?"

"Suppose you tell us?" said Lineham gently. "Perhaps we've got it wrong."

Little by little Lineham teased out the sorry tale. Williams had been working in London and had driven down to Dorset to deliver back to its owner a motor cycle which had been involved in an accident. Charity had picked him up on the train back to Paddington. He had taken her out for a Chinese meal and then they had gone back to his room, where they had spent the night together. The photograph had been taken 'for a lark,' next morning.

"Did you know she was under-age?"

Williams stared blankly at him for a moment, then groaned, put his head in his hands.

"Did you?"

Williams raised his head, eyes blazing. "What do you think? Look, Inspector, I don't want to sound like I've got a swollen head, but I don't have no problems finding birds, see? I don't have to go risking trouble with the law running after little girls. If I'd known, I wouldn't have touched her with a bloody barge-pole!"

"Oh come on, Williams, you must have suspected, surely. After all, she was a virgin."

111

"Virgin!" Williams was shaking his head in disbelief. "I don't know what fairy-tales you've been listening to about her, but believe me, Inspector, someone's been leading you up the garden path."

"Well of course, you would say that, wouldn't you. It lets you off the hook."

"It's the truth!" shouted Williams. "That little bitch knew her way around, I can tell you. That's why . . ." He stopped abruptly.

"That's why what?"

Williams shook his head. "Nothing."

"You were going to say, that's why you didn't believe her when she told you that she was pregnant and that you were the father."

"If you bloody well know it all, why are you going on at me like this?" snarled Williams.

"We want the details," said Thanet. "This is a murder case, remember."

"Ok, OK, I'll give you the bloody details, if it'll get you off my back . . . Like I said, she left next morning and I didn't see her again, not once, from that day to this. There was something about her . . ." He shook his head, as if to erase the memory. "Once was enough, that's all."

"Yet you wrote to her."

"To try and shut her up! She was a real pain, that girl. Kept on and on writing me letters, always the same garbage . . . How much she'd enjoyed herself with me, how much she was looking forward to seeing me again, blah, blah . . . how difficult it was for her because her old man was so strict . . . As if I cared! Far as I was concerned it was over, finito!" A complacent little smile curled the corners of his mouth. "Had other fish to fry, didn't I?" The grin disappeared. "Then she writes and tells me she thinks she might be able to get away over the Bank Holiday. We'd be able to have the whole weekend together, she says. She had it all worked out—what time she'd arrive, where we'd go, what we'd do . . . Well, that did it, I'd had it up to here. This time I did write back and told her straight, I wasn't interested, I'd found someone else, I'd be away that weekend anyway—well, you've read the bloody letter, you know what I said in it."

Throughout this recital Thanet had once again unexpectedly been filled with compassion for Charity. He imagined her

112

romanticising the sordid encounter at Easter until it took on the aura and intensity of a *grande passion,* transforming this shallow, callous youth into everything that was noble and desirable in a man. He saw her eager hopes dashed as the days and then weeks went by without a word in reply, pictured her last attempt to recreate reality from fantasy in her bid to join Williams for the weekend, her shattering disappointment when she at last received the longed-for letter...And then, to cap it all, the mounting panic as she realised that her period was overdue...

"And it was soon after that she drops her little bombshell," said Williams.

"Told you she was pregnant, you mean?"

"Yeah. In a bloody telegram, no less. Probably afraid if she sent a letter I'd chuck it straight in the bin without reading it."

"Claiming you were the father, I presume?"

"You bet. You could've knocked me down with a feather...Oh no, I thought, you're not pinning that one on me, no matter how hard you try."

"So what did you do?"

"What would you have done? I scarpered, of course, moved back home. I knew she'd never find me down here and I was pretty sure I could get my old job back."

Thanet believed him. It was, in fact, precisely what he had expected Williams to do.

"Just one last question, then. Can you give us an account of your movements last Monday evening, between nine and eleven pm?"

"Between nine and eleven," repeated Williams, frowning with concentration. "Monday..." Abruptly, his face cleared and a slow grin spread across his features. "Is that when she...?"

Thanet could see what was coming.

"From eight till midnight I was playing in a group at a disco, here in Cardiff." His fingers jauntily thrummed imaginary strings. "Guitar, Inspector. Go ahead and check."

They would, of course, thought Thanet as Lineham took down the details, but Williams was so cocky in his relief that it would obviously be only a matter of routine. It really did look as though the Welshman was out of the running.

113

He said so to Lineham as they walked back to the car. "We'll get Cardiff to check for us, in the morning."

Lineham did not reply and Thanet looked sharply at him. The sergeant's face was closed, brooding.

"What's the matter, Mike?"

"You knew, didn't you?"

"Knew what?"

"That Williams would be here. That's why you were so determined to come."

"Not knew. Guessed, perhaps."

"How?"

Thanet shrugged. "I just tried to think myself into his shoes, work out how he would react . . . It was very much a long shot."

"But it came off," said Lineham gloomily.

They had reached the car.

"Shall I drive for the first half?" Thanet hoped that Lineham would take the hint and drop the subject. He really didn't feel in the mood for another session of breast-beating by the sergeant.

"I don't mind," Lineham obediently got into the passenger seat and sank into a silence which lasted until well past the Severn Bridge.

"Well, Mike," said Thanet eventually. "What do you think? Think he was telling the truth, about Charity being sexually experienced? Incidentally, odd about that letter, isn't it? That it never turned up. I really did expect to find it in the bag Charity left at Veronica's."

"Hmm?" Lineham made an effort to rouse himself. "She probably tore it up. After all, it wasn't exactly the sort of letter to cherish, was it? She was probably furious he'd given her the brush-off."

"True. Anyway, do you think he was telling the truth?"

"About her sex life, you mean? Yes, I did. Didn't you?"

"Yes. But of course, if he was, the question is, who?"

"Difficult to see how she ever had the opportunity."

"I agree. Mrs. Hodges can't have known anything about it, or she'd have mentioned it, I'm sure."

"Might be one of the masters at school, sir?"

"At a girls' school, Mike?"

"With respect, sir, I think you're a bit out of date. You often find masters in girls' schools these days. As a matter of fact, Louise and I met a master from Sturrenden Girls' Tech at a party recently. Teaches history.''

"You're not going to tell me he wears pebble-lensed specs?"

Lineham smote his forehead in mock self-admonition. "Why ever didn't I think of him before? Of course he does!"

"All right, Mike, cut out the sarcasm. You're right. If there's one master at the Tech, there might be more. We'll get on to the school first thing in the morning.''

"What about the Bible classes?"

"I told you, there are only two boys, and they're much too young. There's Jethro, of course. He often saw her home, apparently—and come to think of it, he's just the type to have a yen for little girls. Inadequate, probably sexually deprived . . . And his wife's enough to make any man impotent. Yes, the more I think about it, the more likely it seems. It could explain why Mrs. Jethro hated Charity so much—and why Jethro himself was so on edge, when I saw him . . .''

Thanet settled down to concentrate on his driving. At Membury they stopped again to refresh themselves with a cup of coffee and a substantial snack. Thanet, aware that it would be too late to ring Joan when he got home, tried to contact her from a phone booth in the service station complex, but without success. Once again, she was out. He gritted his teeth as he slammed the receiver down. He felt as though she was daily floating further and further away from him, like a balloon cut loose from its mooring, and he was helpless to do anything about it.

Now it was his turn to sit in brooding silence and Lineham, preoccupied no doubt with his own anxieties, made no attempt to break in upon his reverie until they were approaching Maidstone.

"Isn't that lightning ahead?"

"I didn't notice." But a moment or two later Thanet saw the distant flicker for himself. "You're right, Mike. Looks as though there's a storm coming up."

Now he had something else to worry about: Bridget. She'd always hated thunderstorms and invariably woke up if there was one during the night. He began to pray that he would get home before it broke. His mother-in-law could sleep through anything.

He made it in the nick of time. The first really loud clap of

115

thunder came as he was running his car into the garage and by the time he emerged the first heavy drops of rain were falling. In his hurry he had forgotten to shut the gate and, cursing, he sprinted back down the drive to do so. He wasn't going to risk a repeat of yesterday's performance, with Ben.

By the time he reached the front door the rain was hammering down and his hair was plastered to his scalp. In the hall he tilted his head, listened intently. Was that a cry? Yes, there it was again.

"Mummyyyy..."

Peeling off his wet jacket as he went, he took the stairs two at a time as outside the lightning flashed and, a second later, there was a deafening crash of thunder. He tossed his jacket in the direction of his bedroom door and went straight into the children's room.

"MUMMYYY..."

Bridget was sitting bolt upright in bed, hands pressed hard over her ears, eyes tight shut, face screwed up. Ben, who had inherited his grandmother's knack, slumbered on undisturbed.

"Sprig..." Thanet plumped down on the bed beside her and gathered her into his arms. Hers at once coiled themslves around his neck and she burrowed her face into his shoulder.

"Daddy..."

He began to stroke her hair with soothing, rhythmic movements. "Hush darling, it's all right, Daddy's here. Don't cry, it's all right..."

Lightning flared and, simultaneously, there was a thunderclap so loud that Thanet's eardrums rang and the house shook. Torrential rain lashed against the windows.

Bridget's body convulsed and she gave a little cry, clung to him even more tightly.

"Don't worry, darling. It's quite safe." He fervently hoped that this was true, that his mother-in-law's house had a good earthing system.

"The house... It *trembled*."

"This house has stood here for hundreds of years, love, and it's going to stand for hundreds more..."

He continued to administer comfort and murmur reassurances while the storm raged overhead and presently the intervals between lightning and thunder began to lengthen as it drifted away. Gradually Bridget quieted and, exhausted by the tensions of the last half an hour, closed her eyes and

116

relaxed against him. When he judged that she was almost asleep, Thanet began to ease her gently down into the bed.

"Don't go 'way, Daddy," she said sleepily.

He told her that he would stay just a little while longer but that the storm had moved away now and that yes, if it returned, he would come to her again.

Suddenly, shockingly, she opened her eyes wide and in them there was the painful honesty of someone who at last faces a long-evaded truth.

"Mummy's never coming back, is she, Daddy?"

"Sprig!" Weakness buckled his legs and he subsided on to the bed again. "Of course she is! In just over two weeks now she'll be home for good. Whatever makes you say such a thing?" Into his weary brain sprang the question: has she heard something I haven't?

"Because she doesn't love us any more."

"Darling, that simply isn't true! Of course she loves us." But the statement had chimed in so exactly with his own fears that he knew he'd sounded unconvincing. For Bridget's sake he tried again. "You *know* she does."

But Bridget was shaking her head, her eyes solemn. "If she did, she wouldn't have gone away..."

"Sprig..." Thanet put his arms around her and lifted her into a sitting position once more, conscious of a sudden spurt of anger against Joan. How dare she cause such insecurity in their beloved daughter? And how dare she put him once again into the impossible position of defending something which, in his heart of hearts, he found indefensible?

Since Joan had started work they had had to deal with many uncomfortable questions from the children and for Thanet, especially, it had been difficult to find convincing answers. For the first ten years of their marriage Joan had apparently been content to remain a housewife, and it had come as a rude shock to find that inwardly she had long been hankering after a satisfying career of her own. Fortunately Thanet had seen the light in time and, having realised that if he persisted in opposing Joan he would most surely lose her, he had at last capitulated and given her his support.

But all along, deep down inside, he had known that, given the choice, he would have preferred it to be otherwise and at a time like this, when his own doubts and fears were more profound than they had ever been, it took an almost superhuman effort to attempt to convince Bridget that hers were unjustified.

But for her sake he did his best, only to find that when at last he crawled into his lonely bed, his own anxieties had proliferated, hydra-like.

Suppose Bridget was right, and Joan wasn't coming back. This might explain why she'd been so elusive of late. Perhaps Bridget had overheard a fragment of conversation between her mother and grandmother, on the telephone.

Or—and in some ways this thought was comforting, in others it made him feel even worse—was it possible that his own anxieties over Joan were becoming so powerful that he was unwittingly communicating them to the children? He had heard of such things happening.

What a responsibility children were, he thought as he tossed and turned, a truly awesome responsibility. You embarked upon "having a baby" without ever really considering that the baby soon becomes a toddler, a child, an adolescent, that it will make impossible demands upon your patience and tolerance, stretch your financial resources until they snap, and bring to an end for ever the twosome for which you abandoned your bachelor state.

He loved Bridget and Ben, couldn't begin to visualise life without them, but there was no doubt that bringing up children was uphill work most of the way. Not just physical work, though in the early years that was demanding enough; equally wearing were the endless decisions to be made, decisions in which mundane things like food, clothes, toys and television programmes became inextricably bound with ethics and morality, so that you were constantly struggling to define your attitudes and justify your behaviour in an attempt to communicate your values to your children.

Then there was the vexed question of discipline: to punish or not to punish? And if so, how? To what degree? It was all so difficult, so complicated. It was much easier, he supposed, if you had a rigid code to follow, like Pritchard. For Pritchard everything was white or black, right or wrong, good or evil. Pritchard would never have to stop and ask himself if he were doing the right thing. Though Pritchard's religion must be cold comfort to him now, when he had lost the daughter he had alienated by it.

Once again Thanet found himself wondering exactly what

118

had happened during that week seven or eight years ago, when Charity had been kept home from school. Whatever it was, it had changed her radically from a lively, mischievous child, whose unacceptable behaviour had no doubt been an over-reaction against too strict a discipline at home, into little more than a zombie. No, not a zombie, he corrected himself, for underneath Charity's rebellion had continued. She had simply bided her time, waited until she had gathered sufficient strength to deal her father a mortal blow, sharpening prematurely the only weapon she possessed, her sexuality.

Furthermore, Thanet was convinced that whatever Pritchard had done to her during that week had not only changed her outward behavior and steeled her antagonism towards him, but had also taught her some bitter lessons which had soured her expectations of life and destroyed her chances of enjoying good relationships with others.

He had to find out what had happened and before he finally fell asleep he determined to put it high on the list of the next day's priorities.

15

Next morning Thanet was riffling hurriedly through the reports which had piled up during yesterday's absence when Doc Mallard put his head around the door and said, "Got it!"

Thanet glanced up abstractedly. "Morning, Doc." Then, as he took in Mallard's air of suppressed excitement, "Got what?"

Mallard glanced back over his shoulder. "Ah, morning, Sergeant." He opened the door wider and advanced into the room, followed by Lineham. "How's your wife?"

"Much the same, thanks, Doc."

"I heard she'd gone into hospital early. What's the problem, exactly?"

The two men chatted about Louise for a few moments and Thanet, anxious to be off, waited with as much patience as he could muster. At last there was a suitable hiatus and he put in quickly, "Got what, Doc?"

"Jethro Pritchard. You know I kept on saying the name rang a bell? Well, I finally remembered." Mallard clasped his hands behind his back and gave a self-satisfied little bounce on the balls of his feet.

"Remembered what?"

"Can't recall the details, I'm afraid. Not surprising, really. Must have been all of—oh, twenty years ago, I'd say."

"What must have been?"

"The Court case."

With difficulty Thanet refrained from saying, "What Court case?" The little doctor, he realised, was enjoying keeping them in suspense. But he did wish he'd get on with it . . .

Mallard glanced from one attentive face to the other and said, "Very unsavoury it was, that I do remember. Something to do with little girls . . . Yes, I thought that would interest you." He glanced at his watch. "Good gracious, I'm late for surgery already."

"But . . ."

Mallard flapped his hand. "Sorry. Told you, can't remember the details. Can't do all your work for you, can I?"

"Thanks, Doc," Thanet called after his retreating figure.

He and Lineham looked at each other.

"Bible classes, indeed!" said the sergeant.

"Let's not jump to conclusions. What I don't understand is that Pritchard—Charity's father—must have known about this conviction. And in that case, why on earth did he trust his brother to see Charity home?"

"Perhaps he thought that being his brother, and her uncle . . ."

"Bit naive, don't you think?"

"Perhaps Jethro convinced him he was on the straight and narrow. After all, if all this happened twenty years ago and he's not been in trouble since . . ."

"But we don't know that, do we, Mike? Anyway, I think the first thing is for you to go through the files, find out exactly what happened. We can't tackle him until we're sure of our facts. You'd better get someone to give you a hand. I really must be off. I only dropped in to the office for a few minutes, just to see if anything important had cropped up . . ."

"You don't call this important?"

"Yes, of course it is, but the point is, I've been wanting a chance to get hold of Charity's mother alone, and on the way in this morning I saw Pritchard in the street, heading for the town. I'd like to catch her before he gets back.''

''How do you know he wasn't on his way to work? Oh, of course, he told us he didn't have to go in for the rest of the week, didn't he? Right, then. Is there anything else you want me to do? I know I've got to check with the school, see if there are any other male teachers . . .''

''Get that house to house on Lantern Street started, concentrating on the earlier times. And go through these reports, see if there's anything interesting.''

''Right, sir. Don't worry, I'll cope. See you later.''

On the way to Town Road Thanet sternly resisted the temptation to consider the implications of Mallard's news. It was a question of priorities. He would have ample time, later, to think about Jethro Pritchard. For the moment it was Mrs. Pritchard he wanted to concentrate on, and he spent the short journey clarifying in his own mind precisely which points he wished to raise with her, and in which order. He only hoped that she had not taken advantage of her husband's absence and gone out.

But he was in luck. Although there was at first no answer to his knock, he thought he saw movement behind the net curtains in the front room, and tried again. A moment later Mrs. Pritchard opened the door.

''Good morning, Mrs. Pritchard. You said I could come and talk to you if I needed your help.''

She hesitated, then stood back. ''Come in.''

She led him into the bleak little sitting room, untying her apron as she went. She laid it over the back of a chair and sat down, folding her hands in her lap. Her meek, waiting stillness, her black dress and the severity of her hair-style combined to give her the simple dignity of Quaker women in the late seventeenth century.

Thanet seated himself opposite her. ''This has been a terrible week for you.''

His sympathy at once brought tears to her eyes, but she blinked them impatiently away, compressed her lips. ''My mother's funeral has been put off until Tuesday.''

Thanet nodded.

''What . . . what about Charity?''

''I'm afraid there'll have to be an inquest first.''

121

"Oh."

She hadn't realised, he could tell from her stricken, resigned look.

"When will that be?"

"On Monday...Mrs. Pritchard, I came to see you because, although I know that this must all be incredibly painful for you, I feel that as Charity's mother you can help me in a way no one else can."

"How do you mean?" It was barely more than a whisper.

"First of all, there's something I must tell you, something which I know will distress you. It will have to be made public at the inquest and that is why I wanted to see you first, to tell you myself. So that you will be prepared."

She was rigid in her chair, bracing herself against what was coming.

"When she died, your daughter had just had an abortion."

Thanet watched with pity as her eyes snapped shut, as if to repudiate this glimpse of a too-harsh reality. He could only guess at the powerful and confused emotions she must be experiencing, but of one thing he was certain: they were all painful.

Suddenly she opened her eyes again. "You don't mean...Are you saying that she wasn't...killed, after all, that she died because of...what she'd had done to her?"

"Oh, no. No, I'm sorry if I misled you. But if it's any comfort at all, I can tell you that she didn't suffer. She died instantly."

Mrs. Pritchard flinched.

"But you must see that because of the abortion, however unlikely it might have seemed to you and your husband, Charity must have been..." How could he tactfully put it? "...on intimate terms with a man."

She ducked her head to hide her embarrassment. "Yes, I can see that," she whispered. Then she looked up and said in a kind of gasp, as if the protest were being forced out of her, "But I just don't see how she could have. I mean...she would never have had the opportunity."

"Nevertheless..."

For a long moment they sat in silence as the indisputable implications of the word sank in.

"Yes," she said at last, with a sigh. "You're right, of course. Nevertheless, she must have."

Again she was silent, thinking, and Thanet waited patiently. Finally she said, "I'm sorry, Inspector, it's no good. I can't think of *anyone*. She just didn't know any men, not...privately, so to speak. Not to my knowledge, anyway. She must have..." She shook her head in sad disbelief. "She must have been deceiving us for some time."

"I know. And you must believe me when I say I'm sorry to cause you additional distress at a time like this."

For the first time she smiled, if that brief, joyless upturning of the corners of her mouth could be called a smile. "You're very kind, Inspector. Not a bit like what I imagined a policeman to be."

Now it was his turn to be embarrassed and he brushed the compliment aside by hurrying on. "So what I want you to do is talk to me about Charity, tell me what she was like, as a person. I think that somewhere along the line things must have gone badly wrong for her somehow, and I feel that if I can understand why, it would help me in investigating her death."

"I don't see how."

"It's difficult to explain, precisely. But I always find that the more I understand about the...victim, of such a crime, the clearer things become."

"I'm not sure, anyway, after what we've just been saying, that I knew her as well as I thought I did."

"I can see that. All the same, she lived in this house with you all her life. I really would be grateful if you would just talk to me about her. Say anything you like."

At last Mrs. Pritchard relaxed a little. She sat back in her chair and gazed at the fireplace with the blank, unseeing gaze of someone focusing on a mental image. "There's not much to tell, really. As I said before, she was quiet, considerate, used to help me with the chores...I never had to chase her, to get on with her homework or do her piano practice." Mrs. Pritchard's eyes flickered briefly in the direction of the piano.

It was shut, Thanet noticed, and the music had been put away, out of sight.

Mrs. Pritchard lifted her hands helplessly. "I just don't know what to say. She never gave any trouble."

This was the opportunity Thanet had been waiting for and he tried not to appear over-eager as he said, "Never?"

Mrs. Pritchard gave a puzzled frown. "What do you mean?" But she avoided his eye, he noticed.

"Well, I understood that when Charity was around seven or eight, she used to be quite a handful at school."

She was staring at him, remembering, and plainly wishing that the conversation had not taken this particular turn. "How did you know that?"

He shrugged. "We pick up all sorts of snippets of information during the course of an investigation such as this. One of the people I talked to was Miss Foskett."

She was silent, waiting, clearly apprehensive.

"I understand that you and your husband went to see her, at her request, to see if anything could be done."

Still she said nothing.

"Miss Foskett said that after that interview, Charity was away from school for a week, and that when she came back, she was a different child..."

Mrs. Pritchard's eyes slid away from his questioning gaze. "It's all such a long time ago," she murmured evasively.

Thanet was sure that the whole episode was indelibly etched upon her memory. He also saw that she was now faced with a dilemma: she wanted to be co-operative, help him as much as she could, but she didn't want to be disloyal to her husband. Her next words confirmed this.

"My husband is a man of very strong religious faith, Inspector."

"I know."

"He... he sees it as his duty to try to stamp out evil wherever he may come across it."

Thanet inclined his head.

"Even when it is in his own daughter." Her voice was no more than a murmur.

"I suppose," said Thanet encouragingly, "he sees any kind of unruly behaviour as the work of the devil."

She looked up, eagerly. "You *do* understand. That's right. That's exactly what he does feel."

"And you agree with him?"

"Of course." But her voice lacked conviction. "Well... to a large extent, yes."

"But not, perhaps, when it came to trying to discipline Charity."

"She was so small," Mrs. Pritchard cried, her sudden

124

passion shocking in its intensity. "She didn't understand. How could she? Oh, she'd been very naughty, I know that, but..."

"So what did he do?"

Mrs. Pritchard moved her feet restlessly as if she would like to get up and run away. Thanet regretted having to press her, but he felt that this incident, so far back in the past, might have been of profound significance in Charity's life, had perhaps shaped and directed her future behaviour to such an extent that it could even have been partly responsible for her death. But it was possible that he had misinterpreted the whole affair and if so, he had to know.

"He punished her, I presume?" he said, as gently as possible.

Mrs. Pritchard pressed her lips together, looking away.

"Did he beat her?" said Thanet, even more softly.

The muscles in her jaw worked and still she refused to look at him.

"Locked her up in her bedroom perhaps? Fed her on bread and water? Told her she'd stay up there for ever if she didn't learn to behave herself...?"

Mrs. Pritchard was shaking her head now as if the movement could shut out his words. Her body was stiff with tension and Thanet hated himself for having to do this. All the same he found himself persisting, almost savagely.

"Said she'd burn in hell, no doubt, if she didn't promise to..."

Mrs. Pritchard clapped her hands over her ears and fell back in her chair.

"Don't!" she cried. She sucked in air as if she were suffocating and then expelled it in a long, slow sigh. Her hands fell away from her ears. "I can't bear it," she said.

What price kindness now? thought Thanet grimly, shaken by his own inhumanity. He felt thoroughly ashamed and asked himself what right he had to deplore the way her husband browbeat her if he himself then proceeded to behave in exactly the same way. Once again, he asked himself if there was some quality in the woman herself which called forth this sort of response in men. And had Charity's revolt against her father's strictures partly been the result of a determination not to become like the mother whose lack of spirit she had come to despise?

So, how should he proceed? Should he leave it, or should he persist? Was his duty to the dead or to the living? Loyalty and obedience to her husband were obviously deeply engrained in Mrs. Pritchard's emotional make-up. What right had he, Thanet, to attempt to break down anyone's moral code? If he were to continue, succeed in overcoming Mrs. Pritchard's resistance, how would it affect her relationship with her husband? Would powerful feelings of guilt cause her even more, unnecessary suffering, or would she perhaps find it a liberating experience, the first step out of the state of resigned submission in which she had lived all her married life?

He had to risk it, he decided. If, after all these years, Mrs. Pritchard still found even the memory of the experience so traumatic, how much more powerfully must Charity have been affected.

But from now on there would be no more bullying. He loathed browbeating witnesses such as this. Already, in the last half an hour, his self-respect had suffered, his image of himself become tarnished, and these things were important to him, he had to hold on to them to be able to feel right about his life, his work.

It would have to be persuasion, then.

"Look," he said gently, "I know how you're feeling, believe me. I can see that the memory is painful to you and that you are constrained by loyalty to your husband. All right, I accept that. I won't push you any further. But I can assure you that I wouldn't be pressing you like this if I didn't feel that it really is important for me to know."

This, he decided, was as far as he was prepared to go. If she still refused, then that was that, he would have to desist.

He waited, and the silence stretched out, on and on. At last he made up his mind that he would give her just ten more seconds. He began to count silently. One, two, three . . .

He had reached nine when she spoke.

"All right, I'll tell you." Her voice was barely audible.

She leant forward in her chair and clasped her hands in her lap, staring down at them as if they could give her strength for the ordeal. Then, taking a deep breath she began to talk in a halting monotone.

When Charity had got home from school that day, Pritchard was waiting for her. He told her to go straight up to her room, where earlier he had spent some time making his preparations. Mrs. Pritchard had had no idea what those preparations were, she only knew she had dreaded Charity's return more than she had dreaded anything in her life before.

Pritchard went upstairs behind the little girl and shut the bedroom door behind them. Mrs. Pritchard, terrified, had crept half-way up the stairs to listen, ready to flee at a second's notice. She knew that her husband would have been furious to think that she was eavesdropping. A few moments later Charity began to whimper.

Mrs. Pritchard looked up. "But he didn't lay a finger on her, I swear it. I'd been so afraid he would lose his temper, but he didn't. In some ways it might have been better if he had. At least it would have been over and done with, then."

A few moments later Charity began crying out, "No. Daddy, no, no, no," over and over again.

Mrs. Pritchard's hands were twisting, squeezing, kneading. "I couldn't think what he was doing to her. I still hadn't heard him say a single word. And then, a few minutes later, I heard him coming to the door, and I ran downstairs, as quietly as I could."

Thanet was imagining it all: the crying child; Mrs. Pritchard on the stairs, hand pressed against her mouth, ears straining; the heavy thud of Pritchard's footsteps crossing the room and Mrs. Pritchard's silent flight to the kitchen.

"He opened the door of the bedroom and called me. 'Hannah?' he said. 'Come up. I want you to hear this.' "

Thanet swallowed. His mouth was dry, his heart-beat accelerated. He had longed to know what had happened to Charity to change her so, but now that he was about to find out he feared the knowing.

Mrs. Pritchard's eyes were screwed up against the pain of the memory and her next words emerged jerkily as if forced out against her will. "He had...he'd tied her up. He'd attached ropes to the four corners of the bed and padded them around her wrists and ankles. She was...she was spreadeagled. She looked so...so helpless, and I shall never forget the look she gave me. It was so full of...terror, and entreaty. She didn't speak—I don't think she could. She just lay there...'Take a good look,' my husband said, 'because it's the last time you'll set eyes on her until she's seen the error of her ways. And as for you, my girl,' he said to

Charity, 'there you'll stay until the Devil comes out of you.'
Then he pushed me out of the room and locked the door
behind me, put the key in his pocket."

Mrs. Pritchard pressed her fingers against her trembling
mouth, then, doggedly, she went on. "He just left her there,
day after day . . . He fed her, of course, or tried to . . . bread
and water, that's all . . . but she wouldn't take them, spat them
out. He said this was a sign that the Devil was still strong in
her . . . But the worst thing was . . . he didn't untie her, not
once, not even to go to the toilet. He just let her lie there in
her own filth . . . She must have hated that, she was always
such a clean little girl."

Mrs. Pritchard's control was slipping now and she bit her
lip, took another deep breath. "In the end, one day while he
was out, I went up to the landing and called through the door.
'Charity, listen,' I said. 'You've got to say you're sorry, do
you hear me? Even if you're not sorry, pretend you are, or
you'll be locked in there for ever. Tell Daddy you'll behave
yourself in future . . . Please, darling, do it for me, do it for
Mummy . . . '"

Now, at last, the tears which she had held in check
brimmed over as she relived the scene outside her daughter's
door. She fumbled blindly for the apron she had folded over
the back of her chair and Thanet realised that she was seeking
a handkerchief. Silently he took one from his pocket and
pressed it into her groping hand. Then he rose, crossed to the
window and stood looking out, giving her a chance to regain
her self-control.

Her story had shocked and revolted him. In his work he
had come across many instances of child abuse, cruelty and
neglect, and the worst, for him, were always the ones in
which "punishment" was inflicted in cold blood. Pritchard's
calculated approach, the prolonged nature of Charity's suffering, filled him with anger and a compassion which extended
only in part to Charity's mother, for had she not stood by and
let it happen?

And yet . . . what did he understand of a woman like Mrs.
Pritchard, conditioned as she was, no doubt, by the rules of
her sect to obey her husband and live cut off from society in
this soul-destroying atmosphere? The Pritchards and their like

128

inhabited a strange, harsh landscape as alien to him as a primitive tribal culture. What right had he to judge or to apportion blame?

Mrs. Pritchard was calmer now, drying her eyes and blowing her nose.

"I'm sorry," she said. "Your handkerchief... I'll wash it."

Thanet smiled at her. "Don't worry about it."

"Inspector..." She hesitated. "These last few days I've wondered... Perhaps I'm being punished for what I did. But she was so little and I was so afraid she was going to... just waste away. Do you think I was wrong, to tell her to deceive him like that?"

"What nonsense! You behaved as any mother would, in the circumstances."

But even as he spoke the thought slid insidiously into his mind: had Charity's mother, in an attempt to save her daughter, unwittingly set her on the path of deception which had led, ultimately, to her death?

Mrs. Pritchard was shaking her head. "I didn't know what else to do. I've thought and thought about it and I just don't know what else I could have done. I couldn't leave it to go on indefinitely, could I?"

Once again, Thanet gave her the reassurance she needed. Besides, it was true that she didn't seem to have had any alternative; loyalty would have prevented her from reporting him to the police and open defiance would have been unthinkable.

"My husband was only doing what he thought was right." But her tone lacked conviction and suddenly she stiffened, cocked her head. For a moment there was panic in her eyes.

"There he is, now." She pushed Thanet's handkerchief out of sight between her skirt and the side of the chair, then smoothed her hair, straightened her shoulders, and stroked her dress into neat, disciplined folds. By the time Pritchard entered the room a few moments later she was apparently quite composed, her face turned expectantly towards the door.

"Ah, there you are, Nathaniel. Inspector Thanet was just..."

But Pritchard was less self-absorbed, more observant than Thanet would have given him credit for. He looked searchingly into his wife's face and turned to Thanet.

"Why has my wife been crying? I told you, I don't want her bothered."

Beneath the belligerence Thanet detected the concern. Better get it over with, he thought.

"Your wife is upset because I brought some rather bad news."

"Well?" snapped Pritchard.

"As you probably know, in cases of unnatural death, there has to be a post mortem. The results of the post mortem on your daughter will be made public at the inquest next week, and I came here this morning because I knew that the findings would be a shock to you, and I wanted you to have the opportunity of hearing them in private." There was no way of cushioning the blow. "She had just had an abortion."

Pritchard seemed to stop breathing and briefly he had no more animation than a waxwork, with painted hair, painted eyes, a painted face. Then he put out a hand and groped behind him for a chair, sank into it as though his legs would no longer bear his weight.

"I don't believe it."

"I'm afraid it's true."

"There must be some mistake."

Thanet shook his head. "No mistake. I'm sorry."

Pritchard stared at him, thinking. Eventually, "Who was responsible?" he said, his eyes beginning now to glitter with anger.

"The father, you mean? We don't know, yet."

"Then shouldn't you be trying to find out?"

"That's precisely what I am trying to do," said Thanet patiently.

"What do you mean?" Pritchard glared at him. "You're not saying you expect us to know anything about it, I hope? You don't think we'd have tolerated any kind of . . . loose behaviour, do you? Oh no, believe me, if we'd had any idea what was going on, we'd soon have put a stop to it, I assure you."

"You are her parents," said Thanet. "I thought that you might perhaps have had some suggestions . . ."

"Well we haven't! To our knowledge, Charity never even knew any men, let alone had any opportunity to . . ." His mouth worked and his nostrils flared in disgust. And then, for so brief a moment that Thanet could almost have thought he had imagined it, Pritchard froze and a name flashed telepathically between them, each syllable as clear and precise as if it had been shouted aloud: *Jethro.*

Pritchard stood up as precipitately as if he had been propelled by some powerful, invisible force.

"I'm sorry, Inspector, we can't help you. Neither my wife nor I wish to discuss this matter any further."

Thanet came slowly to his feet. "Very well, Mr. Pritchard. But if anything does occur to you . . ."

"Then of course we'd be in touch."

The man was hurrying him to the door now. Clearly, he couldn't wait to be rid of him.

The overnight storm had cleared the air, bringing the unseasonable heatwave to an end, and outside the air was cool, almost chill. Thanet shivered as he walked to the car, thinking. He wouldn't mind betting that Pritchard's next move would be to go steaming around to Gate Street and accuse Jethro of seducing Charity—possibly, even, of murdering her. Thanet could be wrong, of course. Perhaps Pritchard had not immediately suspected Jethro. But in case he had, the question was, should Thanet try to get to Jethro first? If he did, he could use the fact that Pritchard was probably on his way to get Jethro to talk. And of course, it was possible that Thanet was misjudging Jethro, in which case he perhaps had a moral responsibility to warn the man of a possible visit from Pritchard.

On the other hand, he didn't want to tackle Jethro until he was in possession of the facts about that earlier conviction—always assuming that Mallard was right, and there had been one.

He'd contact Lineham first, he decided, see if he'd got anywhere with records. Cursing the fact that in his haste, earlier, he had used his own car and not a radio-equipped police car, he drove to the phone box at the end of the street and, with one eye on the Pritchards' house, rang the office.

Lineham sounded pleased with himself.

"Doc Mallard was right, sir."

"Well?" said Thanet impatiently. He wasn't in the mood for a session of Lineham's dramatic pauses.

"In 1966 Jethro Pritchard went down for eighteen months, for indecent assault on a fourteen-year-old girl."

"What was her name?"

"Janet Barker. Address: 4, Davies Street, Sturrenden. I've got the rest of the details here, if you want to hear them."

"Later. Look, I want to see Jethro Pritchard as soon as possible, and I want you with me. How soon can you get around to Gate Street?"

"Five minutes. I'm on my way."

Thanet hurried back to his car. There was still no sign of Pritchard. Good. He drove to Gate Street and parked a little way up the road from number fourteen. On edge in case Pritchard beat Lineham to it, he settled down to wait with as much patience as he could muster.

He didn't have to wait long. Lineham was as good as his word, and a few minutes later his car pulled up in front of Thanet's with a flourish.

"What's the hurry, sir?"

Briefly, Thanet explained. "So it's my guess that Pritchard will be arriving at any minute. Now, I've been thinking, while I was waiting for you. We haven't enough time to get a full confession out of Jethro, and in any case I have the feeling he's the type who'll talk more readily to one person than two. So what I want to do at the moment is soften him up for when I next see him, show him that we know what he's been up to, and then leave him to stew. So we'll look as official as possible—notebook much in evidence and so on. All right?"

"Fine."

"You've not met either of the Jethro Pritchards yet, have you?"

Lineham shook his head.

"A pleasure in store for you, then. Come on."

Mrs. Pritchard answered the door. "He's out," she said in response to Thanet's request, her eyes glinting with satisfaction at being able to thwart him.

"Could you tell us where he is?"

"At the school," she said grudgingly.

Thanet thanked her politely and they turned away.

"Imagine living with that!" said Lineham.

"Don't feel too sorry for him."

"Sympathy could get in the way, you mean? You're a fine one to talk!"

The grinned at each other. Over the years their working relationship had become so finely tuned that there was mutual recognition of the times when it was necessary to fall back on protocol and the times when the barrier of rank simply did not exist. Both of them were aware that it was Thanet, not Lineham, who had to be on his guard against emotional involvement.

"I bet he's pretty pathetic, though," said Lineham. "Child molesters usually are."

"Judge for yourself. There he is."

Jethro Pritchard was approaching. He was walking slowly, head down, shoulders hunched. He hadn't noticed them yet.

"Looks pretty preoccupied," said Lineham.

"He's got reason to be, wouldn't you say? Good morning, Mr. Pritchard."

Jethro stopped dead and his head came up with a jerk. They caught the flash of fear in his eyes before he mumbled a response.

"We wanted a word with you. This is Sergeant Lineham."

Jethro's eyes flickered from one to the other, seeking reassurance and finding none.

"Shall we go into the house?" said Thanet. "Or perhaps you'd prefer to sit in the car. Oh, don't worry, we're not taking you in . . . yet."

Jethro hesitated, caught between two equally unpalatable alternatives: running the risk of his wife overhearing the conversation and being seen to be "helping the police in their enquiries." He chose the latter as the lesser of the two evils. He and Thanet got into the front seats and Lineham scrambled into the back, ostentatiously producing his notebook and leaning it on the back of Thanet's seat, pencil at the ready.

"What's all this about?" said Jethro, with a nervous glance at the notebook.

"Janet Barker," said Thanet. "That's what this is all about."

But his shock tactics hadn't worked. Jethro's watery brown eyes were merely resigned. "I was expecting you to dig that up."

"I suppose you must have been. After all, there is a certain obvious similarity between the two cases."

"What two cases?" faltered Jethro.

"Oh come on, Mr. Pritchard. Janet and Charity, of course."

"I don't understand."

"Don't you?"

133

"No!" cried Jethro. "I don't. Janet was just...well, that was different. But Charity...Charity was killed."

So Jethro had prepared himself for this, had decided to pretend ignorance of Charity's sexual experience. All Thanet's instincts told him that Jethro was guilty of something, but of what, that was the question. Of having seduced Charity? Of having murdered her? Or of both?

Thanet studied the man carefully. Jethro's eyes fell away from his. Sweat beaded his forehead.

"I'm not just talking about Charity's murder, and well you know it," said Thanet fiercely. He had used the ugly word deliberately and had the satisfaction of seeing Jethro wince.

Jethro's ferrety features had sharpened, as if the flesh were melting away, and his sallow skin had taken on a waxy, yellowish hue. He moistened his lips with the tip of his tongue.

"I don't know what you mean," he muttered.

"Don't you, Mr. Pritchard? Oh, I think you do...Where did you go after Bible classes, you and Charity? Did you stay at the meeting hall? Go to the school? Or perhaps you came here, when your wife was out and your mother safely in bed..."

"I don't know what you're talking about, I tell you," said Jethro frantically.

"I don't think your brother is too pleased, that you should so have abused his trust. He's very upset, naturally. In fact, I have the feeling he'll be along at any minute, to...shall we say, discuss the matter with you."

Jethro cast a desperate glance back along the street.

"Well, I think that's all for the moment, Mr. Pritchard." Thanet leaned across and released the door handle. "Out you get."

"I can go?" Jethro was bewildered.

"For the moment. But make no mistake about it, we'll be back."

Thanet waited until Jethro had got out and then said quietly to Lineham, "See you back at the office."

They left Jethro still standing on the kerb, gazing after them.

Thanet was quite pleased with the way the interview had gone. Now, what he needed was more evidence against Jethro. He would have to run a second house to house check in Gate Street. It was surprising how often a second check paid off. And it would be worth finding out exactly what time the meeting at the school had ended, and making enquiries in the row of houses opposite. He already knew that Jethro had been out and about for part of the relevant time, but if they could find someone who had actually seen him leave the school that night, and could prove that he had lied . . .

He said so to Lineham as they climbed the stairs to the office together.

"I'll get someone on to it right away, sir."

Thanet picked up a sheet of paper which had been left in a prominent position on his desk.

"A message from Carson . . . ah . . ."

"He was still trying to get through to the school when I left. What does it say?"

"You were right. There are four masters at the school. One of them is in his thirties, has fair hair and wears pebble-lensed specs. What's more, guess what he teaches?"

"Music!" said Lineham, with a flash of inspiration.

Thanet gave a slow, satisfied nod.

"Music."

16

Leslie Mathews, music master at Sturrenden Technical School for Girls, lived in a large Victorian house on the main Ashford Road. Once the home of a prosperous Sturrenden tradesman, the place now had a sad, neglected air, the row of bells a mockery of the generous life-style for which it had been designed.

Thanet twice pressed the bell marked Mathews and waited, but no one came.

"He's out, by the look of it."

"Unless the bell's not working," suggested Lineham.

"Better go up and see, I suppose."

Mathews lived on the top floor. The front door was unlocked, they discovered, allowing people to come and go as they pleased, and Thanet and Lineham climbed the three long flights of stairs tutting at the lack of security. The distant throb of pop music grew louder as they rose.

Facing them at the top was a door with a china plaque. A garland of flowers surrounded the legend, *Roger lives here.* The capital R would have graced a mediaeval manuscript, thought Thanet. It was an elaborate affair of precise brushstrokes and graceful curlicues.

"Very pretty, I'm sure," said Lineham's sarcastic voice in his ear.

A second door, a few paces to the right along the narrow landing, bore a roughly-torn scrap of paper tacked to the door with a drawing pin. DAVE, it proclaimed in sprawling capital letters. This was where the music was coming from and it was now so loud that Thanet could feel the floorboards vibrating beneath his feet.

By contrast, the card on Mathews' door was reassuringly orthodox: a small oblong of white pasteboard with the surname only written in neat, italic script. Thanet wondered how Mathews got on with his neighbours.

There was no answer to their knock.

"Dave?" said Lineham.

Thanet nodded and they moved back along the landing. Lineham had to hammer on the door with the side of his fist to make himself heard above the din and when at last it was flung open a tide of sound swept out to engulf them. How could anyone bear to shut himself in a confined space with that level of noise, Thanet wondered. It would be his idea of hell.

Dave was unshaved, unwashed (by the smell of it) and undressed, save for a skimpy towel draped around his waist. Over his shoulder Thanet glimpsed a tumbled bed and a girl's face.

Dave hadn't appreciated the interruption.

"What d'yer want?"

"Mathews," bellowed Thanet, pointing along the landing.

"How the hell do I know where he is!" And Dave made to slam the door.

Thanet put his foot in the gap and produced his ID.

Dave glowered at it, muttered something and rolled his eyes.

"Hang on."

Leaving the door ajar he went back into the room, switched off the tape and returned a moment later with a dressing gown slung around his shoulders.

"OK," he said resignedly. "But make it quick. I'm otherwise engaged, as no doubt you've noticed." And he gave a salacious wink.

"We wanted a word with Mr. Mathews," said Lineham, "and he seems to be out."

"So?"

"Have you any idea where he might have gone?"

"Half term, isn't it? Could be anywhere."

"Where, for example?"

The man shrugged. "How should I know? Now, if you don't mind . . ."

"But we do," said Lineham. "So why not give us a suggestion or two and we'll leave you to . . . get on with it."

Dave grinned. "How can I refuse an offer like that? OK, let's see. Tried little Miss Prim and Proper yet?"

Charity? Thanet wondered. Surely Mathews hadn't brought her here.

"His fiancée," said Dave. "Er . . . what's her name . . ." and he snapped his fingers in the air, once, twice. "Eileen," he said triumphantly. "That's it. Eileen."

"Eileen who?"

"Something to do with hunting. That's how I remember names, see. There's a word for it. Let me see now. Hunting . . . hunting . . . got it! Chase. Eileen Chase. That do you?" And he began to close the door.

"Where does she live?" said Lineham quickly.

"Sorry, haven't a clue."

"And her job?"

"Teaches. Same school as him."

Lineham thanked him and let him go. The music blared out again behind them as they clattered down the uncarpeted stairs.

"So, what now, sir?"

"Might as well go and see Eileen Chase, if we can get her address. If she and Mathews are engaged, there's a chance he might be with her. And anyway, I'm curious about her, aren't you?"

A phone call to the school produced the address and they drove to the quiet residential area on the far side of Sturrenden where, according to the secretary, Eileen Chase lived with her invalid mother. It was a nineteen-thirties development of semi-detached houses, each with its small front garden sporting a minute lawn and the ubiquitous rose-bed. Shangri-La was distinguished from its neighbours by a beautiful Nelly Moser Clematis. Thanet paused for a moment to admire the fountain of huge, pale pink flowers with their distinctive carmine bar before approaching the tiny front porch.

Once again there was no answer to the knock.

"Not our day, is it?" said Lineham, turning away in disgust.

Thanet held up his hand. "Just a minute." His head was cocked to one side, listening.

"I can't hear anything."

Thanet gave a quick, admonitory shake of the head, then pointed to the ground.

Lineham looked down. The single step up into the porch had been converted to a ramp. He looked chagrined. "Of course, the mother . . . I didn't notice."

Now he knew what they were listening for and a moment or two later they heard it: the faint, rhythmic squeak of a wheelchair approaching.

Then the door opened, on the chain.

"Yes?" The segment of face was at waist level.

"Mrs. Chase?"

"That's right."

"Nothing to be worried about, ma'am. We're just on a routine enquiry. Police officers."

"Why aren't you wearing your uniforms?"

"Plain clothes police, ma'am."

"I want to see your identification."

"Certainly." Thanet extended his card and a hand emerged through the crack, plucked it from him. Then the door closed.

Thanet caught Lineham smothering a grin. He didn't blame him. What if the old lady didn't open up again? Thanet found himself imagining the farcical scene in which he confessed to the Super that he'd been relieved of his warrant card by an old lady in a wheelchair.

The door opened again, wide, this time.

Mrs. Chase was tiny, and painfully thin, the bone structure of face and hands clearly visible beneath the pale, almost transparent skin. Her shoulders were hunched and she had to twist her head sideways and back at an unnatural angle to look up at her visitors. There was a rug over her knees and her face was heavily scored with lines of pain and ill temper—scarcely surprising, Thanet thought. He had heard of people who managed to endure the most horrific lives with sweetness and good humor, had even met one or two of them, but suspected that if he himself were ever to find himself in such a position he would lapse at once into peevishness and self-pity.

She held out his card. "You can't be too careful these days, you know."

"Quite right, ma'am. It's very sensible of you, to take precautions."

Especially, he thought, in her position. One of the most abhorrent recent manifestations of violent crime was the upsurge of attacks on the most vulnerable members of society, the old and the handicapped, often in their own homes.

"What do you want?"

"We're trying to find Mr. Leslie Mathews—your daughter's fiancé, I believe. He wasn't at home, so we thought he might be here."

At the mention of Mathews' name she had pursed her lips and a look of intense dislike had flitted across her face. Now there was satisfaction in her voice as she said, "What's he done?"

"As I said, ma'am, this is just a routine enquiry. We think Mr. Mathews might be able to help us."

She squinted up at him and Thanet guessed that she was trying to work out how best to turn this unusual situation to her own advantage.

"You'd better come in," she said at last.

"If you could just tell us whether or not Mr. Mathews is with your daught—"

"Come in, I said." Her sharpness revealed that she was not accustomed to being thwarted. With astonishing deftness she swivelled the wheelchair and set off down the passage. Thanet and Lineham had no option but to follow.

The room into which she led them looked as though someone had taken a gigantic broom and swept all the furniture to the edges of the floor. This was presumably to allow Mrs. Chase freedom of movement in her wheelchair, Thanet thought, but the effect was curiously disturbing, as though the stage had been cleared for some major upheaval or confrontation. A gas fire was full on and the atmosphere was suffocating.

"That's better," she said. "Chilly out there. Sit down." She waved a hand at a settee against the wall and both men complied. At once she manoeuvred her chair into a position squarely in front of them and only a few feet away, thus giving herself the psychological advantage of being able to look down on them. And who could blame her, Thanet thought. He could understand such stratagems becoming second nature to someone in her position.

He decided deliberately to relinquish the initiative, see where she led them. Lineham glanced at him, obviously wondering if Thanet's continuing silence indicated that he wanted the sergeant to take over the questioning. Thanet gave an almost imperceptible shake of the head. Lineham sat back.

"I knew it!" said Mrs. Chase. "I knew there was something. As soon as I set eyes on him, I could tell there was going to be trouble. I warned Eileen, but she wouldn't listen." Her mouth twisted. "Mooning about like a love-sick schoolgirl. At her age!"

"How old is your daughter, Mrs. Chase?"

"Thirty-seven. I ask you! She should know better, have some dignity. What's more, he's four years younger than she is. Disgusting, that's what I call it. Engaged, indeed!"

"When are they hoping to be married?"

"They haven't deigned to inform me, yet."

"They'll live here, I suppose?" What an appalling prospect, thought Thanet. Mathews must be either a brave man or an insensitive one even to contemplate such an idea.

"So they say. Going to convert upstairs into a self-contained flat. Eileen says it won't make any difference to me, she'll be able to do for me everything she does now, but I can't see it, myself, when she's got a husband to fuss over."

And this, Thanet thought, was no doubt the root of the trouble. Understandably. This late blossoming of her daughter's love-life must have filled Mrs. Chase with terror. Thanet couldn't like the woman, but he could sympathise with her predicament.

"Why do you want to see him?" Mrs. Chase's eyes were suddenly avid, alight with the hope that Thanet might be able to throw her a life-line, that her daughter's romance was about to be still-born.

"I'm afraid I can't tell you that... He is out with your daughter, I presume?" He wouldn't put it past the old woman deliberately to have led him up the garden path in the hope of extracting information from him.

"Oh yes, he's out with her all right. Gallivanting, as usual."

"Where have they gone, do you know?"

"For a walk, that's all I know. They only left about twenty minutes ago."

Thanet glanced at his watch. A quarter to two. He suddenly realised that he was hungry. He and Lineham hadn't yet had any lunch.

"What time will they be back?"

"Half past three, they *said*. But they're usually late."

Thanet could understand why. With Mrs. Chase's hostility waiting to ambush them the moment they stepped through the front door, there could be little incentive to be punctual.

"Your daughter has been at home all over the half-term holiday?"

"If you can call it being at home, yes. Spent most of it up in her bedroom. I was looking forward to having a bit of company for a change, but no, all over the weekend she was going around looking as though the world had come to an end. To tell you the truth, I thought they might have split up. No such luck, unfortunately."

"She didn't see Mr. Mathews at all, over the weekend?"

"No. Wouldn't tell me why, either. Just said he was away and she didn't want to discuss it. And then, on Monday night he turns up, large as life, at ten o'clock at night." Her nose wrinkled in disgust. "He'd been drinking, too. I could smell it the minute he walked into the room. But her... she's got no pride. When the doorbell went she couldn't get there quick enough. And when she came back in with him... you'd have thought someone'd given her the crown jewels."

"Did Mr. Mathews say where he'd been, over the weekend?"

"I didn't wait to find out. As soon as I saw the condition he was in, I made Eileen put me to bed."

Her look of gloating satisfaction told Thanet that Mrs. Chase would have prolonged this process as much as possible, in order to keep the lovers apart.

"Is that what you want to know?" she said eagerly. "What he was doing over the weekend?"

Thanet stood up. "I'm afraid I can't tell you that, Mrs. Chase."

"You're not going?"

"We must, I'm afraid."

Why was it that this sort of person always brought out the worst in others, Thanet wondered, as he experienced a brief and shameful sense of satisfaction at her disappointment.

"But you'll come back, at half past three?"

"Possibly." But he had no intention of allowing himself to be manoeuvred into interviewing Mathews in the presence of this woman. He an Lineham would wait outside, catch the couple as they returned home. And if the man was innocent of any involvement in Charity's death, well, Thanet only hoped that by coming here he hadn't handed Mrs. Chase another weapon with which to make her daughter's life a misery. One of the unfortunate results of a criminal investigation is that its effects spread outwards, like ripples on a pond, disrupting the lives of the innocent as well as the guilty.

He and Lineham had something to eat at a little sandwich bar on the edge of Sturrenden—it was too late, by now, to go to a pub—and by a quarter past three were in position, parked a little way up the road, where Mrs. Chase would not be able to see them.

At twenty to four Lineham nudged him. "There they are."

Walking slowly towards them was a youngish couple, holding hands, feet dragging like children facing a particularly unpleasant day at school. They were talking, engrossed in each other, and as they drew nearer they saw that the man was wearing pebble-lensed spectacles.

Thanet and Lineham got out of the car and went to meet them.

"Mr. Mathews?"

The intrusion was a shock and they stopped, startled, surprise changing to apprehension when Thanet introduced himself.

"We'd like a word with you in private, if we may."

Mathews and Eileen Chase edged closer to each other, as if Thanet were threatening to rip them apart by force.

"My fiancée and I have no secrets from each other."

Mathews fitted the description: medium height, fair hair,

142

thinning at the temples. His clothes were nondescript—fawn cords and a green sweatshirt.

Thanet shrugged. "As you wish. Is there somewhere quiet nearby, where we can talk?"

Mathews looked questioningly at Eileen and she said quickly, "There's the park." She was small and slight with a high, bony forehead and slightly protruding eyes. Her shoulder-length hair was caught back in an Alice band, in a style which gave her a curiously immature, little-girl look, an impression heightened by her dress, a shirt-waister in green and white checked gingham.

She and Mathews led the way to a pair of wrought-iron gates a little distance away on the other side of the road. Apart from some children playing on the swings in the recreation area, the place was deserted.

"Over there will do," said Thanet, indicating a small paved area backed by hedges, where two wooden benches were set at right angles to each other.

They all sat down, Mathews and his fiancée watching Thanet apprehensively.

"I won't beat about the bush, Mr. Mathews," said Thanet. "We are investigating the murder of Charity Pritchard and we understand that you and she travelled down from London together on Monday night."

This was no news to Eileen, Thanet noted. She merely looked calmly at Mathews, waiting for his reply.

"No! Yes...well, not exactly."

"Oh come, Mr. Mathews. Either you did or you didn't."

"Well, we did travel down on the same train, but it was purely a matter of chance. We just happened to get into the same compartment at Victoria."

"You sat together?"

"Yes...Well, it seems silly, if you see someone you know on a train, not to sit with them, doesn't it?"

"Depends on whether you *want* to sit with them, surely," said Lineham. "I know some people I'd run a mile to avoid."

"I didn't have much choice about it. She came and sat opposite me, and I could hardly have moved away without being downright rude."

"Rather awkward," said Thanet.

"Quite."

"I mean, I suppose you really have to be very careful, a man in your position."

"What do you mean?"

"Well, a male teacher in an all-girls school," said Lineham. "And an unmarried one at that . . . Bound to be the occasional schoolgirl crush to fend off, surely?"

Mathews cast a panic-stricken glance at Eileen and her grip on his hand tightened. Thanet wondered how much the girl knew, whether it would be worth trying to question her alone. It would probably be a waste of time, he decided. Her loyalty to Mathews was patent.

"Did Charity have a crush on you, Mr. Mathews?" he said softly.

There was a brief silence. Mathews and Eileen did not look at each other, but Thanet was aware of the current of sympathy and strength flowing from the girl to her fiancé through those linked hands. She may not have looked a force to be reckoned with, but Thanet knew that a woman who falls in love for the first time relatively late in life will probably be prepared to fight tooth and nail to keep her lover.

Mathews leaned forward slightly, his eyes so magnified by the lenses of his spectacles that Thanet found it impossible to read their expression.

"What, exactly, are you implying, Inspector?"

It was a good try at indignation, but it lacked that note of conviction imparted by genuine innocence. Up until this moment Thanet had been uncertain of the precise nature of the relationship between Mathews and Charity. He was well aware that Mathews could have been telling the truth, that he and Charity had met by chance on that train, and that Mathews' nervousness might have been based on nothing more than the knowledge that this unfortunate coincidence might appear to implicate him in the murder of a girl who had been no more to him than one pupil among many.

But now, suddenly, he was certain: Mathews and Charity had had a sexual relationship and, what was more, Eileen Chase had known about it.

"Not implying, merely asking, Mr. Mathews."

It would be best, now, if Mathews were left wondering just how much the police knew. Thanet changed tack.

"I understand that you were away for the whole weekend?"

Mathews shifted uneasily on the seat. "That's right."

"Would you mind telling us where you went?"

For some reason, this was the wrong question. Mathews relaxed a little. "By all means. I was walking. In the Chilterns."

What was the question he should have asked? Thanet was frustrated to find that he didn't know.

"Alone?"

"Yes. I was camping out. I do, from time to time. Does you good to get right away from civilisation."

Especially with problems like yours, thought Thanet. "Can you think of anyone who might remember seeing you—when you stopped to buy food, whatever?"

"Not offhand."

It was pointless to waste time trying to get the man to come up with verifiable details at this point. This was clearly a no-danger area for Mathews. "Perhaps you could think about it, give us a ring... And now, if we could just go back to Monday evening again..."

"I really don't see what else I can tell you. As I said, we met by accident, travelled down in the same compartment, and that's it."

"You left the train together," said Thanet.

"Well, naturally..."

"*And* left the station together," said Lineham.

Thanet leaned forward. "Of course, what we're really interested in, is what happened then."

"Happened?"

So far Eileen Chase had not said a single word throughout the entire interview. Now, the strain was beginning to tell. The taut muscles of her jaw betrayed the force with which her teeth were clamped together.

"What did you do, when you left the station?" Lineham took up the questioning at Thanet's signal.

"I went to see my fiancée." Mathews glanced at Eileen for confirmation and she gave a quick, taut nod.

"Arriving at her house at what time?"

"About..." Mathews stopped.

Would the temptation to lie, give himself a false alibi, prove irresistible, Thanet wondered.

Mathews turned to the girl. "What time was it, darling, did you notice?"

She hesitated. Then, "Ten o'clock," she said, looking straight into his eyes.

The message was clear. *Tell the truth as far as possible*, she was saying. Of course, there was Mrs. Chase to take into account. Would Eileen have lied, if she lived alone, Thanet wondered.

Mathews looked back at Lineham. "If Eileen says it was ten, then it was."

"So what were you doing in the meantime? The station is only ten minutes walk from here."

"I stopped at a pub, had a drink or two. Any law against that?"

"None. Which pub?"

Mathews hesitated. "I'm sorry, I don't know."

"You don't *know*?"

"I don't make a habit of going to pubs. I've no idea what most of the pubs in Sturrenden are called. I just happened to be passing this one and felt like a drink, so I went in."

"Where was it?"

"Somewhere between here and the station."

"You really can't be more precise than that?"

"No . . . I wasn't feeling well."

"You were ill?"

"Not exactly. Just a bit under the weather . . . Well, if you must know, I was trying to make up my mind about something."

"What?"

"I'm sorry, I can't tell you that. It's a private matter."

Some unspoken communication passed between him and the girl, and Thanet saw her fingers tighten on his again. She was backing up his decision not to speak. There was no point in pressing the matter.

Lineham had understood this. He raised his eyebrow at Thanet. *Shall I push him?*

No, Thanet returned.

"How long did you stay in this pub, Mr. Mathews?" said Lineham.

"I'm not sure. But if I left the station about nine and didn't get here until ten, it must have been three-quarters of an hour or more."

"Did you see anyone you know?"

"Not that I can recall."

"And how many drinks did you have?"

"Two, three perhaps."

"Beers?"

"Whiskies." Mathews lifted his chin defiantly, as if defending his right to drink whatever he wanted.

Lineham glanced at Thanet, relinquishing the questioning.

Thanet allowed a long pause, leaning back in an almost leisurely manner and giving Mathews a long, assessing stare. "You must see, Mr. Mathews, that all this uncertainty about your movements does leave you in a most unfortunate position. I'm surprised that in the circumstances you haven't taken the trouble to retrace your steps and discover exactly which pub you did go into."

"But why should he!" Eileen Chase could keep silent no longer. "It never entered our heads that my fiancé would have to answer all these . . . ridiculous questions, just because of a chance meeting on a train!"

"Miss Chase, your loyalty does you credit. But it shouldn't blind you to the facts. And those are that on Monday evening Charity Pritchard travelled down from London with Mr. Mathews, was seen leaving the station with him and shortly afterwards was murdered. No, wait a minute," he went on as she opened her mouth to protest. "You really must see that in the circumstances it is no more than our duty to question Mr. Mathews closely, especially as he is so vague as to his movements. But there is one way in which you might be able to help him."

"How?"

"Do you happen to have a photograph of him?"

As he had guessed, she had one in her wallet. It was a good likeness, too.

"Thank you. We'll get someone to check the pubs and see if we can find someone who can corroborate his story."

"Inspector," said Mathews, "can I ask you something?"

"Go ahead."

"It's obvious, from all these questions, that Charity was killed some time after she left the station that evening. Do you know exactly when?"

Thanet didn't see why he shouldn't tell him. "Not to the minute. But some time between 9:35 and 10:40."

"I see." Mathews' response was carefully neutral, but underneath there was suppressed excitement. "And how was the earlier of the two times fixed?"

So that was it. "As you have guessed, because that was the time at which she was last seen alive."

"But in that case, I'm in the clear, surely! If she was seen alive after we parted?"

"I'm afraid we won't be able to accept that unless we can find someone who can verify that you were elsewhere between 9:35 and 10."

"This is absolutely monstrous!" said Eileen Chase. Her pale skin was stained with pink and her prominent eyes bulged with anger. "To suggest that Leslie could have . . . He's the kindest, most gentle person imaginable." She cast him a glance of pure adoration. "He'd never do such a thing, never."

"Maybe not, in normal circumstances. But murder never is committed in normal circumstances, not by ordinary people, anyway. They are driven to it by a compulsion outside their everyday experience. Oh yes, someone had a powerful reason for wishing Charity dead, Miss Chase, and believe me, I am going to find out what that reason was. And when I do . . ." Thanet rose, and his tone suddenly became casually conversational, "well, when I do, I shall have found the murderer, shan't I? Good day."

Mathews and Eileen Chase sat as if turned to stone as the two detectives walked away across the park.

17

Thanet flexed his spine and massaged the dull ache in the small of his back. Whenever he was tired or under stress it seemed to become worse, an unwelcome distraction when he was least equipped to cope with it.

It was a quarter past six and he was alone in the office. He had dispatched Carson to check Mathews' alibi at all the pubs between the railway station and Eileen Chase's house, and had then insisted that Lineham go and visit Louise.

"You can't miss two nights in a row."

"But what about all those?" Lineham had gestured at the piles of unread reports on Thanet's desk.

"They won't run away. Go on, hurry up, or you'll be late. I could do with a breathing space anyway."

Which was true. Thanet felt as though his brain were so clogged with information that it had almost ceased to function. What he really needed now was to go home and have Joan thrust a drink in his hand and insist he relax for a while before supper. He closed his eyes, visualising her smile, the touch of her hand on his arm, the luxury of sinking into an armchair and knowing that she was there, moving about in the next room. How little we appreciate these simple pleasures while we have them, he thought. His longing for her presence was almost a physical pain, an ache deep inside him. Just to hear her voice again . . .

He opened his eyes, stared at the telephone. Why not? It might be a good time to catch her. He found that, without making a conscious decision, he was dialling.

"Could I speak to Mrs. Thanet, please?"

He braced himself for a familiar, "I'm afraid she's out," but it didn't come.

"Just a moment, I'll see if she's in."

The seconds ticked away and Thanet found that he was holding his breath, hope ebbing with every moment that passed. She wasn't back yet, had already gone out, was spending the evening with a friend . . . Fiercely he repudiated the threatening fantasy of a friend who was not only male but physically attractive, intelligent, sympathetic, enlightened . . .

"Hullo?"

Joan's voice, as familiar to him in its every inflexion as his own face in the mirror.

"Got you at last!" As soon as the words were out of his mouth, he could have kicked himself. His attempt at light-heartedness sounded merely reproachful.

"Luke!" If Joan had noticed, she chose to ignore it. "Darling, how lovely to hear you! We always seem to be missing each other, these days. How are you? How are the children? How's the case going?"

"Fine, fine and not so fine, in that order. What about you?"

"Exhausted! You remember the remand home where I did my last placement? Well, they've had an epidemic of mumps

149

there, and as two of the staff had gone down with it—it's an especially virulent strain, apparently—Geoffrey and I have been going back in the evenings to help out.''

Geoffrey Benson was also on the training course. Thanet had never met him.

''I see.'' Thanet tried to ignore the red light flashing in his brain. ''Sounds as though you've been having a hectic time. I should think we'll all seem as dull as ditchwater when you get back home.''

Joan must have picked up the underlying anxiety beneath his attempt to tease her, for her reply was vehement.

''Nonsense, darling. I can't tell you how I'm longing to be home again, start leading a normal life again.''

Had she meant it? To Thanet her tone was strained, as if she were trying to convince herself as well as him.

Thanet gave her the latest news of Louise and then she said, ''But tell me how the case is going. Properly.''

''It's going, and that's about all I can say at the moment. At least I'm not completely stuck yet.''

''Anyone definite in mind?''

''Not really. We could take our pick from about half a dozen possibilities.''

''Sounds complicated.''

''It is, a bit. Joan . . . I do miss you.''

''And I miss you too, darling.''

''But . . .'' How to describe the immensity of his need, this hunger for her mere presence? Over the years I've got out of the habit of expressing such feelings, he thought desperately, and the words just won't come easily any more.

''Anyway, it won't be long, now, will it, Luke? Only another couple of weeks . . . I suppose your back's playing up?''

How well she knew him. ''A little.''

''Where are you?''

The question surprised him. ''In the office. Why?''

''Anyone else there?''

''Not at the moment.''

''In that case, why don't you lie down on the floor for a little while, do your exercises, relax.''

''Here? What if someone came in?''

''Couldn't you say you didn't want to be disturbed for a bit? There'd be nothing unusual in that, surely?''

"I could, I suppose..."

"Then do it. You'd feel miles better, afterwards. Promise?"

"Well..."

"Luke!"

"Oh, all right. I suppose it might be a good idea."

"Of course it would. Look, sorry darling, but I'm afraid I must go now. I've got to get back to the Home. I was just leaving when you caught me."

"Well I'm glad I did."

"So'm I." She blew him a kiss down the line. "'Bye, darling. I love you."

"I love you, too."

The line went dead and Thanet replaced the receiver, sat staring at it for a full minute before pressing the buzzer on his desk.

"I don't want to be disturbed for a half an hour."

"Right, sir."

"Not for any reason, is that clear?"

Allowing himself the luxury of a slight groan, Thanet stood up, rubbing his back, then carefully lowered himself to the floor. The carpet, though thin, was at least clean. The pain flowered as taut muscles met the hard, unyielding surface, then began to ebb as the tension started to seep away.

Thanet worked conscientiously through the exercises which his physiotherapist had given him, then began the relaxation routine: tighten leg muscles... relax. Arm muscles... relax. Shoulder... neck... jaw... He began to breathe deeply and regularly. In... out. In... out. Veronica... Mrs. Chase. Jethro... his wife. Mathews... Eileen Chase.

Which of the six could it be?

He was pretty certain that Veronica was out of the running. She was too passive, too self-pitying, a victim rather than an assailant. He couldn't see her being sufficiently devious to plan a murder in cold blood, nor sufficiently aggressive to strike out in anger with the degree of force that had hurled Charity against that unfortunately placed piece of jagged metal. And so far there hadn't been so much as a whisper of anyone seeing her outside the house that night.

Memo: check through the files again, to be sure on that point.

Mrs. Hodges, now, was a different matter. Not by nature an aggressive woman, she would certainly be capable of ex-

151

tremes of behaviour in defence of her one ewe lamb, Thanet was sure. Yes, she should definitely be considered a suspect—it was quite possible, as Lineham had suggested, that she had followed Charity and killed her *before* returning to the house and greeting Thanet and Lineham as though nothing had happened. After all, there was only her word for it that Charity had still been alive at that point. The house to house reports covering that earlier period should be on his desk by now. Thanet resisted the urge to get up at once and check through them. He needed a little more time, first, to order his thoughts properly.

Then there was Mathews. Now here was another promising suspect. His motive was powerful. If, as Thanet suspected, he had indeed had a sexual relationship with Charity, then his whole career would have been at stake. No one was going to employ a teacher who had not only seduced a pupil—and an under-age one, at that—but had driven her to seek an abortion without her parents' knowledge or consent. If any of this had ever come out, Mathews would have been finished and so long as Charity was alive the threat of exposure would remain.

Then there was the possibility that Charity had threatened to tell Mathews' fiancée about the baby, and that he had killed her to prevent her doing so. Eileen Chase clearly adored Mathews and Thanet thought that she would probably be willing to forgive him anything, so long as she could keep him. But, would *he* have known that?

Thanet thought back over the afternoon's interviews and tried to work out exactly what had been going on between the engaged couple. Mrs. Chase had said that all over the weekend Eileen had gone around "looking as though the world had come to an end." And Mathews had gone away on a walking trip because "it does you good to get away from civilisation." Everything pointed to a quarrel before the weekend, a reconciliation afterwards.

A quarrel about Charity?

Say that it had been about her. Say that Mathews had decided to confess to Eileen—or say that Eileen had found out about the relationship and had decided to confront Mathews with it ... No, the latter was unlikely, Thanet decided. If

Eileen had found out, then it would have been more in character for her to say nothing for fear of rocking the boat, and hope that the affair would die a natural death.

So, say that Mathews had decided to confess, and had told Eileen that he felt he was no longer worthy of her and that their engagement was off. She would have protested, Thanet was sure, but the outcome had nevertheless been that Mathews had gone away alone for the weekend. In his chosen solitude he had obviously thought things over and decided that he really didn't want to lose Eileen, and that if she was prepared to forgive him he would be a fool not to bow to her generosity. When he got back he would go at once to see her and ask her to take him back.

Then, on the train, he had met Charity, had found himself in the position of having to travel down with her.

This was where the scenario became blurred. After leaving the station Mathews could have left the girl and headed straight for Eileen's house, as he claimed, stopping to boost his courage with a couple of drinks on the way.

Or he could have followed Charity and killed her.

Thanet couldn't really see Mathews setting out to murder in cold blood, but say that he had been provoked into it? Say that Charity, still in a precarious emotional state after the thoroughly unpleasant experience of having had to seek and undergo an abortion without any moral support whatsoever, had told Mathews that she intended to expose him to the Education Authorities? He would have argued, begged, pleaded and, if he had not succeeded in persuading her to change her mind by the time they left the station, could have walked home with her to continue the argument. Would he have risked being seen with her in public? Only if he was desperate, Thanet decided. Which he might have been. There was no word of their having been seen together in Sturrenden that evening after they left the station, but that didn't necessarily mean that they hadn't been . . .

"Sir?"

Someone was shaking him by the arm.

"Sir! Are you all right?"

Lineham's concerned face hovered over him.

"Of course I am, man." Thanet was furious at being discovered stretched out on the floor. Careful, even in his haste, not to undo the good work, he rolled over on to his side

153

and climbed cautiously to his feet. "I'm still breathing, aren't I? Anyway, I thought I gave orders not to be disturbed for half an hour."

"That was at six twenty-five. And it's a quarter past seven now. When I saw you on the floor I thought..."

He must have fallen asleep. "Never mind what you thought," snapped Thanet. "You were wrong, weren't you. I was simply... meditating. Complete relaxation is highly conducive to meditation."

"I must remember that, sir. Shall I put a directive up on the noticeboard?"

Thanet opened his mouth to make a sharp retort, caught Lineham's eye and grinned. "All right, Mike, so you caught me out."

"Back, sir?"

Thanet didn't know whether to be relieved or angry, that his sergeant had so immediately understood.

"You're not my nursemaid, Mike, and don't you forget it. How's Louise?"

Lineham's face sagged. "Still putting up a good front. We're both so bloody cheerful..."

"Did you have a word with the Sister?"

"They think it might be tomorrow—the induction, I mean. They haven't told Louise yet, thought it might send her blood pressure up even further."

"It hasn't come down at all, then?"

Lineham shook his head gloomily. "Slightly higher, in fact."

"Look, are you quite sure you wouldn't prefer to be off the case at the moment? I could easily..."

"No! Thank you, sir, but no."

"All right. But if you change your mind..."

"Thanks. Have you... er... had time to go through any of those, yet?"

"No need to be so tactful. No, I haven't. I told you, I was thinking."

"Come to any conclusions?"

"Not really." Thanet briefly outlined the thoughts he had had before dropping off to sleep. "That's as far as I got."

"What about Eileen Chase? If she'd had the whole weekend to brood over Mathews chucking her because of Charity, she could have decided to have it out with the girl herself."

"Slipped out of the house without her mother knowing, you mean? Yes, I'd thought of that."

"Mrs. Chase might well have been watching television and thought Eileen was still up in her room, moping."

"But how would Eileen have known how to find Charity?" Lineham shrugged. "No idea. But it's still possible, isn't it! I should think she'd be prepared to go to almost any lengths to keep him."

"Then there's Jethro . . . No, I've had enough of speculating for the moment. Let's get down to these reports."

They divided the pile between them and Thanet lit his pipe before settling down. He felt much refreshed by his brief dereliction of duty. Therefore it hadn't been dereliction at all, he decided.

He began with the forensic report. He had glanced through it before, but now he checked it more thoroughly. His first impression had been correct: there was nothing of any significance in the findings. Just as well, perhaps. If there had been, and Charity's father had blurred the issue by that untimely but understandable intervention, Thanet and Lineham would have been in serious trouble for not having managed to stop him. But the fact that there was no evidence of a preliminary struggle did support the theory of a blow struck in anger—and therefore an unpremeditated crime.

Thanet relit his pipe, which had gone out, and started on the Lantern Street reports.

There was nothing. No one, at any time during that evening, had seen either Veronica or Mrs. Hodges outside the house. This did not of course necessarily mean that neither of them had been out—for one thing, so many of the Lantern Street houses were unoccupied that it might be quite easy to miss being seen—but it did mean that there was absolutely no evidence as yet to support Lineham's theory.

"Sir!"

The note of excitement in Lineham's voice brought Thanet's head up sharply.

"That second house to house we asked for, in Gate Street . . ."

"Well?"

"They haven't quite finished it yet, but some of the reports are in."

"And?"

155

"As usual, they found several people who'd been out the first time they called, and one of them was the daughter of a Mrs. Wells, the Jethro Pritchards' next-door neighbour, at number twelve. The girl—she's nineteen—says that just after half past nine that night there was a persistent knocking at the Pritchards' front door. She knew Mrs. Pritchard must be in, because if ever Mrs. Pritchard goes out in the evening, it's Mrs. Wells who old-lady-sits, so when the knocking went on and on she wondered what was up and went to look out of the window."

Thanet found Lineham's habit of giving an interesting piece of information a dramatic build-up either engaging or infuriating, according to his own mood at the time. Now, he almost expected the sergeant to say, "And guess who it was!"

"Get on with it, man," he snapped.

Lineham leaned back in his chair, confident of the impact of his next words. "It was the Jethro Pritchards' son!"

"Their son!" Thanet digested this piece of news in silence for a moment and then said, "I wonder why no one has mentioned him before."

"According to the girl—and I quote, 'Caleb's the black sheep of the family. Got himself chucked out because he couldn't stand all that boring old religious stuff.'"

"Just how black, I wonder. How old is he?"

"Twenty, she says."

"Twenty . . . and Charity's cousin. What do you think, Mike?"

"Well, he was obviously in the area at the right time, wasn't he?"

"Quite. Did Mrs. Jethro open the door to him eventually?"

"Yes. But he didn't go in. The girl stayed at the window, hoping for a bit of drama, I suppose. Or because she fancies him."

"Hmm. Interesting. We'll have to find out more about him, obviously. Have you come across anything else, on Jethro or his wife?"

"The same girl confirms that Jethro did arrive home at ten fifteen, sir."

"Does she, now . . . Well, we'll go around first thing in the morning, find out where this young man is living, whether he and Charity kept in touch. And I'd also like to know why they haven't told us about him before."

"Because we didn't ask?"

"Well, we're going to ask now."

18

When Thanet drove into the car park next day, Doctor Mallard was just getting out of his car. It was a sparkling morning. The weather seemed to have settled down again into its seasonal norm and a stiff breeze chased little puffs of cotton-wool cloud across a sky of soft, luminous blue.

"Morning, Luke. Lovely day."

"Morning, Doc. Beautiful, isn't it?"

"Bit late, aren't you?"

"Had to transfer my family back home, after the half-term holiday. We've been trying to get things tidied up a bit, at my mother-in-law's."

"When's Joan coming back?"

"Another fortnight, yet."

"And she'll have completely finished her training, then?"

"Yes."

Mallard laughed. "Thank god, eh? By the way, did you know that young Louise is having her induction this morning?" He glanced at his watch. "Correction, she'll have had it by now."

"Yes, I'd heard. What are her chances?"

"Excellent, I'd say. But the baby—well, we'll just have to wait and see."

Thanet stopped. "You mean, there really is a chance it might not survive?"

"Unfortunately, yes. These toxaemia cases are so unpredictable, it's impossible to tell, in advance."

"Does Lineham know this?"

"Oh, he knows, all right. And, I'm sorry to say, so does Louise, having been a nurse herself. It can't help her particular problem."

No wonder Mike has been so distracted over the last few days, Thanet thought. He remembered guiltily the occasions

157

when he had felt impatient or irritated with the sergeant. "You think I ought to insist Lineham has the day off? I've offered him a few days' leave, several times, but he's refused to take them."

"I should leave it to him to decide. He's probably better off working than worrying himself sick. And nothing'll happen for hours yet, anyway. Does he intend to be present at the birth, do you know?"

"I'm pretty sure he does."

"Then I should say that as long as he keeps in touch with the hospital it would be better to keep him busy until labour is well established."

"Right, I'll do that. Thanks, Doc."

Pausing in the office only long enough to scoop up a gloomy-looking Lineham, Thanet set off for Gate Street. Charity's mother was just coming out of Jethro's house. She started when Thanet greeted her.

"Oh . . . Good morning, Inspector. I didn't see you."

She looked harassed. Hair was escaping from her normally immaculate bun, and her black cardigan was buttoned up askew.

"We're just going to have a word with your sister-in-law. We didn't realise, until last night, that she has a son."

Mrs. Pritchard squinted at him, shielding her eyes from the sun. "Caleb?"

"Yes. Why has no one mentioned him, do you know?"

"His parents have nothing to do with him, now. We've all lost touch with him, since he moved away from home."

"Charity, too?"

"Oh, yes. They never got on, anyway, even as children . . ." She closed her eyes, swayed slightly. Thanet put out his hand to steady her.

"Mrs. Pritchard, are you all right?"

"Yes . . . yes. Thank you, I'm fine. It's just that I'm not sleeping too well, that's all . . . " Her voice trailed away and there was an awkward silence. Then she gave him a quick, nervous glance. "Inspector . . . "

"Yes?"

She hesitated, then shook her head. "Nothing. I must be getting home." And she turned, set off down the street with a slightly unsteady but dogged gait.

"Think I ought to see her home, sir?"

158

Thanet was still watching the receding figure. She was walking rather more briskly now.

"I think she'll be all right."

"She looked just about at the end of her tether, to me."

"Scarcely surprising, is it?"

Thanet knocked at the door of number fourteen. He had already decided that as far as Mrs. Jethro Pritchard was concerned, it was pointless to waste time on the tactful approach. Her hostility so far had been unremitting and it was a surprise, therefore, to find that he was greeted by a baring of the teeth that was clearly intended to be a smile.

"Good morning, Inspector. Come in, won't you?"

He and Lineham raised eyebrows at each other behind her back and followed her into the sitting room.

"Do sit down." She brushed an imaginary speck of dust off the arm of one of the chairs. "I'm afraid I haven't got around to cleaning in here yet, today."

"It looks fine to me."

By now Thanet had guessed the reason for this sudden change of attitude: Mrs. Jethro Pritchard was afraid.

Charity's father had probably come storming around, as Thanet had expected, and had accused Jethro of seducing his niece and causing her to seek an abortion. With both brother and wife against him, Jethro had no doubt crumbled, confessed. Now, Mrs. Pritchard was afraid that she and her husband were about to be plunged into a scandal far worse than the one they had weathered before, a scandal involving not only incest but, possibly, murder. Thanet couldn't like the woman, thought it very likely that a measure of the responsibility for her husband's aberrations lay at her door, but he couldn't help feeling a twinge of pity for her now. She had seated herself opposite him, solid knees clamped together, hands clasped tightly in her lap. She was waiting for the axe to fall.

Or was it possible that her fear was on her son's behalf?

"Is your husband at home, Mrs. Pritchard?"

"No. He's at the school."

"There's a question I wanted to ask you both."

She said nothing, seemed almost to stop breathing.

"Why didn't you tell me you had a son?"

For a moment she looked at him blankly, as though she must have misheard. Then she shook her head a little, as if to clear it. "I'm sorry . . . ?"

159

Thanet repeated the question.

Her mouth became a thin, hard line. "Our son is dead to us, Inspector."

Thanet said nothing, and eventually his silence forced her into a reluctant explanation.

"He has chosen to walk with the ungodly."

"He left the Children of Jerusalem?"

"Yes."

"How long ago was this?"

"Eighteen months or so."

"When we asked you if Charity knew any young men, you said no."

"I told you, Inspector. Our son is dead to us. As far as we are concerned, he doesn't exist."

"How did Charity get on with him?"

"Not very well. They never really took to each other."

"Did they ever meet after Caleb left home?"

"How should I know? He leads his own life, now. He has nothing to do with any of us."

"Then why was he knocking at your door on Monday night, Mrs. Pritchard?"

"Who told you that?" Her eyes sparked with anger. "They had no right. Spying on people . . ."

"They had every right, Mrs. Pritchard. A duty, even. This, I would remind you, is a murder case . . . What did he want?"

"How should I know?"

"But you let him in."

"I did not! As soon as I saw who it was I told him once and for all that I didn't want him coming around here bothering us, with his long hair and greasy jeans . . ."

"He must have said why he'd come."

"I told you, I didn't ask!"

And from this evasion she would not budge.

"Could you tell us where he lives?"

"I've no idea."

"Where he works, then?"

"Works! That's a joke! Works!" She leaned forward, her eyes hot and bitter. "Work is sacred, Inspector, which as far as my son is concerned is a very good reason for not doing any."

This was all Thanet could get out of her.

"Right, Mike," he said, when they were back in the car.

160

"I want you to find Caleb and talk to him. You might get his address from Jethro, at the school. If not, well, you'll just have to use your initiative. If you think it necessary, bring the boy in for questioning. Use your own judgement. You can drop me off at the office, first. Oh, and Mike, you'll no doubt be giving the hospital a ring from time to time. When they say that Louise is ready for you to join her, let me know, then drop everything and go. Understood?"

"Yes, sir. Thank you."

There were more reports on Thanet's desk. He lit his pipe and settled down to read them. Within minutes he was on his feet again. He wanted to see Jethro. At once.

On his way to the school he thought about the new information which had just come in. A woman who lived opposite Holly Road Primary School had worked late in her front garden on Monday evening. She had been keeping an eye on the time, because she wanted to watch a television programme which began at 10. People had begun to stream out of the school just before 9:30 and within ten minutes or so the place had been deserted. Last of all, just before a quarter to ten, she had seen Jethro come out, locking the school gates behind him.

It was only ten minutes walk from the school to Jethro's house, and yet he had not arrived home until 10:15. What had he been doing, during that half an hour? Charity had left the Hodges' house at 9:35. Had their routes converged?

Suppose that Jethro had somehow managed to scrape together the money to pay for Charity's abortion, and had been anxious to know that everything had gone according to plan. She might well have told him what time she hoped to arrive home. They could even have arranged to meet. Jethro would have been on tenterhooks to know that the operation had been a success, full no doubt of good resolutions never to land himself in the same mess again. But suppose Charity had seen things differently? Suppose that she had decided to keep up the pressure, demand more money for her continuing silence? Jethro might well have lashed out at her in an explosion of anger, disappointment and fear.

In any case, he certainly had some explaining to do.

Thanet ran him to earth in one of the cloakrooms, fixing a leaking lavatory cistern. His left eye was almost invisible in an area of swollen, discoloured flesh.

"I'd like a word. Where can we talk?"

Jethro groaned. "Not again! Your sergeant only left a few minutes ago." Reluctantly, he led the way to a little cubbyhole of a room equipped with a sagging armchair and an electric kettle. A crumpled newspaper lay on the arm of the chair. Thanet picked it up and noted with interest that it was today's and that it was folded back at the racing page, and marked. Jethro was evidently a backslider in more ways than one.

"Your brother's been to see you, then." Thanet nodded at the black eye.

Jethro's hand instinctively began to move towards his bruised face, then stopped. "I don't know what you mean."

"Oh come, Mr. Pritchard. You won't convince me you got that by walking into a door."

"A ladder, as a matter of fact."

"Oh, a ladder, was it? Well, I'm afraid I don't believe you. In fact, I'm beginning to think I can't believe a word you say."

"What do you mean?"

"Look, I've had enough of beating around the bush. I'll give it to you straight. We know that you had a sexual relationship with your niece, we know that she became pregnant, we know you gave her money to enable her to procure an abortion and on top of all this, we now know that you lied to us about the time you left here the evening she died. We have a witness, Mr. Pritchard, a nice, solid witness. In view of all this, if you were me, what would you think?"

Thanet paused for a moment. There was a sheen of sweat on Jethro's forehead and the empurpled area of flesh was vivid against skin the colour of grubby linen.

"I . . ." But he couldn't continue.

"Exactly. Now, this witness states that she saw you lock the school gates behind you at around 9:45 that night, instead of after 10, as you claimed. And that quarter of an hour to twenty minutes make a lot of difference, Mr. Pritchard. In fact, you could call it of paramount importance."

Thanet paused again, but Jethro was still speechless.

"Charity, you see, left Mrs. Hodges' house at 9:35—ten minutes before you left here. It would have taken her around ten to fifteen minutes to reach the entrance to the alley . . . which leaves you with about five minutes in hand to get to the place

162

where she was killed. If you hurried, you could have done it easily. What did you do, Mr. Pritchard? Hang around in that alleyway, hoping to catch her on her way home? Or had the meeting been arranged before she left?''

''No!'' Jethro burst out. ''It wasn't like that, Inspector, I swear it wasn't. We hadn't arranged . . . I didn't meet her, I swear I didn't. I didn't even see her.''

He was sweating profusely now, and he dragged a dirty handkerchief from his pocket, mopped at his forehead.

''I'm sorry. I don't believe you.'' But it was interesting to note that Jethro had denied none of the other allegations. This, Thanet decided, was the moment to set the record straight, while Jethro was still terrified of being arrested for murder.

''You don't deny the rest of what I said?''

Jethro hesitated and for a second Thanet thought that he was going to hold out after all. Then, slowly, he shook his head.

''What's the point?'' he said, wearily. ''You've got it all worked out, haven't you? If I do deny it you'll only keep on and on until I give in . . . But I didn't kill her! I swear I didn't!''

''You admit, then, that you seduced her, that she told you that she was pregnant, and that you gave her money to procure an abortion?'' Briefly, Thanet regretted Lineham's absence, that he had no witness to Jethro's confession, but the thought did not trouble him unduly; Jethro was too weak a character to stick to a retraction, even if he chose to back-pedal when it came to the point of making an official statement. But if he knew his man, alongside Jethro's admission would run a need to justify himself. He was right.

''Maybe I did, but it wasn't my fault. It was her.'' Jethro was even managing to work up some indignation against the dead girl. ''She was a real little whore . . . Putting her arms around me and rubbing herself against me . . . Sitting on my lap and wriggling so I thought it would drive me mad . . . Believe me, she was asking for it—begging for it, even. And once we had . . . she couldn't get enough of it, I can tell you. She was mad for it. She frightened the wits out of me. She'd want it anywhere—up against the wall of the alley, in the kitchen of my own house, even, with my mother sitting there with her back to us and my wife coming down the stairs . . .''

Jethro was shaking as he relived the state of fear Charity

163

had induced in him. And Thanet believed him. It was difficult to reconcile that child-like, innocent-seeming figure in the alley with the nymphomaniac Jethro was describing, but Thanet was sufficiently experienced by now not only to recognize the ring of truth when he heard it, but to know that even the most beautiful apple can be rotten at the core. Fleetingly he remembered a local murder case. A fourteen-year-old girl had helped her middle-aged lover to plan and execute the murder of his former mistress and in his summing-up the judge had said that he wished to make it clear that this was not, as many people might think, a case of an older man leading a young girl astray, that she was, in his opinion, the most truly evil person he had ever encountered in all his years on the bench.

Had Charity been another such?

Now that Jethro had started talking he couldn't seem to stop. He went on and on detailing times and places and Thanet let him, knowing that with every word Jethro was making it more and more difficult to go back, later, on what he was saying. Eventually, though, the flow of sordid detail sickened Thanet and he cut through the torrent of accusation, self-pity and self-justification.

"Pretty unbearable, was it?"

Pathetically grateful that Thanet appeared to understand, Jethro agreed that yes, it had been.

"How unbearable?" said Thanet softly. "Unbearable enough to make you want to take active measures to prevent it going on indefinitely? Unbearable enough to make you decide to kill her?" But even as he spoke he was asking himself if Jethro would have had the guts.

Too late, Jethro saw the trap into which he had fallen. His one good eye gazed at Thanet with a fixed, frantic stare. Then, with a groan, he lowered his face into his hands, shaking his head from side to side in despair.

"Well?" said Thanet sternly. "I'm waiting."

Still no reply.

Thanet stood up. "Very well, Mr. Pritchard, if you can't satisfy me as to your precise movements between 9:45 and 10:15 on Monday night, then I shall have to ask you to accompany me to the police station."

Jethro lifted a face like a trapped rabbit's. "No! Look, Inspector . . . If I . . . If I did tell you where I was, during that half an hour, can you give me your word my wife won't find out?''

What was coming now? "That depends," said Thanet cautiously.

"On what?"

"On whether the information has any relevance to the case.''

"Well, it hasn't . . . Or at least, only for me . . . Look, sit down, Inspector, and I'll tell you.''

Thanet sat.

Even now Jethro procrastinated. He blew his nose, made a show of putting his (now revolting) handkerchief away, sat up a little straighter.

Thanet folded his arms in an exaggerated gesture of patience.

"My wife'd kill me if she knew . . . I was in a pub,'' said Jethro, with the air of someone confessing to a major crime. "With my son.''

So that was it. If Mrs. Jethro knew that her husband had not only committed the sin of imbibing alcohol—and in a public house, at that—but had also been fraternising with the son who was "dead" to her, Jethro's life would be hell on earth.

"You'd arranged to meet?"

Jethro shook his head. "I bumped into him soon after leaving the school. He was coming to look for me. He'd been to the house, apparently, but my wife . . . I keep on trying to patch things up between them, but it's no good, she won't listen.''

"She told him where you were?"

"Oh no. He just came along on the off-chance. Well, there aren't many other places I could be. He knows I come here sometimes, even when the school is closed . . . just to keep an eye on things.''

Jethro's eyes flickered around the tiny, shabby room with a proprietorial air. This, Thanet realised, was his sanctuary. Though it was still beyond him to understand how Jethro, with a conviction for indecent assault on an under-age girl, should have managed to get a job in a school in the first place. Perhaps he had somehow managed to suppress the information?

"Which pub did you go to?"

165

"The King's Head. In Denholm Street. We usually do, when we have the chance."

Well away from this area, then—presumably to minimise the chance of Mrs. Jethro finding out. Did this mean that, if Jethro was telling the truth, he was in the clear?

Thanet's brain moved into top gear, inventing and discarding one scenario after another—Jethro had met and killed Charity before meeting Caleb... after leaving him, later on... they had done it together...

This was the point at which Jethro dropped his bombshell.

"We had a lift."

"A lift?" An independent witness? "Who from?"

"Friend of my son's. Came by just after we met, gave us a lift over to the King's Head. We all had a drink together. Then he ran me home. Nice young chap."

"Name?"

"Pete."

"Pete who?"

Jethro shrugged. "Dunno. Never heard his last name. Caleb—my son—would know, I expect."

"You gave your son's address to Sergeant Lineham?"

"Yes."

Thanet left in a dispirited mood. They'd check, of course, but it really did look as though that was the end of one of his most promising suspects. And he wasn't getting very far with the others. In default of any shred of evidence against Mrs. Jethro, Mrs. Hodges or Veronica (whom Thanet had never really seriously considered anyway), it looked as though the list was now reduced to two. All he needed now was to find Carson's report on his desk confirming that every moment of Mathews' time was accounted for, from the moment he left the station to the time he arrived at Eileen's house, and the case would come to a grinding halt.

Thanet tried to reassure himself that this had happened before, that it did not necessarily mean defeat, that sooner or later something would turn up, some scrap of information hitherto ignored or unavailable... Nevertheless, Thanet loathed finding himself in the position of having to rely on such stray crumbs. All the while there were leads to follow up it was possible to feel optimistic, but when there were none it was difficult not to sink into a mood when he could think only of all the unsolved murders still in the files of every police force in the country, and wonder if he himself was this time going to have to admit defeat.

But back at the office a surprise was awaiting him.

"There's a Mr. Mathews and a Miss Chase to see you, sir. They've been waiting nearly an hour."

A confession? Hope burgeoned once more.

"Where are they?"

"Interview room two."

"I'll see them right away."

19

Mathews had armoured himself in respectability: dark suit, white shirt, sober tie. Eileen, too, was formally dressed in a fawn linen suit, cream blouse with Peter Pan collar. They both stood up when Thanet came into the room.

"What can I do for you?"

They glanced at each other. Eileen gave a small, encouraging nod.

Mathews' Adam's apple moved jerkily in his throat. "I...we thought we ought to clarify the position."

"Shall we sit down, then?" Thanet checked: the police-woman who had come to take notes was ready.

"I don't know where to begin." Mathews looked helplessly at his fiancée.

Eileen edged her chair closer to his and took his hand. "Begin with why we decided to come," she said softly.

Mathews clutched her hand in both of his, like a talisman. "It's just that...Well, we're not exactly stupid, Inspector. We appreciate the position I'm in. We know that you're bound to be looking for a *man* in connection with Charity's death, in view of..." His courage failed him and once again he cast a desperate glance at Eileen.

"In view of the fact that she'd just had an abortion, Inspector," she said calmly. "As my fiancé said yesterday, we have no secrets from each other. It's obvious that there would

167

have been a post mortem and that in the circumstances you would look first for the father of that child.''

Mathews had gained strength from her intervention. "It was clear from your questions, yesterday, that I was high on your list of suspects, so we thought that if we came and told you everything, you would believe me when I said I was innocent.''

"Of the murder, Leslie means." Eileen leaned forward in her chair, the protuberant eyes bulging earnestly. "You must believe that.''

So they had come to confess to the lesser crime in the hope of exonerating themselves from the greater. Well, we'll see, thought Thanet.

"What do you mean by 'everything'?" he said cautiously.

Mathews' face was suddenly flooded with scarlet. "The child was mine.''

So, candidate number three for the paternity of Charity's baby. Thanet wondered what Mathews would say, if he knew about the other two.

His confession made, Mathews suddenly became voluble. "As I said, it was obvious, yesterday, that you suspected the truth. And we thought it would only be a matter of time before you started to put pressure on me, ask for blood samples and so on. So, to be honest, we thought it would look better if I came in of my own free will and confessed— to being the baby's father, that is. But the murder . . . Inspector, I swear I had absolutely nothing to do with that. When I heard . . . I just couldn't believe it. And I'd travelled down from London with her, just before! I knew how bad it would look, so at first, I . . . we thought it would be best if we kept quiet.''

"You helped Charity arrange for the abortion?"

"No. She fixed it up herself, said she didn't need any help from me. Only the money." Mathews released Eileen's hand and wiped his palm on his trouser leg.

"How much?"

"Two hundred pounds.''

Charity, it seemed, had had a talent for capitalising on even the most unpromising situations. Just before Thanet left Jethro had told him that he, too, had given Charity two hundred pounds—money he had won betting and had tucked away "for a rainy day,'' unknown to his wife. It was not surprising, then, that even after paying for the abortion Charity had had over a hundred and fifty pounds left—and there would have been more, Thanet reminded himself, if she had managed to squeeze money out of the young Welshman.

All in all, Thanet found that he was liking Charity less and less with every day that passed.

"You know which clinic she went to?"

Mathews shook his head. "She wouldn't tell me. Somewhere in London, that's all."

"You arranged to meet on the train, on Monday night?"

"No! That was pure chance, I swear. If I'd known she was catching that one . . . She was the last person in the world I wanted to see, I assure you. As I said, she got on after me, came and sat opposite."

"How did she seem?"

"Very quiet. Tired, I thought. Well, that would be understandable . . ."

"What did you talk about?"

"We didn't talk, not really. I just asked her if it had gone off all right and she said yes. She dozed, most of the way. To tell you the truth, I was relieved. It was a pretty embarrassing situation."

"I can imagine. And when you got to Sturrenden?"

"As I told you, we parted outside the station. And that was the last I saw of her."

"Excuse me for a moment, will you?"

He left them exchanging an apprehensive look and hurried up to his room. Before proceeding he needed to find out if Carson's report was in. He shuffled through the reports he had not yet had time to read that morning and found the one he sought. His eyes skimmed the single sheet of paper, his spirits plummeting.

The landlord of the Red Lion, in Cresset Street, remembered Mathews coming in soon after nine. He was firm on the time because his daughter, who helped behind the bar, had left for a disco at nine. The landlord hadn't been too pleased to be left single-handed to cope with the Bank Holiday crowd. He'd first noticed Mathews just after she left. He remembered him partly because he was not a regular, partly because of the orange rucksack he carried, and partly because he had looked so depressed. He had spoken to no one, had consumed several whiskies and was walking unsteadily when he left at about ten to ten. At no point during the three-quarters of an hour had Mathews left the bar.

And Eileen's mother, who could have no possible reason to lie, had been quite definite about the time of Mathews' arrival that evening: ten o'clock. So Mathews simply wouldn't have had time either to have followed Charity after leaving the station or to have intercepted her on her way home.

Thanet tossed the report on to the desk with an exclamation of disgust. There was no point in questioning Mathews any further at present, he might as well let the couple go. He was at the door when the phone rang. It was Lineham.

"Any luck, Mike?"

"I found him, sir. Caleb. Got his address from Jethro, as you suggested. Jethro's got a lovely black eye, by the way."

"Yes, I know. I've seen it. What did Caleb say?"

"No wonder Mrs. Jethro Pritchard has disowned him. Guess what he does for a living?"

Thanet was in no mood for games. "Just tell me, Mike, will you?"

"He's a one-man band! You know, blow through a comb, play an accordion, clash the cymbals with a string attached to one foot . . ."

"I get the picture."

"I rather liked him, actually."

"And, let me guess, he spent the relevant time having an innocent drink in the King's Head with his daddy."

"That's what Jethro says?"

"Yes."

"So does Caleb. And I'm afraid it looks pretty cast-iron. There's a third party who bears them out."

"The chap called Pete?"

"Peter Andrews, yes. I've been to see him, too. He's a mechanic at Potters, in Biddenden Way."

"Reliable, you think?"

"I'd say so, yes. He says he picked them both up just along the road from the school, drove them to the King's Head, had a drink with them and then took Jethro home—the old boy was getting a bit agitated in case his wife got wind of what he'd been up to. Andrews gave him a peppermint to suck and dropped him off at the corner of Gate Street, just before 10:15."

"When the girl next door saw him arrive home."

"He could easily have gone out again."

"There's been no whisper of that, from anyone. Just a moment."

A policewoman with a slip of paper in her hand had just come into the room, looking urgent.

"A message for DS Lineham, sir. Switchboard said you were on the phone to him."

"Well?"

"The hospital rang. His wife is asking for him."

"Thank you."

Thanet relayed the information to Lineham, told him to take the rest of the day off and returned to interview room two.

"Right, well I think that's all, for the moment."

Mathews and Eileen exchanged a disbelieving glance and then looked up at Thanet in mingled astonishment and hope.

Eileen was the first to find her voice. She came slowly to her feet as she said, "You mean, you believe us? That Leslie had nothing to do with Charity's death?"

"His alibi has been checked. That's why I left you, just now. I thought that the report was probably in, but I hadn't had time to look at it before talking to you earlier. Mr. Mathews seems to be in the clear."

Mathews stood up and he and Eileen looked at each other, transfigured by joy. Then Eileen turned back to Thanet, the radiance fading. "We needn't have come and told you all this after all, then. I should have thought...we should have waited...how stupid of me. I panicked, I suppose."

Thanet noted the varying pronouns with interest.

Mathews put an arm around her shoulders. "Never mind, darling. It doesn't matter, now...except that...Inspector, may I ask...?"

"Go ahead."

"Will there...In view of the fact that Charity is dead...will there be a prosecution?"

"For unlawful intercourse, you mean? Extremely unlikely, I should think. After all, you can't have a prosecution without evidence and as the main witness—as you so rightly point out—is dead, I can't see that it would have much chance of success. And I imagine that you have learnt your lesson."

"Oh, I have," breathed Mathews fervently. "Believe me, I have." And in a daze of incredulous happiness, they left.

Thanet watched them go, glad that this case had had at least one positive outcome. Mathews, he was convinced, was no pervert, had merely been too weak, too flattered, perhaps, to resist a young girl's determined advances.

For by now Thanet believed that in the case of each of her "lovers," it had been Charity who had initiated the affair. With young Williams she had failed to shape matters as she would have wished, he had been too experienced for her, but Mathews and Jethro had, he was sure, been as clay in her manipulating fingers.

Yes, he thought as he returned to his office, there was no doubt about it, his feelings towards the girl had undergone a considerable change since the moment he had first stumbled upon that pathetic figure huddled in the alley. Then, he had seen her as innocence destroyed, now he felt that despite her tender years she had herself been a destroyer, totally lacking in compassion, loyalty or finer moral feeling. He had no idea whether or not her awakened sexual appetite had truly been as gross as both Jethro and the young Welshman had claimed it to be, but in any case, Thanet was more certain than ever that Charity had consciously used that sexuality to strike back at her father in retaliation for the long years of tyranny.

How heady must her sense of power have been, while she explored its deadly potential. But unfortunately for her it proved to be a weapon she could not control. She had become pregnant. How had she reacted? Would she have been in despair, as most girls of her age in her position would have been? Probably not, Thanet thought. She would have been much more likely to have been furious with her own body, for having dared to betray her. In any case, she had not lost her head. She had been determined to turn even this situation to her own advantage.

But unwittingly she had set in motion the forces which would ultimately destroy her.

To Thanet's mind, the saddest aspect of Charity's life was that she had evidently come to believe that to possess power over others was the road to fulfillment. Lacking generosity of heart she had failed to inspire it in those around her, and she had died without ever having experienced the joy of giving and receiving in love. Of all the people he had met on this

172

case, not one, apart from her parents, had expressed any affection for her and it seemed that no one else would mourn her passing.

But it was still Thanet's task to find out who had killed her and he took a piece of paper and once more wrote down the names of his suspects. Then he sat brooding over it. Every one of these people had suffered because of Charity. The question was, which of them had decided to retaliate? And, even if he could find out, how could he prove it? It looked as though his two most likely candidates, Jethro and Mathews, were out of the running. With uninvolved third parties to support their stories, there didn't seem to be much likelihood of proving their guilt. And all four women—Veronica, her mother, Eileen Chase and Mrs. Jethro—well, so far there was not a single scrap of evidence to connect them with the crime.

So, where did he go from here? Thanet sighed. The answer was all too familiar: back to the files. Past experience had taught him how easy it was mentally to dismiss something as unimportant, only to find later that it was a tiny but crucial piece of the jigsaw. Somewhere in those mounds of documented facts and statements he might find a chance remark, an innuendo, perhaps even something left *un*said, which could point him in the right direction.

At the moment, he'd be glad to be pointed in any direction.

20

Thanet closed the last of the files, sat back in his chair and massaged his temples. It was nine o'clock and after the long hours of reading his head was aching, his back stiff and his eyes gritty.

And it had all been for nothing.

No bells had rung, no new insight had rewarded his dogged determination to finish the task he had set himself.

He had missed Lineham, too. Normally they did this particular job together, pausing to comment, suggest, argue, speculate with the unconscious ease of long association.

173

Deprived of this stimulation and of Lineham's value as a sounding-board, Thanet had gradually found himself sinking into a stupefied inertia; ideas either failed to flow or seemed too uninspired to warrant more than passing consideration.

Reminded of the sergeant, Thanet now rang the hospital. After a short delay he was informed that Louise's labour was progressing satisfactorily but that the birth was not yet imminent. No hope of Lineham returning to the office tonight, then. Thanet stood up and stretched. Time he gave up and went home.

Despite the open window the room was stuffy, stale with tobacco smoke. Thanet folded his arms on the window sill and leaned out, taking in deep breaths of fresh air. The street below was almost deserted, the shop fronts illuminated for the hours of darkness ahead, but above the roof-tops the light still lingered in an oyster-shell sky streaked with apricot and rose. It all looked very peaceful and yet, somewhere out there a murderer walked free, growing daily more confident, perhaps, that his crime would remain unsolved.

As well it might, thought Thanet despondently. Where have I gone wrong? What have I left undone? What have I missed? There must, surely, be something. Perhaps it was merely a question of viewpoint. Thanet was still convinced that this had been no casual killing. There had been no robbery, no sexual assault, no struggle. But the blow which had sent Charity reeling against that wicked piece of iron had caught her unprepared. So what, exactly, had precipitated it?

Thanet stared unseeing over the chimneys of Sturrenden, transported by his imagination back to the narrow alley where Charity had met her death.

Scenario one: Charity and the murderer were walking side by side along the footpath. Tempers were rising, the killer's anger building inexorably towards flash point.

Thanet frowned and narrowed his eyes, as if intense concentration would reward him with a glimpse of the killer's face.

With whom would Charity have been quarreling?

With Veronica, because Veronica was refusing to go along with Charity's schemes, ever again?

With Mrs. Hodges, because she had discovered the reason for Charity and Veronica's "friendship," and was making it

174

clear that she was not going to allow her daughter to be blackmailed and browbeaten any longer?

With Eileen Chase, because she wanted Charity to leave Mathews alone in future?

With Mathews, because . . . No, Mathews was now in the clear, remember. And so was Jethro.

With Mrs. Jethro, then, because she had found out about her husband's relationship with Charity and was determined that she and her husband were not going to suffer the ignominy of another court case?

Thanet was no nearer enlightenment and he shook his head wearily. What was the point of going on? But he couldn't leave it alone. Obsessively, he returned to the darkness of the alley.

Scenario two: the murderer was lying in wait for Charity, poised to spring as the hurried, echoing tattoo of her footsteps came closer and closer . . .

Well, if that was how it had been, Thanet simply couldn't visualise either Veronica or her mother crouching there in the shadows with murder in her heart. Eileen Chase? Well, possibly. Thanet was by now even more convinced that Eileen would fight tooth and nail to preserve her last chance of happiness. Mrs. Jethro, too, would be a determined and formidable adversary.

But, would either of them be prepared to kill?

In any case, there was no evidence against either of them, and besides, the manner of Charity's death argued against it having been a premeditated crime. If murder had been planned in advance the killer would surely have come equipped with a weapon, and none had been either used or found.

No, that blow had been struck in anger, Thanet was sure of that. So . . .

Scenario three: Charity's murderer comes hurrying along the footpath, either to meet her or to catch her up. For whatever reason he is already in a precarious emotional state, keyed up to challenge her or to present her with an ultimatum, perhaps. They meet, he speaks and then . . . Ah yes. Then she responds in such a way (with scorn? contempt? defiance?) as to cause his self-control to snap.

If indeed it had happened like that, which of his suspects was most likely to fit the bill? All of them, he decided dejectedly. So he was no further forward. But wait! Perhaps he had been too limited, too blinkered in his thinking. Perhaps this was why he hadn't got anywhere. True, there had so far been no hint of anyone else caught up in Charity's toils, but that did not necessarily mean that such a person did not exist. Perhaps Thanet had not even met him yet. Or . . . perhaps the murderer was someone with a familiar face, someone they simply hadn't thought of casting in this role?

The wail of a fire engine somewhere over to his right briefly penetrated Thanet's absorption and he automatically turned his head, seeking the glow which would indicate its destination. There was nothing, but the strident signal of danger must have touched the alarm button in his subconscious, because he was suddenly remembering that incident with Ben a couple of days before.

In a kaleidoscope of recollected sound and vision he saw the bicycle rolling towards the open gate, heard the roar of the approaching tractor, his own frantic shouted warning. Again, Ben somersaulted over the handlebars, lay motionless upon the green of the grass verge and, in a miracle of resurrection, scrambled unharmed to his feet. Thanet relived his own relief, anger, shame as the palm of his hand cracked against Ben's tender flesh.

"How many times have I told you never to ride down that drive when the gate is open?"

A face that was already familiar . . . someone in a precarious emotional state . . .

Illumination was blinding and Thanet straightened up with such a jerk that he struck his head on the lintel. The combination of physical pain and mental dazzlement disoriented him and he staggered, clutching at the windowsill to steady himself.

After a few moments, when he felt more in control, he returned to his desk and sat down, rubbing the back of his head.

Was it possible?

That unique response, familiar to every parent, of intense anxiety instantaneously transmuted into relief and then into anger when the danger is over . . . Was this what had brought about Charity's death?

Had she been killed by her own father?

176

Thanet's mind raced as he began to test this new theory against the events of that night.

He had never seriously considered Pritchard as a suspect because Pritchard had reported Charity's disappearance before the crime was committed and because Thanet had therefore had the impression of having had the man under his own surveillance for the entire evening. But now he realised that this was not so. For twenty minutes or so, while Thanet and Lineham were visiting Mrs. Hodges, Pritchard had been left at home alone, on Thanet's own suggestion.

Say that Pritchard, unable to bear the inactivity, had decided to go and look for his daughter along the footpath.

Here was a new scenario indeed: Pritchard advancing slowly, fearful of stumbling at any moment across his daughter's body. After the long hours of slowly mounting tension he is keyed up to an almost unbearable pitch of anxiety. Then he thinks he recognises the footsteps approaching. Hope burgeons. Can it possibly be Charity?

It is, and at once, now that he is assured of her safety, anxiety is transformed into an overwhelming rush of anger. He demands to know where she has been. And Charity?

What does Charity do?

She, too, is in a state of tension. She knows, from Mrs. Hodges, that she has been found out, that there is no possibility this time of covering her tracks, of fobbing her father off with evasions or half-truths. Pritchard is going to want to have chapter and verse, corroboration of her story down to the last detail. And although her rebellion has long been in the making, she is not yet ready for open confrontation. At fifteen she is not equipped for independence and cannot hope to throw off the shackles of home in the same way as her cousin Caleb.

She really has only two options: to try to brazen it out, or to attempt to forestall him by jumping in first with profuse apologies and a plea for forgiveness. In her weakened state it was quite possible, Thanet thought, that she would have opted for the latter, but in any case he was pretty certain that all the way home she would have been bracing herself for the meeting and rehearsing the part she would play.

And then, suddenly, while she was still unprepared, there her father was. It was easy to imagine the rest. Thanet remembered the way he himself had shrunk from the power and impact of Pritchard's rage in the kitchen that night. One false word from Charity—or even no response at all—and after the long hours of fear and tension Pritchard's self-control would have snapped. One hard slap would have been enough...

But would Pritchard have left his daughter's body lying there? Not if he had realised the extent of the damage he had done, but it was extremely unlikely that he should have known of the existence of that broken latch and it was possible that after striking Charity, unable to trust himself further, he had at once wheeled blindly away and hurried home to await her return.

Thanet now remembered that when he and Lineham had arrived back at the Pritchards' house after seeing Mrs. Hodges, Pritchard had been waiting in the hall. At the time, Thanet had assumed that this was because the man was eager to hear their news, but perhaps he had only just got home and had really been waiting for Charity to turn up. And when Thanet had assured him that Charity was safe, Pritchard's relief—which Thanet had attributed to the information that Mrs. Hodges had recently seen the girl—could have been because he thought that Thanet was saying that he had seen Charity *since* the scene in the alley, and that no harm had been done. And then, when Pritchard had realised that this was not so...this must have been the point at which he had begun to be afraid that that blow had done more damage than he had intended.

Thanet mentally reviewed the remainder of the events of that evening and saw that all along Pritchard's behaviour had been entirely consistent with this new interpretation of events. It was Thanet's own assumptions as to the man's motivation, his own misinterpretations of Pritchard's behaviour, that had led him astray.

Yes, the more he thought about it, the more convinced he became that he had hit upon the truth. He had always felt that Pritchard's sanity was balanced on a knife-edge, imperilled by religious fanaticism and dangerously unrealistic expectations of those about him. Thanet still believed that in his own way Pritchard had loved his daughter and had genuinely tried to do what he believed to be best for her. In Pritchard's eyes Charity had been a brand to be plucked from the burning and it had been his duty, however unpleasant, to ensure her salvation. How shattering it must have been to find his worst fears confirmed, to see Charity lying dead in that alley and to realise that he himself had killed her. Scarcely surprising, then, that his raw, agonized exhibition of grief had been almost too painful to witness.

What effect would the realisation that he had killed his own daughter have had upon such a man? Would he be crushed by guilt, sorrow and remorse—or would he seek to justify himself?

Thanet remembered what Miss Foskett had told him, recalled Mrs. Pritchard's account of Charity's harsh punishment all those years ago, and wondered: would Pritchard have tried to persuade himself of his innocence by trying to convince himself that in striking out at Charity he had really been attacking the devil that was in her?

Thanet had come across religious fanaticism before and was only too well aware of its capacity for self-deception and delusion. Nevertheless the man would have realised that the police would not be prepared to accept this excuse as justification for murder and would have been on tenterhooks in case they discovered the truth—or, for that matter, in case anyone discovered the truth.

Mrs. Pritchard, for instance?

Thanet suddenly recalled Mrs. Pritchard's appearance when he had seen her leaving her sister-in-law's house, this morning. She had looked distraught, on the verge of disintegration. He had attributed her distress to natural shock and grief, but what if it had had a more sinister origin? He remembered now that she had seemed to want to tell him something, but had held back. And he, intent upon his errand, had made nothing of it. Assuming that Pritchard had indeed killed his daughter, what if Mrs. Pritchard had begun to suspect the truth?

Thinking back to his previous conversation with her, Thanet began to wonder if he himself could have been responsible for arousing such suspicions. He still believed that this whole tragic train of events had been set in motion when Charity had been cowed into apparent submission by her father's harsh and misguided treatment. He had not actually said so to Mrs. Pritchard, but it would not have been too difficult for her to work it out for herself after he left. What if, having done so, she had finally shed her stubborn loyalty to her husband and begun to blame him for what had happened? Not for the

179

murder, of course. Thanet was certain that at that point Mrs. Pritchard would not have suspected him of that. But she could have begun to hold him responsible for setting Charity on the wrong road, the road which had led her to deceit and, finally, to death.

And if so, Thanet was sure that her attitude to her husband would have changed. Mrs. Pritchard had loved her daughter. Once she had begun to blame Pritchard for Charity's death her change of attitude would have filtered through into her behaviour. What if Pritchard had misinterpreted the reason for that change? What if he had assumed that his wife had begun to suspect him of Charity's murder? Thanet could envisage only too well a conversation begun at cross-purposes and ending, on Mrs. Pritchard's part, in horrified enlightenment. And although she may at one time have been prepared to justify her husband's behaviour, Thanet could not believe that she would now be prepared to do so. To condone punishment was one thing, but murder, and of her own child . . . No, she would have been bound to condemn him.

And how would Pritchard have reacted to that? Here, surely, was a highly explosive situation. Had Thanet unwittingly put Mrs. Pritchard herself in danger?

Thanet rose and began to pace about the room. If only he were able to discuss all this with Lineham. Perhaps the entire fabric of the case he had built up against Pritchard was no more than the product of an over-heated imagination. But he didn't think so. There was an essential rightness about it which both elated and appalled him. Because if he were right, Pritchard was not to be trusted and Mrs. Pritchard must be warned, convinced of the necessity of removing herself to safety.

Was he being alarmist? Should he go and see her now, tonight? Or should he sleep on it, wait till morning?

But if he did, and harm came to her, he would never forgive himself for not having tried to prevent it. He would go. At least, then, he would be able to gauge the emotional temperature, see how things stood between them.

He hurried out to the car park.

21

Well before he reached Town Road Thanet realised that, somewhere in the quiet residential area ahead, something was amiss. An ambulance overtook him, its blue light flashing, and he began to notice small knots of pedestrians hurrying in the same direction. He was aware of the strange osmosis by which news of disaster spreads, and he began to feel as though he and all these others were being sucked into the same maleficent vortex.

He was driving with the window open and simultaneously he smelt smoke and remembered the siren he had heard shortly before leaving the office. A fire, then. Impatiently, he repudiated the idea that there could be any connection between his mission and the emergency ahead. But he failed to convince himself. If his theory was correct, Pritchard had been living on a short fuse. What more likely than that the situation had now exploded?

He turned the last corner before the entrance to Town Road and saw that ahead of him the sightseers had come to a halt against a cordon of uniformed police, like detritus washed against a sea wall. Abandoning his car he jumped out and shouldered his way through the crowd, ignoring the indignant protests from all sides. Within seconds he had been recognised and was allowed through. Noting with a sinking sense of inevitability that the furious activity ahead was indeed centred on or near the Pritchards' house, he set off at a run. All along the street the inhabitants of Town Road had come out on to the pavements to enjoy their grandstand view.

It was the Pritchards' house. And the fire had really got a hold. The doorway was an orange gateway to hell and long, forked tongues of flame licked hungrily at the brickwork through window spaces from which the glass had long since exploded. Arching jets of water were being directed into the house through every opening, but the firemen had no doubt been hampered in their task by the fact that these houses had no rear access. The fire could be fought on one front only, and it seemed that someone must be trapped inside, for the men were now setting ladders against the eaves.

Thanet knew better than to approach the station officer in charge of operations at this particular moment. Human life came first, curiosity could be satisfied later. Though what prospect there could possibly be of saving anyone trapped inside that inferno, Thanet could not imagine.

Out of breath, he skidded to a stop beside the two ambulancemen and showed them his warrant card.

"What's happening?"

"Some crazy bastard's trapped inside. They went in, to try and get him out, but he'd barricaded himself in the attic. Now they're going to try and break in through the skylight."

Thanet looked up. The small black oblong of glass set into the roof was still black. The fire, then, had not yet penetrated there. Pritchard—for it must be he—still had a chance, if he chose to take it. No one can rescue a man determined not to be saved.

Thanet put the question he dreaded to ask.

"Where's his wife?"

He was scanning the faces of the watchers now, seeking Mrs. Pritchard's slight, submissive figure, that distinctive, old-fashioned bun.

"Got out just in time, apparently. When she couldn't stop him splashing petrol around she ran to the phone box and rang the fire brigade. By the time she got back, the place was well alight. He's a real nut-case, if you ask me."

Petrol. That would account for the ferocity of the blaze, the speed with which the fire had gained hold. And, now that the word had been mentioned, Thanet could smell the sharp, pungent tang of it in the air.

But Mrs. Pritchard was safe, thank God, and now he spotted her, an island of immobility in the shifting, restless crowd on the far pavement. She was gazing intently upwards, the knuckles of one hand pressed against her mouth. Thanet had just begun to move towards her when there was a collective groan from the crowd, audible even above the roar and crackle of the flames.

The black oblong in the roof was now illuminated by a flickering glow from within. The fire had reached the attic. The redness was increasing in intensity with terrifying speed, the fire feeding itself no doubt upon the accumulated clutter of a disused attic, tinder-dry from years of storage. And according to the ambulancemen, Pritchard himself had accelerated matters by piling it all into one place, against the door.

Thanet hoped that it would not become the man's funeral pyre.

One of the firemen had now almost reached the skylight, which was two-thirds of the way up the roof slope. Suddenly it was flung open and Pritchard heaved himself out. The fireman steadied himself and put up his hand to grasp Pritchard's, but Pritchard ignored him, turning his back and scrabbling to secure first one foothold then another on the upper edge of the window frame. Spreadeagled against the roof, his body contracted in readiness to spring and then launched itself upwards in a desperate lunge, hands clawing for the roof ridge.

Along with the crowd behind him, Thanet caught his breath, tensed himself for the inevitable fall.

But it didn't come. With an agility born surely of desperation, Pritchard had somehow managed to secure a handhold, had hauled himself up and was now attempting to stand. Slowly, arms outstretched like a tightrope walker, he managed it, teetering slightly as he straightened up. He stood for a moment steadying himself and staring down at the furious activity below, then lifted his face to the sky.

"God is my witness!" he cried.

The words floated faintly down to the silent watchers in the street below. Then something must have collapsed in upon itself in the attic, for almost at once and so swiftly that it was over almost before it had begun, a fountain of sparks erupted from the skylight opening, spraying out in all directions, and tongues of fire spread with lightning speed up Pritchard's legs and body and along his outstretched arms.

Some of the petrol, Thanet realised, must have splashed on to the man's clothing.

For a brief, appalling moment, Pritchard stood in flames against the sky, a horrific parody of the cross which he had always denied. Then, with an agonised scream, a seething, writhing mass of fire, he slid diagonally down the roof, cartwheeled over the edge and landed with a sickening thud in the street below.

Mrs. Pritchard started forward with a cry as firemen rushed to put out the flames. Thanet caught her by the arm.

"I should give them a few moments."

She stared blankly up at him for a moment, as if wondering who he was, and then she recognised him, gave a little nod. But she did not speak, simply stood watching the activity around her husband's body, hands pressed to either side of her face.

The flames were already extinguished, the ambulancemen carefully transferring Pritchard to the waiting stretcher.

Thanet touched Mrs. Pritchard's arm. "I'll go and ask how he is."

Pritchard was still alive, apparently. Just.

"Should think he'll be dead on arrival, though."

"His wife'll want to go to the hospital with him," said Thanet.

"OK. But hurry."

Thanet helped Mrs. Pritchard into the ambulance and then jumped in beside her. She didn't seem to register his presence. She still hadn't said a single word and throughout the brief journey sat staring into space.

Shock, thought Thanet. And who could wonder? Mother, daughter, husband, home, all lost within the space of one short week. The only way to survive such an experience must be at first to blank out reality, to curl up inside yourself like a snail in a shell and stay there until some instinct tells you that you can now begin to cope with life again.

They were almost at the hospital when the attendant who had been keeping a watchful eye on Pritchard glanced up and caught Thanet's eye. His expression of regret and slight shake of the head were enough to tell Thanet that Pritchard was dead. Mrs. Pritchard had not noticed the brief exchange of glances. Better to break the news when they were no longer cooped up with her husband's body, Thanet decided.

He waited until a whispered request had produced a small, private room and a cup of tea from a sympathetic night sister.

"It's bad news, I'm afraid, Mrs. Pritchard."

His tone had forewarned her. Suddenly she was alert, her eyes wary.

"Your husband. He died, on the way to hospital."

For a second she froze. Then her cup began to rattle in its saucer. Thanet reached out, took it from her, set it on the table.

"There was nothing they could do. I'm sorry."

She gave a fierce nod, pressed her shaking hands together. "Just give me a few moments."

Thanet waited in a sympathetic silence, admiring her effort at self-control.

At last she flung back her head, took several deep breaths. When she looked at him again he flinched from the pain in her eyes.

"He was... unbalanced," she said, forcing each word out with difficulty. "Perhaps even..."

But she could not bring herself to say it. Thanet said nothing, waited. If Mrs. Pritchard needed to talk, who else was there to listen? Her sister, perhaps, but she was far away in Birmingham. And as for her brother-in-law Jethro, or his wife... no one in a vulnerable state could possibly seek either comfort or understanding there.

"You know he...?" Again, she could not put it into words.

He had to help her. "Charity, you mean?"

She nodded. "He didn't mean to... It was an accident." Then, fiercely, as if even now it mattered to her that her husband should be exonerated of evil intent, "You must believe that," she cried.

"I do."

But his acceptance was not enough. Now that she had begun she had to continue, to justify, elaborate, explain. "It was while he was waiting for you to come back from Mrs. Hodges' house..."

It had all happened exactly as Thanet had thought: the impulsive decision to go and look for Charity along the footpath, the lashing-out in anger, the immediate return to the house, confident that Charity would soon come creeping home in a properly chastened frame of mind. And when she didn't, the growing fear that he had hit her harder than he had intended to, that she was lying unconscious, perhaps, in the alley—and, finally, the genuine grief and agony of mind when at last he saw her, dead...

"I had a feeling there was something wrong, right from the beginning," said Mrs. Pritchard miserably. "He was upset, of course, that was only to be expected, he really loved her, in his own way. But there was more to it than that, I was sure of it and then, when we heard that Charity had been... carrying on with someone, it was almost as if he was glad! He began to go on and on about how bad she was, how the Devil had been in her right from the day she was born... And in the end it dawned on me that what he was really saying was that it was a good thing she was dead, that he was talking as

185

though whoever did it had done something . . . *praiseworthy*."
Her voice cracked in disbelief.

"Looking back, now, I can see that he was trying to justify
himself, but that was when I began to wonder . . . when I
began to be afraid . . ." She pressed her knuckles hard against
her mouth, in that characteristic gesture of hers, as if she
were trying to batten down the horrific memory of her
dawning suspicions.

"I didn't know what to do. I couldn't believe it, but the
more I thought about it, the more I saw that it would make
sense. I began to feel that if I couldn't talk to someone about
it, I'd go out of my mind. But I couldn't think of anyone to
go to, anyone who'd understand. This morning, when I saw
you, I almost told you then . . . But how could I? You're a
policeman. I just couldn't betray my own husband. And
yet . . . If he had done this terrible thing . . ."

She could control her distress no longer. Suddenly her face
crumpled and the tears began to stream down her face.

Thanet thrust a handkerchief into her hand, patted her on
the shoulder and said, "I'll be back in a moment." He left the
room, granting her that which she had so far denied herself,
the luxury of abandoning herself to grief. Quickly, he arranged that she should be kept in hospital overnight. She
would, he was assured, be given a sedative that would ensure
her a good night's sleep. Then he returned to her.

Her eyes were red and swollen, her face puffy, but she had
stopped crying and was looking calmer. She nodded grateful-
ly when he told her of the arrangements he had made, but
protested when he said that he thought it would be best for
her if they continued their conversation tomorrow.

"I'd much rather finish telling you tonight. Otherwise, I
shall just lie awake, going over and over it in my mind."

"If you're sure . . ."

"I am. Truly."

"Very well." He sat down again.

"I was trying to explain to you how I was feeling this
morning . . ."

"You were in an impossible situation."

She nodded, blew her nose. "I'd never want to live
through these last few days again."

But you will, thought Thanet sadly, you will. In your
imagination you will live them again and again. Perhaps the

memory will gradually fade, the pain become less acute, but they'll be with you till the day you die.

"By this evening I felt I couldn't stand it any longer . . . the doubts, the suspicions . . . I felt I just had to *know*. And there was only one way of finding out, really. I knew he'd be angry, but honestly, I was past caring . . .

"At first, I didn't dare ask him straight out if he'd killed her, so he didn't know what I was talking about—or perhaps he did know, and was just pretending to misunderstand. So in the end, I asked him outright. He . . . he just stared at me, and for a minute I thought he was just going to walk out on me. Then he started . . .

"He went on and on about how evil Charity had been, how the Devil had always been in her, how he thought he'd got rid of it when she was a little girl, but he hadn't, and it had been there, lurking inside her all these years, waiting for its chance to come out into the open at last . . . Then he began to cry, said how much he'd loved her, that he hadn't meant to hurt her, not Charity, his little girl . . . He begged me to believe that. But I must see, he said, that it was all for the best . . .

"I just couldn't speak, couldn't say anything, and in the end he began to get angry with me. He said he could see I didn't believe him, but he could prove that he had been right to do what he did. If God hadn't wanted Charity to die, she wouldn't have, he said, and God would give me a sign to show me that he'd only been acting as God's instrument. If our eye offended we should pluck it out, he said, and if the evil lay in our only child, then our only course was to sacrifice that child on the altar of duty . . . He went on and on and I couldn't bear it. I kept on thinking of Charity, of how much I'd loved her, how God would surely never have asked that of me . . . And in the end I put my hands over my ears. He was beside himself with rage then, grabbed my arms and forced my hands down. I would listen, he said, whether I liked it or not. He'd told me he could prove that he was innocent of evil and he would do so. Then he rushed out of the house."

Thanet could guess what was coming.

"When he got back he was carrying this huge can of petrol. He wasn't shouting any more, he was quite calm. God would be his witness, he said. Like Shadrach, Meshach and Abednego he would walk through the fire unharmed and I would see at last that every word he had been saying was God's truth. All the while he was talking he was splashing the petrol about, everywhere . . . in the bedrooms, down the staircase, in the sitting room . . . He was cool, methodical, and now I was the one who was screaming, begging him to stop. He just shook me off and went on with what he was doing . . . ''

Thanet already knew the rest, but he went on listening, patiently, as Mrs. Pritchard told the remainder of her tragic tale. When she had finished she closed her eyes and leaned back in her chair, exhausted, as motionless as a mechanical doll that has run down.

Thanet waited for a little while and then said gently, "He must have been in torment over the last few days."

She opened her eyes and there was gratitude in them, for his understanding.

"He was. I think he knew, really, that there was no justification, never could be any justication for what he had done. He was desperate to convince himself otherwise—well, you saw him yourself, tonight. In the end I don't think he could have gone on, not knowing. I think he just had to find some way of giving himself the final proof.''

Had Pritchard known, in the last, few agonising moments of his life, that he had been deluding himself, Thanet wondered. Perhaps Mrs. Pritchard was right and deep down inside he had known all along that he was, and had come to feel that he could not live with the knowledge.

Mrs. Pritchard had closed her eyes again. Now that she had unburdened herself, perhaps she would be able to rest. Quietly, he left the room, went to fetch the Sister.

Before she was led gently away Mrs. Pritchard attempted a smile. "Thank you for listening to me."

Thanet touched her shoulder and left.

Outside, on the hospital steps, he paused to take in great lungfuls of fresh air. He felt as though he were sloughing off the claustrophobic, unnatural atmosphere of Pritchard's world and emerging into a universe where sanity was the norm and optimism possible again. His car, he remembered, was still parked near Town Road and he decided that the walk would do him good. For once he would break his own rule and leave writing up the day's reports until tomorrow.

In the car, the pace of his driving reflected the exhaustion that was beginning to steal over him and by the time he turned into his own driveway he could think of nothing but falling into bed and sinking into oblivion. He couldn't be bothered to put the car away, but left it in the drive. As he trudged wearily to the front door he was surprised to see a line of light around the sitting room curtains. His mother-in-law was usually in bed long before this. There must be something on television she especially wanted to see, he decided, as he let himself in. Yes, the sitting room door was ajar and he could hear the murmur of conversation.

As he shut the door behind him the sound cut out.

"Luke?"

He stood stock still. Joan's voice? Surely he had imagined it. There was a movement within the room, a shadow across the band of light spilling into the hall, and the door opened wide.

Joan stood silhouetted in the doorway.

He wanted to believe it, but he couldn't. She wouldn't be home for two more endless weeks. This vision had been conjured up by his own tiredness, need and longing.

"Darling? Are you all right?"

The light in the hall clicked on and now he had to believe the evidence of his own eyes. Joan really was here, only a few steps away. Without a word he opened his arms and she came into them, smiling, kissing his cheek and then laying her head against his shoulder. He folded his arms around her, burying his face in the springy golden curls, breathing in the unique smell of her.

She *was* real, she *was* here.

Even in the days of their courtship, when to see and hold her had been his paramount need, Thanet could not remember feeling quite like this. It was as if the body pressed against his was truly the other half of him and only in her presence was he complete. He closed his eyes and let the joy and peace wash over him.

They stood for a moment or two longer and then she leaned back in his arms and wrinkled her nose at him. "You smell like Bonfire night."

If only she knew why, Thanet thought. Briefly, the horrifying image of the burning cross that had been Charity's father flashed across his mind and he was pierced by a painful shaft of pity for them all—for Pritchard, for Mrs. Pritchard and for Charity, their ill-starred daughter, doomed by heredity and environment to her brief, unhappy life and untimely death. With an effort he wrenched his thoughts back to the present and essayed a smile. "Do I?"

She was watching his face. "What is it, darling? What's happened?"

He shook his head and kissed the tip of her nose. "Tell you later."

She waited for a moment to see if he would say anything more and, when he didn't, stepped back a little. Smiling, she lifted her hands as if to display herself. "Well . . . surprised?"

"Let me pinch you, see if you're real." Gently, he squeezed her chin between thumb and forefinger, clowned surrender. "You're real!"

She was laughing now, tugging him into the sitting room, talking all the while.

"I decided I just couldn't last out another fortnight, so this afternoon when two of the staff at the Home were pronounced fit for duty again, I said, 'That's it, I'm off to see my poor neglected family' . . . Look, I've made you coffee and sandwiches."

Thanet allowed himself to be pushed gently into a chair, fussed over.

Joan poured him some coffee, then sat back and studied him critically. "Just as well I did come home, by the look of it. You look terrible. I don't know whether to feel gratified or horrified, that you obviously can't survive without me!"

Thanet leaned across to kiss the tip of her nose. "Gratified, of course. What else?"

She dropped her bantering tone. "Case going badly?"

He shook his head. "It's over."

"Want to talk about it?"

"Tomorrow." Time enough, then, to plunge back into the murky depths of the Pritchards' life, relive the grim events of the last few hours. For tonight he just wanted to savour the pleasure of having Joan home again, to relish the relief of knowing how wrong he had been ever to suspect that she had been slipping away from him. He knew her too well for her to succeed in a face-to-face pretence; her joy at being home equalled his.

The telephone rang.

Joan groaned. "Oh *no*. Not tonight. Here we go . . . Down to earth with a bang."

She knew that his conscience would never allow him to leave it unanswered, and she watched with resignation as he heaved himself out of his chair.

"Lineham here, sir. It's a boy!"

"Mike! Congratulations! How's Louise?"

"Fine. They've knocked her out now, as a precaution against something called—I think—eclampsia—but they say she'll be all right, there's absolutely nothing to worry about."

"That's marvellous."

"They say the baby's fine, too. Yelling his head off."

"What are you going to call him?"

"Richard."

"Nice name."

"Well, just thought I'd let you know. Got some more phone calls to make now, of course. See you tomorrow."

"Right. Thanks for ringing."

Thanet turned to Joan. "Mike, as you'll have gathered. It's a boy. And both Louise and the baby are fine."

"Wonderful. What a relief!"

"Certainly is. Tell you what, we'll go and see Louise tomorrow, smuggle in some glasses and a bottle of champagne. I feel like celebrating."

He held out his hands, tugged Joan to her feet and put his arms around her once more. The case was over, Louise and baby were doing well, Joan was home. What more could he want?

At moments like this he felt that life itself was a celebration.

DOROTHY SIMPSON is a former French teacher who lives in Kent, England, with her husband. Their three children are now all married. Her fifth, Luke Thanet novel, LAST SEEN ALIVE, won the 1985 British Crime Writers' Association Silver Dagger award. Her other books are SUSPICIOUS DEATH, ELEMENT OF DOUBT, DEAD ON ARRIVAL, PUPPET FOR A CORPSE, SIX FEET UNDER and THE NIGHT SHE DIED. Her ninth Luke Thanet novel, DEAD BY MORNING, is coming soon from Bantam.

If you enjoyed this book
you will enjoy Dorothy Simpson's
other books for Bantam
which include her ninth
Inspector Luke Thanet novel,

DEAD BY MORNING

Here is an exciting preview
of this suspenseful new mystery,
to be published in the fall of 1990.

Turn the page for a sample of
DEAD BY MORNING
by Dorothy Simpson.

Thanet lifted the edge of the curtain aside and peered out into the dark street. 'It's nearly half-past twelve. Where can she be? She's never been as late as this before. And—yes—it's beginning to snow, look!'

Joan joined him at the window. 'So it is. The temperature must have risen.'

Earlier on it had been freezing hard.

She returned to her seat by the fire. 'Darling, do come and sit down, you're driving me mad prowling about like that.'

'How you can sit there so calmly I just do not know. She's always home by half-past eleven. Anything can have happened.' Thanet, who had seen far more than his share of broken bodies during his years in the police force, blanked off hideous images of Bridget mutilated, injured, suffering appalling pain or even now dying, perhaps. He plumped down beside Joan on the settee and, leaning forward, put his elbows on his knees and his head in his hands.

Joan put her hand on his shoulder. ' "Anything" includes perfectly ordinary things like being delayed at work, Tim's car not starting, being held up because they witnessed an accident . . .'

Their daughter Bridget was now nearly seventeen. She had managed to scrape one or two respectable grades in her GCSEs last summer and, always keen to have a career in cookery, was taking a year off to gain some practical work experience in the kitchens of a local restaurant before starting a year's Cordon Bleu course in September. Tim was one of the waiters, and gave her a lift home each night that their stint of duty coincided.

Thanet's shoulder twitched impatiently. 'Yes, I know . . . But in that case, why hasn't she given us a ring?' Perhaps Tim wasn't as trustworthy as he had appeared. A married man with two children, he had seemed a decent enough young man, but what if his offer of lifts for Bridget had had an ulterior motive, what if . . . ?

Thanet jumped up and crossed to peer out of the window once more. 'It's coming down more heavily now.'

The snow was already beginning to lie, mantling the ground with a thin gauzy veil of white. Huge soft wet flakes swirled around the fuzzy orange globe of the street lamp on the pavement outside their house and hurled themselves silently against the windowpane like moths attracted to the light, melting from the contact with the warm glass as they slid down. Thanet peered hopefully down the street. Nothing.

'We should have refused Tim's offer, insisted on fetching her ourselves.'

'That would have looked really churlish, as he actually has to pass our house on his way. Anyway, it's ridiculous turning out late every night if we don't have to.'

'Better than having to sit here and wonder where she is and what's happened to her.'

Joan laughed. 'It looks as though you're in for a really bad time.'

'What do you mean?'

'Don't look so alarmed! I simply mean that this is only the beginning. We've been unusually lucky up to now but no doubt this is only the first of many, many nights over many, many years when we're going to lie awake waiting for the sound of her return, wondering where she is, if she's all right . . .'

'How can you make so light of it?'

'I'm not making light of it. It's just that I . . . well, I'm a little more resigned to it, I suppose. I can remember how my own parents used to fuss when I was late home after going out with you.'

'Do you? Did they? I never knew that.' Thanet took her hand, momentarily distracted.

'They certainly did. But I wasn't going to tell you, naturally. It would have made me sound like a little girl, to be fussed over.'

He grinned. 'The ultimate insult.'

'Exactly. And that's precisely how Bridget will take it if she gets home and finds us sitting here like a reception committee.' Joan stood up, decisively. 'So come on, let's go to bed.'

'But . . .'

'Luke! Come on.'

Grudgingly, he allowed himself to be persuaded upstairs. 'But I'm not going to let it go, mind. If she's going to be late like this she really must let us know.'

'All *right*. I'll speak to her about it. Tactfully.'

Thanet caught her eye and grinned. 'Not too tactfully.'

She smiled back. 'Agreed.'

They had just got into bed when outside in the street a car door slammed. A few moments later they heard the front door close. Quickly, Joan switched off the bedside light. When Bridget had crept past their door on the way to her room, Joan said, 'That wasn't all that was worrying you tonight, though, was it?'

Thanet turned to face her in the darkness. There was no point in denying it. 'No,' he admitted.

'Draco again.'

' 'Fraid so.'

'Why didn't you say?'

'I should think you're sick and tired of hearing about him.'

'Nonsense. It enlivens my days no end.'

He could hear the laughter in her voice.

'Seriously, though,' she said. 'What's he been up to this time?'

'That's the trouble, we're not sure. There're all sorts of rumours flying around. Some new campaign he's planning . . . But one thing's certain, it's sure to make life even more uncomfortable for the rest of us.'

Just over a year ago Superintendent Parker had retired and Goronwy Draco had taken over at divisional headquarters in Sturrenden, the small country town in Kent where Thanet lived and worked. The new Superintendent was a fiery, dynamic little Welshman who was firmly of the opinion that a new broom should sweep clean as quickly as possible. Suffering under the new regime of regular morning meetings and tighter control, Thanet had grudgingly to admit that under Draco's ever-watchful eye divisional headquarters at Sturrenden had become a much more stimulating place to work. Enlivened by newly decorated offices and higher standards of cleanliness and efficiency, the place now crackled with a new energy and there had been a gratifying increase in crimes solved and villains safely ensconced behind bars. Draco may not be popular, but he certainly got results.

Thanet sighed. 'I expect we'll survive.'

As soon as he opened his eyes next morning he was aware of the difference in the quality of the light. There must have been more snow overnight. He hoped that the fall had not been heavy. Snow was very picturesque but it brought problems. However hard the local authority tried, it never seemed to make adequate preparation for bad weather. A mere skim of snow brought its crop of traffic jams and minor accidents; anything over six inches, severe disruption. And of course, there was the cold. Thanet hated the cold and the tip of his nose told him that the temperature in the bedroom was at a far from acceptable level. February was definitely bottom of his personal popularity chart of favourite months. He allowed himself the indulgence of a few more moments in the warm cave that was the bed, then braced himself and slid out, careful not to allow a gush of cold air to disturb Joan, who was still sleeping peacefully. He padded across to the window. Might as well know the worst.

Despite his dislike of the inconvenience snow brought in its wake he could not escape the inevitable sense of wonder at its transforming beauty. Beneath its mantle of pristine white, his familiar world preened itself in the first rosy light of a clear winter dawn. He peered at the roof of the garage, trying to gauge the depth of the fall: not more than a few inches, by the look of it. Good. It shouldn't take too long to clear the drive, with Ben's help. And the gritting lorries had been out last night, so the roads shouldn't be too bad.

Three-quarters of an hour later, fortified by the porridge that Joan had insisted on making, he and Ben had almost reached the front gate. Up and down the road warmly clad figures shovelled and swept drives and pavements. In the road cars seemed to be making slow but steady progress.

Joan appeared at the front door. 'Luke? Telephone.'

'Finish it off, will you, Ben?'

Ben, thirteen, gave a reluctant nod.

'Sergeant Pater,' said Joan, handing over the receiver.

The Station Officer. Something out of the ordinary, then, to necessitate an early morning call, in view of the fact that Thanet was due at headquarters in half an hour or so.

'Thanet here.'

'Morning, sir. Just had the report of a body in a ditch at the side of the road, out at Sutton-in-the-Weald. Found by a man walking his dog.'

As in his last case, Thanet thought. If you were a dog owner you certainly seemed to run a greater risk of stumbling over a corpse than most.

'You've reported it to the Super?'

'Yes, sir. He says he's going out there himself.' Pater's tone was carefully non-committal.

'Ah.' Thanet's heart sank. This was new. What was

Draco up to now? He remembered wondering, when Draco first arrived, just how long the new Superintendent would be content to sit behind a desk. All that restless energy needed numerous outlets. Thanet hoped that active participation at ground level wasn't going to be one of them. It would be impossibly inhibiting to have Draco breathing down his neck.

'Apparently there's been quite a bit of snow out there, fifteen inches or so, with some pretty deep drifts in places, so it's going to make transport a bit tricky. The Super's put through a request to the Council to clear the road as soon as possible and he's asked for a couple of Land Rovers to be laid on for you. He wants you to meet him here and he'll go out with you.'

'I see. What time?'

'Eight-thirty.'

'Right, I'll be there. Have you contacted Sergeant Lineham?'

'I'll do that next, sir. I'll arrange for the SOCOs and the CCTV sergeant to come in the other Land Rover, and pick up Doc Mallard on the way. I thought I'd let you know first.'

So that Thanet wouldn't be late for Draco, no doubt.

'Thanks.'

Grateful that he had already had breakfast and that the driveway was clear, Thanet put on thick socks, wellington boots, sheepskin jacket, gloves and woolly hat in anticipation of hours of standing around in the snow. 'I feel like the Abominable Snowman,' he said as he kissed Joan goodbye.

She grinned. 'You look like him. Here.' She handed him a Thermos.

'Thanks, love. Oh, hang on. Better take some shoes, in case. I can't go tramping in and out of houses in these.'

'Sure you wouldn't like me to pack a suitcase for you?'

'All very well for you, in your nice, centrally heated office.'

Joan worked as a Probation Officer in Sturrenden.

'Courtroom actually.'

'Courtroom, office, what's the difference, it'll be *warm.*'

'Stop grumbling,' she said, pushing him out of the front door. 'Go on, you don't want to keep Draco waiting, do you?'

Thanet rolled his eyes. 'Heaven forbid.'

As he got into the car he realised that he had been so put out by the prospect of Draco's presence that he had forgotten to ask whether the body was that of a man or a woman.

It was another couple of hours before he found out.

The journey out to Sutton-in-the-Weald had been irritatingly protracted. The first few miles hadn't been too bad but then the snow had begun to deepen and a little further on they had caught up with the snow plough sent out at Draco's request. After that they had resigned themselves to travelling behind it the rest of the way, at a snail's pace. Fortunately a local farmer with a snow-clearing attachment on the front of his tractor had eventually turned up coming the other way and after a certain amount of manoeuvring they had been able to proceed more quickly.

There then followed a long wait for the second Land Rover bringing Doc Mallard and the Scenes-of-Crime officers. Meanwhile, there had been little to do. The body lay in a roadside ditch backed by a high stone wall, only a few yards from the lion-topped pillars at the entrance of the driveway to Longford Hall Country House Hotel. From the road nothing could be seen but the upper surface of a sleeve in distinctively bold black-and-white checked tweed, lying along the edge of the ditch as it had been uncovered by the dog. Although the arm was patently stiff with rigor mortis, PC Yeoman, the local policeman who had been first on the scene, had understandably cleared the snow from the man's face, to make quite sure that he was dead. The rigid features, pallor of the skin and open, staring eyes had told their own tale and thereafter he had left well alone, winning Thanet's approval by erecting a temporary barrier of sticks stuck into the snow and linked by string.

Despite his years in the force Thanet had rarely been able to overcome a dread of his first sight of a corpse, but today, uncomfortably preoccupied by Draco's presence, he had approached the body with no more than a twinge of trepidation and, gazing down at the dead face set deep in its ruff of snow, he felt no more than his usual pang of sorrow at a life cut short. Blurred as the man's features were by snow, it was difficult to estimate his age with any accuracy, but Thanet guessed that he had been somewhere between forty and sixty. Time, no doubt, would tell.

No further attempt had yet been made to clear the snow from the rest of the body. Thanet wanted photographs taken first. Not that he thought this very important. Covered with snow as it was, the body had obviously been placed or had fallen into the ditch before or around the time the snow started. Still, one never knew. It paid to be scrupulously careful and, with Draco taking in every move, Thanet had every intention of playing it by the book.

In any case, the marks in the snow told their own story: a scuffled, disturbed area betrayed the dog's excited investigation of this interesting and unusual find and there were two sets of approaching and departing footprints, belonging to Mr Clayton, the dog's owner, and PC Yeoman. Thanet, Draco and Lineham had been careful to enquire which were Yeoman's tracks, and to step into his footmarks when they approached for their brief inspection of the body.

As yet the snow had kept most people indoors and there had been little traffic up and down the road. Half an hour ago a tractor had begun clearing the hotel drive and any minute now Thanet expected someone to arrive and demand an explanation of the activity just outside the gates.

'Where the devil are they?'

Draco, who along with Lineham and Thanet had been stamping up and down the road in an attempt to keep warm, was finding it difficult to contain his impatience. 'They should have been here half an hour ago.'

'Perhaps Doc Mallard was out on a call.'

Draco snorted, two dragon-like puffs of condensation emerging from his nostrils. Short, square and dark and sporting an astrakhan hat and a heavy, fur-lined overcoat, he looked like a Russian statesman awaiting the arrival of foreign dignitaries. The backdrop of snow served to heighten the illusion.

'Like some coffee, sir? I've got some in the Land Rover.'

'Thank you. Excellent idea. Should have thought of it myself.'

'My wife's, actually.'

Thanet fetched his Thermos from the Land Rover and he, Draco and Lineham took it in turns to sip the steaming liquid. Lineham had been very quiet so far, subdued no doubt by Draco's presence. Thanet had to suppress a grin at the memory of Lineham's face when he had seen Draco climb into the Land Rover. The sergeant evidently hadn't been warned.

A vehicle could be heard coming down the hotel drive and a moment later a Range Rover pulled up between the stone pillars. A man and a woman jumped out.

'What's going on here?'

It was, unmistakably, the voice of authority, cultured and self-assured. Its owner, clad in country uniform of cords, thick sweater, Barbour and green wellies, was in his late forties, tall and well built with slightly receding dark hair and slate-grey eyes which quickly summed up the situation and unerringly selected Draco as the person to approach. 'What's happened?'

Draco handed the Thermos cup to Thanet and, drawing himself up to his full height, announced, 'Superintendent Draco, from divisional police headquarters at Sturrenden . . .'

But the man wasn't listening. He had caught sight of the arm in its boldly checked sleeve and his expression changed. 'My God, that's . . .'

He spun around, putting out his hand to prevent the woman behind him from coming any closer.

'What is it, Giles? What's the matter?'

Clear, ringing tones, another Barbour and more green wellies. A beautiful woman, this, a little younger than her husband, in her early forties, Thanet guessed. She, too, was dark, her long hair swept back into a thick French plait, accentuating the classic bone structure of her face. She would look much the same, he thought, twenty years from now.

'I think you ought to get back into the car, darling,' said her husband.

She shook off his restraining arm impatiently. 'What do you mean, what are you talking about?'

The movement gave her a clear view of the arm for the first time and she gasped. 'My God, that's Leo's coat.'

Draco stepped forward. 'Leo?'

'My brother.' Her gaze was riveted to the arm, her eyes appalled. She clutched at her husband, who put an arm around her. 'Is he . . . ?'

'Dead?' said Draco. 'I'm afraid so. If it is your brother, I'm sorry that you had to learn of it like this.'

'But why are you just standing around drinking coffee, for God's sake! Why aren't you trying to get him out? You can't just leave him there!' She grabbed the stick marker nearest to her, tugged it out of the snow and, tossing it impatiently aside, started towards the ditch.

The three policemen darted forward to stop her, but it was her husband who grabbed at her coat and tugged her back. 'No, Delia. Can't you see? If it is Leo, there's nothing anybody can do now.'

'But it's awful! It's . . . inhuman, just leaving him buried in the snow like that!' She turned on Draco, her eyes blazing. 'How dare you!' Her contemptuous gaze swept around the little group of policemen and returned to Draco. 'The Chief Constable is a personal friend of ours. I shall report you to him. Immediately!'

Thanet studiously refrained from looking at Lineham.

She turned to her husband. 'Come on, Giles. We'll go back to the house and get something done about this absurd situation.'

And with another furious glance at Draco she swung herself up into the car and sat gazing stonily through the windscreen as her husband manoeuvred the Range Rover around and drove off.

'A lady who's used to getting her own way, I presume,' said Draco, apparently unruffled. 'You're going to have your hands full with her, Thanet.'

Just what Thanet had been thinking. Though the prospect intrigued rather than dismayed him. He raised an eyebrow at PC Yeoman. 'Who are they?'

'Mr and Mrs Hamilton, sir. Owners of Longford Hall. She runs the hotel, he runs the estate.'

'There are the others now, sir,' said Lineham.

'About time, too,' growled Draco.

Doc Mallard's half-moon spectacles glinted through the windscreen as the Land Rover drew up.

'Where the devil have you been?' snapped Draco as Trace, the SOCO sergeant, got out, followed by his team.

Mallard accepted Thanet's steadying hand. 'My fault, I'm afraid, Superintendent. Blame it on a doctor's irregular lifestyle. I was out at a confinement. Woman was on her way to hospital, but the ambulance

got stuck in the snow. Luckily I just got there in time.'
He beamed. 'Bouncing baby boy, mother and child
both right as rain, I'm glad to say. Nothing like bringing life into the world to cheer you up, you know.'

'I'm sure.' Draco turned to Trace. 'Well, let's get on
with it now you are here. If we have to stand around
out here much longer we'll all turn into blocks of ice.'

BANTAM MYSTERY COLLECTION

Kinsey Millhone is...

"The best new private eye." —*The Detroit News*

"A tough-cookie with a soft center." —*Newsweek*

"A stand-out specimen of the new female operatives."
—*Philadelphia Inquirer*

Sue Grafton is...

The Shamus and Anthony Award winning creator of Kinsey Millhone and quite simply one of the hottest new mystery writers around.

THE MYSTERIOUS WORLD OF AGATHA CHRISTIE

Acknowledged as the world's most popular mystery writer of all time, Dame Agatha Christie's books have thrilled millions of readers for generations. With her care and attention to characters, the intriguing situations and the breathtaking final deduction, it's no wonder that Agatha Christie is the world's best-selling mystery writer.

☐ 25678	**SLEEPING MURDER**	$3.95
☐ 26795	**A HOLIDAY FOR MURDER**	$3.50
☐ 27001	**POIROT INVESTIGATES**	$3.50
☐ 26477	**THE SECRET ADVERSARY**	$3.50
☐ 26138	**DEATH ON THE NILE**	$3.50
☐ 26587	**THE MYSTERIOUS AFFAIR AT STYLES**	$3.50
☐ 25493	**THE POSTERN OF FATE**	$3.50
☐ 26896	**THE SEVEN DIALS MYSTERY**	$3.50